"What I'm trying to say is that
I want a one-night stand."

She met his gaze, clearly waiting for his reaction.

He opened his mouth and then closed it again.

"I want you," she said softly.

"For tonight," he clarified.

"Yes."

Ignoring the unmistakable flash of disappointment—
What the hell is that about?—he pulled her inside, kicked his door shut, and gently pushed her up against the wood and cupped her face. "You need to be sure."

"I am." She blinked. "Are you? Because it's okay if you're not. I can find someone else. I can make a list."

This stopped him. She could make a list? Of who? Not important, he told himself. *Shake it off.* "You're not going to need a list for this, Bailey."

She stared at him. "No?"

Hell no. "I already told you that I want you. Now I'm going to show you." He gave her a few seconds to absorb that before he leaned in and kissed her, putting every ounce of his want and need into it.

"Shalvis knows all the right buttons to push...The flubs and flaws are hilarious, the grief feels credible, and the sparks fly in this solid, light romance from the always-reliable Shalvis."
—*Publishers Weekly*

"Top Pick! 4½ stars! The first Cedar Ridge book is flaw-less. This author knows romance, and readers can always expect her to deliver humor, heat and a kick-ass story."
—*RT Book Reviews*

"Fans of the Lucky Harbor series will be thrilled to know this series starts strong...*Second Chance Summer* has Jill Shalvis's trademark humor and deadpanned responses combined with some wonderful sexy times."
—FictionVixen.com

It's in His Kiss

"Shalvis combines humor, sparkling repartee, believable characters, and highly sensual sex scenes to make this book work on every level."
—*Publishers Weekly* (starred review)

"4½ stars! Top Pick! Shalvis never ceases to amaze readers with her fun-loving, sultry romances and this addition to the Lucky Harbor series will knock your socks off!"
—*RT Book Reviews*

"Another successful light, sexy contemporary romance from Shalvis, with storytelling that mixes humor and emotion."
—*Kirkus Reviews*

Once in a Lifetime

"Readers will cheer."
—*Washington Post*

It Had to Be You

"Engaging writing, characters that walk straight into your heart, and a town you can't wait to revisit make this touching, hilarious tale another heart-warmer worthy of Shalvis's popular series."
—*Library Journal*

Forever and a Day

"4½ stars! Top Pick! Shalvis once again racks up a hit."
—*RT Book Reviews*

At Last

"A sexy, romantic read...What I love about Jill Shalvis's books is that she writes sexy, adorable heroes...The sexual tension is out of this world. And of course, in true Shalvis fashion, she expertly mixes in humor that has you laughing out loud."
—HeroesandHeartbreakers.com

Lucky in Love

"Shalvis pens a tale rife with the three *H*'s of romance: heat, heart, and humor. *Lucky in Love* is a down-to-the-toes charmer."
—*RT Book Reviews*

Head Over Heels

"[A] winning roller-coaster ride ... [a] touching, character-rich, laughter-laced, knockout sizzler."
—*Library Journal* (starred review)

"The Lucky Harbor series has become one of my favorite contemporary series, and *Head Over Heels* didn't disappoint ... such a fun, sexy book."
—USAToday.com

The Sweetest Thing

"A Perfect 10! Once again Jill Shalvis provides readers with a sexy, funny, hot tale."
—RomRevToday.com

"Witty, fun, and the characters are fabulous."
—FreshFiction.com

Simply Irresistible

"Hot, sweet, fun, and romantic! Pure pleasure!"
—Robyn Carr, *New York Times* bestselling author

"Heartwarming and sexy ... an abundance of chemistry, smoldering romance, and hilarious sisterly antics."
—*Publishers Weekly*

My Kind of Wonderful

JILL SHALVIS

GRAND CENTRAL
PUBLISHING

NEW YORK   BOSTON

Copyright © 2015 by Jill Shalvis
Excerpt from *Nobody But You* copyright © 2015 by Jill Shalvis

Grand Central Publishing
Hachette Book Group
1290 Avenue of the Americas
New York, NY 10104

www.HachetteBookGroup.com

Printed in the United States of America

OPM

First Edition: December 2015
10 9 8 7 6 5 4 3 2 1

Grand Central Publishing is a division of Hachette Book Group, Inc.
The Grand Central Publishing name and logo is a trademark of Hachette Book Group, Inc.

The Hachette Speakers Bureau provides a wide range of authors for speaking events. To find out more, go to www.hachettespeakersbureau.com or call (866) 376-6591.

The publisher is not responsible for websites (or their content) that are not owned by the publisher.

My Kind of Wonderful

Chapter 1

The wind whistled through the high Colorado Rocky Mountain peaks, stirring up a dusting of snow as light as the powdered sugar on the donut that Hudson Kincaid was stuffing into his face as he rode the ski lift.

Breakfast of champions, and in three minutes when he hit the top of Cedar Ridge, he'd have the adrenaline rush to go with it. As head of ski patrol, he'd already had his daily before-the-asscrack-of-dawn debriefing with his crew. They'd set up the fencing and ropes to keep skiers in the proper runs and safe. They'd checked all the sleds to make sure their equipment was in working order.

Now he had time for one quick run before they ran rescue drills for a few hours, and then he was on to a board meeting—aka fight with his siblings. One run, ten glorious minutes to himself, and he was going to make it Devil's Face, the most challenging on the mountain.

Go big or go home. That was the Kincaid way.

Just then the radio at his hip chirped news about a

report of someone in trouble at the top of Devil's Face, and Hud shook his head.

So much for a few minutes to himself.

Ah, well, it was the life, his life, and he'd chosen it. At the top of the lift, he hit the snow at a fast clip. He'd seen a lot here on their mountain and even more on his monthly shifts as a cop in town. It was safe to say that not much surprised him anymore.

So when three minutes later he found a girl sitting just off center at the top of Devil's Face, her skis haphazardly stuck into the snow at her side, he didn't even blink.

Her down jacket was sunshine yellow, her helmet cherry red. She sat with her legs pulled up to her chest, her chin on her knees, wearing ski boots as neon green as neon green could get and staring contemplatively at the heart-stopping view in front of her.

Hud stopped a few feet away so as to not startle her, but she didn't budge. He looked around to make sure this was the person of interest. Sharp, majestic snow-covered peaks in a three-hundred-sixty-degree vista. Pine-scented air so pure that at this altitude it hurt to breathe. There was no one else up here. They were on top of the world.

Not smart on her part. The weather had been particularly volatile lately. Right now it was clear as a bell and a crisp thirty degrees, but that could change in a blink. High winds were forecasted, as was another foot of snow by midnight. But even if a storm wasn't due to move in, no one should ski alone. And especially no one should ski alone on Devil's Face, a thirty-five-hundred-foot vertical run that required a great deal of skill and in return promised dizzying speeds. There was a low margin for error up here where one little mistake could mean a trip to the ER.

Even Hud didn't ski alone. He had staff all over this place—a few of them at the ski patrol outpost only a few hundred yards away, another group at the ski lift he'd just left, even more patrolling the resort boundaries—all of them connected to each other by constant radio contact.

"Hey," he called out. "You okay?"

Nothing.

Hud glided on his skis the last few feet between them and touched her shoulder.

She jerked and craned her neck, at the same time pulling off her helmet and yanking out her earbuds. Tinny music burst out from them loud enough to make him wonder if she still had any hearing at all.

"Sorry," she said. "Did you say something?"

Not a girl but a woman, and without her helmet, Hud realized he'd actually seen her before. Earlier that morning she'd been in the parking lot, sitting on the back bumper of her car and pulling on her ski boots, all while singing along with the radio to the new Ed Sheeran song. He couldn't tell now behind her dark sunglasses, but he knew she had eyes the color of today's azure sky and that she shouldn't give up her day job to become a singer because she couldn't hold a tune. "I asked if you're okay," he said.

She removed her sunglasses and gave him a sassy look that said the question was ridiculous.

She'd worn a tight ski cap beneath her helmet, also cherry red, with no hair visible and enough layers of clothing that she was utterly shapeless. But that didn't matter. Her bright eyes sparkled with something that looked a whole lot like the best kind of trouble.

He'd been running ski patrol for years now and had been a cop for long enough that he was good at reading

people, often before they said a word. It was all in the posture, in the little tells, he'd learned.

Such as all the layers she wore. Yes it was winter, and
yes it was the Rocky Mountains, but thirty degrees was
downright balmy compared with last week's mid-teens.
Most likely she wasn't from around here.

And then there was the slightly unsure posture that said
she was at least a little bit out of her element and knew it.
Her utter lack of wariness told him something else, too, that
probably wherever she'd come from, it hadn't been a big city.

None of which explained why she was sitting alone on
one of the toughest mountains in the country. Maybe . . .
dumped by a boyfriend after a fight on the lift? Separated
from a pack of girlfriends and just taking a quick break?
Hell, despite appearances, maybe she was some kind of a
daredevil out here on a bet or whim.

Or maybe she was simply a nut job. As he knew,
nut jobs came in all shapes and sizes, even mysterious
cuties with heart-stopping eyes. "So are you?" he asked.
"Okay?"

Her smile faded some. "Do I not look okay?"

Hud had a sister and a mom, so he recognized a trick
question when he heard one and knew better than to touch
it with a ten-foot pole. Instead, he swept his gaze over her
but saw no visible injuries. Then again, he couldn't see
much given all the layers. "You're not hurt."

"No, that's not the problem." She paused. "I guess
you're probably wondering what is the problem."

"Little bit," he admitted.

She rolled her eyes. "Did you know that people who don't
understand ski maps, or maps at all, shouldn't ski alone?"

"*No one* should ski alone," he said, but then her words

sank in and he pulled off his sunglasses and stared at her in incredulous disbelief. "Are you saying you're on Devil's Face, the most challenging run on this mountain, because you misread the ski map?"

She bit her lip and tried to hide a rueful smile, which didn't matter because her expressive eyes gave her away. "I realize this is going to make me look bad," she said, "but yes. Yes, I'm here because I misread the map. If you must know the truth, I had it upside down."

Upside down. Jesus. "We color-code the things, you know. Even upside down, green is still for beginners, blue for intermediate—"

"Well, I know that much!"

"This run is black—a double-diamond expert," he said. "It's marked all over the place." He pointed to a sign three feet away.

CAUTION: DOUBLE DIAMOND. EXPERTS ONLY!

"I saw that," she said. "Hence my thinking position because trust me, I wasn't about to be stupid on top of stupid."

He let out a low laugh. "Good to know."

"And you should also know that I'm not a complete beginner. I've taken ski lessons before, at Breckenridge." She grimaced. "Though it's been a while."

"How long is a while?"

She bit her lower lip. "Longer than I want to admit. I thought it'd be like getting on a bike. Turns out, not so much. But if it helps, I realized my mistake right away and I really was just taking in the view. I mean, look at it . . ." She gestured to the gorgeous scenery in front of her, the stuff of postcards and wishes and dreams. "It's mind-boggling, don't you think?"

The wonder in her gaze mesmerized him. A little surprised at himself, he turned to take in the view with her, trying to see it through her eyes. The towering peaks had a way of putting things into perspective and reminding you that you weren't the biggest and baddest. A blanket of fresh snow stretched as far as the eye could see, glistening wherever the sun hit it like it'd been dusted with diamonds.

She was right when she said it was mind-boggling. He tried to never take this place for granted, but the truth was that he did. Interesting that it'd taken a pretty stranger to shake him out of his routine and make him notice his surroundings. He turned his head and met her gaze. Yeah. He was definitely noticing his surroundings.

She smiled into his eyes. "I figured after I got my fill of the view, I'd just head back to the ski lift and ask if I could ride it down. No harm, no foul, right? But then came problem number two."

"Which is ... ?" he asked when she didn't continue.

"I broke my binding, and while I've got lots of stuff in all these pockets, I'm not packing any tools. I think I just need a screwdriver or something. I thought I'd locate a ski patroller."

"I am ski patrol," he said.

Looking surprised, she ran her gaze up and down the length of him. Usually when a woman did such a thing it was with a light of lust in her eyes, but she didn't seem overly impressed.

He looked down at himself. "I'm not in my patrol jacket," he said. "I was hot from putting up the fencing..." Why the hell was he defending himself? Shaking his head, he removed his skis and walked to hers. He laid out the one she pointed to and took a look. Yep, she'd broken a binding. "The hinge failed," he said.

She crouched next to him and the scent of her soap or perfume came to him, a light, sexy scent that made him turn his head and look at her.

But what held his interest were those baby blues. They were wide and fathomless, and he found himself utterly unable to look away.

As if maybe she was every bit as transfixed as he, she blinked slowly. "Can we fix it?"

We? "I could rig it enough to get you down the mountain if I had a piece of wire." He pulled out his radio. "I'll just call for—"

"Oh, I've got it." She rose and pulled a small notebook from one of her pockets. Attached to it was a paper clip. She pulled it loose and waved it proudly. "I've a piece of wire right here, see?"

"Nice." He took the paperclip, straightened it, then used it to thread through the binding and twisted it in place. During the entire two minutes this took, she remained hunkered at his side, leaning over his arm, her soft, warm breath against his neck, taking in everything he did.

She sucked in a breath. "You're . . ."

When she didn't finish the sentence, he turned his head and watched her gaze drop to his mouth, which was only a few inches from hers.

"Handy," she finished softly.

"And you're . . ."

She smiled. "Stubborn? Annoying?"

"Set to go," he said.

She laughed and he smiled. "I'll help you back to the lift," he said.

"Oh, I'm good now, thanks to you." Rising, she nudged her ski into place so that she could secure her boot into it. She struggled with that for a minute, unable to snap her ski in, the effort causing her arms to tremble a little bit.

Hud started forward but she stopped him with a raised hand and he checked himself.

Ski number two took her longer because she had a balance problem. He lasted until she started to fall over and then all bets were off. Again he moved toward her but at the last second she managed to catch herself on her pole. When she finally clicked that second ski in, she lifted her head and flashed him a triumphant smile, like she'd just climbed a mountain.

"Got it!" she said, beaming, swiping at her brow like maybe she was sweating now. "See? I'm good."

"You were right about the stubborn," he said. "But not the annoying."

"Well, you haven't given me enough time." And with another flashing smile, she pushed off on her poles.

In the wrong direction.

Hud caught her by the back of her jacket. Even with all those layers, she was surprisingly light. Light enough that he could easily spin her around and face her in the right direction, which was a hundred and eighty degrees from where she'd started.

She laughed and damn, she really did have a great laugh, one that invited a man right in to laugh along with her. "Right," she said, patting him on the chest. "Thanks. *Now* I'm good."

At his hip, his radio was buzzing. His guys were checking in, getting ready for their high- and low-angle rope rescue drills. Hud was supposed to run the exercise, but he wanted to make sure the woman got safely on the lift first.

"Sounds like you have to go," she said.

"I do." But when he didn't move, her brows went up. "You're cute," she said. "But you do know that even an intelligent person can screw up reading a map, right? That despite whatever it looks like, I really don't need a keeper."

Wait a minute. Did she just call him *cute*? He'd never once in his life been called cute.

Taking in his expression she laughed, like he was funny. "It was a compliment," she said.

Not in his book. His radio crackled again. Dispatch this time, making sure he'd located the "troubled" skier. "I've got her," he confirmed, eyes narrowed in on the skier in question. "It's handled."

The dispatcher went on to fill him in on two other incidents. Hud told her how to deal with them both and then replaced the radio on his hip.

"Okay," his wayward skier said. "I stand corrected. You're not cute. You're kinda badass with all that bossy 'tude. Happy now?"

Happy? More like dizzy. "Let's just get you to the lift," he said. Calm. Authoritative. The same tone that people usually listened and responded to.

Usually...

"I'm good now," she said, and with a wave pushed off on her poles, thankfully heading directly toward the ski lift.

Not surprisingly, she wasn't all that steady. This was because she kept her knees locked instead of bending them, incorrectly putting her weight on the backs of her

skis. Whoever had given her those lessons at Breckenridge should be fired.

But she hadn't asked him for tips. And he no longer
worked at the ski school.

She'd be fun to teach, though. The thought came unbidden and he shrugged it off. All he cared about was that
she was on the right path now, leaving him free to take
Devil's Face hard and fast the way he'd wanted.

Except…Her helmet lay in the snow at his feet, forgotten. He had no idea how anyone could forget the eye-
popping cherry-red thing against the white snow, but
she had.

And so had he, when he rarely forgot anything. It
was those pretty eyes, that sweet yet mischievous laugh,
both distracting as hell. "Hey," he called after her. "Your
helmet."

But she must have put her earbuds back in because she
didn't stop or turn back.

Hud scooped up the helmet and, giving Devil's Face
one last longing look, headed toward the lift as well,
catching up with her halfway there.

She'd stopped and had her weight braced on her poles.
Bent over a little bit, she was huffing and puffing, out of
breath. They were at well over eight thousand feet and
altitude could be a bitch. It affected everyone differently,
but breathlessness was the most common side effect.

Although an uncomfortable and worrisome thought
came to him that maybe it wasn't the altitude at all. When
he'd lifted her before, she'd been light, almost…frail.
People didn't realize it took a lot of strength and stamina
to ski, and he was nearly positive she didn't have either.
He put a hand on her shoulder.

She whirled to face him, saw the helmet dangling off his finger, and pulled out an earbud with an apologetic smile. "Sorry, I think the altitude's getting to me. I really should've gotten some caffeine down me before facing the mountain." She slid on the helmet. "Thanks, Prince Charming."

"Huh?"

"You know, Cinderella," she said. "The prince had her slipper and you had my helmet... Never mind," she said with a pat to his arm when he just stared at her. "Ignore me. Probably I should've put far more practical things on my list than skiing in the Rockies."

And then before he could ask her what the hell she was talking about now, she'd tightened the strap beneath her chin, put her hands back into the handholds at the top of her ski poles, and pushed off.

He watched her head for the lift that would carry her back to safety, thinking two things. One, he really hoped she knew how to stop. And two, she was definitely a nut, but possibly the prettiest, most bewildering nut he'd ever met in his entire life.

Chapter 2

Bailey Moore considered it a win-win when she got herself situated on the lift without breaking another binding, falling on her face, or making a fool of herself. Especially since her concentration had been shot thanks to the mountain hottie she'd just skied away from.

Don't you dare look back, she told herself firmly. There's absolutely no reason to. Not a single one...

She totally looked back.

And there he was on his skis like they were an extension of his own body, as if the rugged badass mountains behind him had nothing on him.

He was watching her as well, or so she assumed since his dark lenses were aimed her way. She waved at him.

He didn't wave back but the very corners of his mouth turned up. Then he planted his poles, executed a lithe jump to turn his skis in the other direction, and skied off with an effortless motion that Bailey knew she could never in a million years of lessons hope to replicate. It was . . . well, incredibly sexy.

But as Bailey also knew, the sexy ones weren't the keepers. For the most part, they'd never been disappointed or hurt by love or life, and as a woman who'd faced it all at one time or another, she had no patience for the weak, shallow, or clueless.

And actually, she had no patience for this line of thinking at all. She had other things to concentrate on. Laughing a little at herself, she turned her head to take in the top of the peak as the lift carried her away from it. It had been the top, the very tippy top, and the stunning view suddenly made her glad for her map incident.

She'd never seen anything like it. Most anywhere you stood in Colorado, you were surrounded by mountains— towering, rugged, intimidating alpine peaks that you had to tip your head back to see and that always seemed to frame the entire world.

Not on Devil's Face. For the first time, *she'd* been the highest point, and everything below her—the world—was at her feet. And as someone who until very recently had never been in control of her own destiny, it staggered her.

In a really great way.

The lift hit a snag and jerked. Bailey gasped and grabbed the steel bar in front of her for all she was worth. With nothing below her but thick pines and an endless blanket of snow, she could do nothing else. There wasn't a building in sight, not even the comforting view of the base lodge.

When the lift jerked again, her hand ached from the tight grip, but she didn't let go. If she was going down, she was going down holding the sissy bar all the way. And wouldn't that be pretty effing ironic if after all she'd been through, she was about to expire right here, now, alone on a mountain?

And if by some miracle she didn't die from the fall, her mother would kill her.

But miraculously the lift held firm and she lived to breathe another day. Ten minutes later she glided off without so much as a hitch. Perfect execution, she thought proudly and looked around, really wishing Mountain Hottie could see her now, that *anyone* she knew could see her.

But nope, just her.

She'd grown up in a tiny mountain town just south of Denver, about two hours from here and though just about everyone she knew was a big skier, she was not. She'd been concentrating on other things. Today, the wind hitting her face, the sun warming her cheeks, and the feeling of being in control—for once—had all given her a small taste of what she'd wanted for herself. And after her business meeting, she hoped for a bigger taste.

Beaming, she straightened on her skis and glanced over at the base lodge. She could see the entire north-facing wall. Unlike the rest of the building, which was sided with wood and glass, gorgeous and rustic looking, the north wall was smooth stucco. Easier to maintain than wood, but plain looking and, frankly, boring.

She'd been hired by the resort's publicist to paint a mural there.

Painting was important to her, very important. She earned a living as a graphic designer, but painting reminded her of her grandma, whom she still missed so very much. One of her earliest memories was of sitting on a stool in her grandma's studio with the sketch her grandma had given her to paint. Sort of a paint-by-numbers but personalized.

Don't worry about staying inside the lines, Bailey darling... Just go for it.

That's what Bailey intended to do.

Excited, she skied—okay, plowed—her way to the lodge. Luckily it was only a hundred yards or so and relatively flat, but that meant she had to use her poles. By the time she made it to the stairs of the lodge, she was sweating and shaky. When she finally managed to release her boots from her skis, she dropped to her knees to gasp in air. Probably she should add an exercise regime to her list.

Stat.

Hand to her pounding heart, she panted for air and changed her mind. Maybe she was grateful no one could see her right now. That's when she lifted her head and... came face-to-face with Mountain Hottie. Of course, because heaven forbid she run into him two minutes ago when she'd been on her skis and looking good.

How he'd beaten her down the mountain, on his own power no less, she hadn't the foggiest. "Hey," she said, trying to act like she wasn't breathing like a locomotive on its last legs. Or dripping sweat. Staggering to her feet, she casually leaned over her poles, surreptitiously trying to catch her breath.

"Hey," he said. Not breathing like a locomotive. Not sweating. In fact, not out of breath or exerted at all, the bastard. "The binding held."

"You wouldn't have let me go if you'd thought it wouldn't," she managed.

"True." He paused. "You going to yell at me again if I want to know if you're okay?"

She managed a snort. "I didn't yell at you."

His mouth quirked a little as he stood there all wind-tousled perfection, clearly yanking her chain in his own oddly stoic way.

And in her own *not* stoic way, she kind of liked it. She straightened. "For the future, I'm always okay," she said. "So you don't have to ask me that question again."

"It's my job."

Oh. Right. Ski patrol.

"Want to tell me why you're so touchy about being asked if you're okay?"

Nope. She really didn't. It was a trigger for her, not surprising given how many times over the past ten years those three simple words—*are you okay*—had been asked of her. Now when someone brought it up, what she really heard was all the pity the words usually conveyed.

And she hated pity with the same level of loathing she saved for all creepy-crawlies, kale, and men in open-toed shoes of any kind. "Let's just say it annoys the crap out of me."

"Duly noted," he said. "Next time I'll query you about the weather. Or if you've had a real ski lesson yet."

Look at that, Man of Few Words did have a sense of humor. And she liked that. A lot. She liked *him* for some odd reason, not that *that* was going anywhere. "You have a name?"

"Hudson Kincaid. You?"

"Bailey Moore," she said as his radio went off. Without taking his eyes from her, he cocked his head and listened, then turned down the volume. "I've got to go."

Good. Maybe when he was gone she could stop making a fool of herself.

He started to turn away but then stopped and gave her one more long look. "Stay off the top."

"Sir, yes sir," she said, and saluted him.

Another smile threatened the corners of his mouth. "If only I thought you meant that," he said, and then he was gone.

Bailey let out a slow, shaky breath. What had just happened? It'd been so long since she'd had any sort of interaction she wasn't exactly sure.

Liar. That was flirtation and you started it.

And she'd liked it.

But man, she was rusty. *Sir, yes sir?* Seriously, she needed some practice being normal.

She struggled a few minutes to gather up her skis and poles into one of the long lines of ski stands.

It took a few more minutes to pull off her helmet and figure out how to lock it to her skis. Man, this sport looked so much easier on TV. Everyone always appeared to glide so effortlessly down the mountain and then carried their skis on their shoulders like it was no big deal. It really was deceiving. Still, she was challenging herself and that felt... well, amazing. She glanced at her phone to check the time and was gratified to see she was half an hour early for her meeting. She'd use it to feed the beast, which had been grumbling loudly all morning.

The cafeteria wasn't crowded, most likely due to it being a weekday. Bailey loaded a tray and sat down in a secluded corner of the place, cozied between a half wall and a huge wall of windows where she could see the incredible view.

You almost, nearly, sort of skied down that, she thought with pride. She could also see that huge blank wall, as it was one of the walls designating the outside eating area. It was protected from the elements by being half dug into the hill behind it and also a huge extended patio roof. She stared at that wall, trying to envision her mural on it.

It was going to be amazing.

She was stuffing her face, nearly moaning with pleasure because the food was incredibly good, when her phone buzzed an incoming text. Her meeting place had been changed to another address in town.

Damn.

It took her nearly half an hour just to turn in her rental skis and get to her car. By the time she drove into Cedar Ridge from the ski resort, she was already ten minutes late, but even that didn't dampen her excitement.

Hud jerked awake when his phone buzzed in his pocket. He blinked the boardroom into focus and also his siblings' faces, ranging from amused to pissed off. "Shit," he muttered.

"Yep," his sister Kenna agreed from her place across the table where, if he went by the jelly beans layered all over him, she'd been tossing them at him as he snoozed. "You fell asleep," she said. "When you opened your mouth and started snoring, I wanted to go for a bull's-eye but Gray wouldn't let me. He was afraid you'd choke."

Gray, the oldest Kincaid sibling and ruler of their universe—at least in his own mind—shrugged at Hud. "No one here wanted to take over ski patrol," he said, "so your premature death would've been annoying. We boring you?"

"Shit," Hud said again, and straightened in his chair. Hell yes, they'd bored him, right to sleep, not that he could say so and keep his teeth. But the truth was, he had two speeds—ninety miles an hour and fast asleep. "And I don't sleep with my mouth open or snore." He looked to Gray for confirmation.

Gray backed him and shook his head. Nope, Hud didn't sleep with his mouth open or snore.

Hud nodded. That's right, he didn't. He stood and... sent a waterfall of jelly beans cascading to the floor.

Kenna chortled, pleased with herself.

Realizing his phone was still buzzing, Hud pulled it from his pocket, saw the number for his mom's nurse, and immediately answered. "Is she okay?"

At the question, his siblings' easy, relaxed attitude vanished. Everyone sat straight up and watched Hud's face carefully, good humor gone.

"She's fine," Jenny, the head nurse, told Hud. "But I really think you need to take away that credit card you gave her. Carrie isn't so good with credit, as you well know."

Hud rubbed his temple at the truth of this statement. The card was for emergencies because he knew what it was like to feel stuck and helpless. But he and his mom had different ideas on the definition of "emergency." Last month she'd ordered two matching kid bikes, the exact bikes he and his identical twin Jacob had once begged her for—when they'd been eight years old. And then a week ago she'd ordered the drum set Hud had wanted for his birthday. His tenth birthday.

Kenna had commandeered the damn thing and now used it late at night to drive him crazy.

"What did she order now?" he asked Jenny.

The nurse hesitated.

Not good. Hud's mom loved the Internet and the nurses let her have Wi-Fi access because it was a great babysitter. "Jenny," he said a little tightly. "What did she buy?"

"A woman."

Following her GPS, Bailey parked in front of a building adjacent to the hospital.

A nursing/support facility.

Checking in at the front desk, she found that she was expected and was given a guest pass.

She was guided to a room where people in wheelchairs were exercising. Their instructor at the front of the room was in a wheelchair too. She wore a headband, leotard, and leg warmers and had her class rocking out to "Hit Me with Your Best Shot" by Pat Benatar.

When she caught sight of Bailey, she waved and ended the class. "That's enough for our seated Jazzercising class today, gang," she called out. "Same place tomorrow. I'm bringing Sting and Queen."

"In person?" one of the other elderly women asked hopefully.

"Unfortunately, Sting didn't return my calls and Freddie's dead, but hey, we all gotta go sometime." The teacher rolled toward Bailey and then shocked the hell out of her by standing up. "Hiya, I'm Carrie. Great to meet you."

"You're not . . . ?" Bailey gestured to the wheelchair.

"Oh no. I just teach in the chair because they're elderly. Plus they're all—" She broke off to look around and make sure no one was looking at them. "A little . . ." She circled a finger around her ear, the universal sign for crazy. "But very sweet, each of them. Well, except Tony. Don't turn your back on him, because he's got octopus hands.

Anyway, they don't all need the chairs but I insist because sometimes they fall asleep and it's less disruptive to the class to have them just nod off rather than fall over. The domino effect isn't pretty. Follow me."

Bailey followed her to a room at the end of the hall— a patient room. There, Carrie kicked off her shoes and climbed into the bed.

She was a patient here.

"Whew," Carrie said. "Nap time. But this first. You're my first choice for the Cedar Ridge project."

Bailey looked around, more than a little confused. "You're the publicist for Cedar Ridge Resort?"

"Actually..." Carrie paused. "'Publicist' might not be the exact right word."

Oh boy. Knees weak, Bailey sank into the guest chair facing the bed. "And what would be the right word exactly?"

"Mom," Carrie said.

"I don't understand."

"Cedar Ridge is family owned. It's been a rough few years for the resort and the Kincaids. We need a boost."

"Rough?" Bailey asked.

"Yes." Carrie rubbed her temple. "The details don't matter. What does matter is family. Memories. And what better way to preserve both of those things than a big picture to share with the world."

"The mural," Bailey said.

"The mural." Carrie beamed. "One big pic to depict our favorite memories to share with everyone."

"Okay," Bailey said, thinking of her own personal favorite pic, one she kept as her wallpaper on her phone. It was herself, her mom, and her grandma in her grandma's studio, all covered in paint and laughing together. "I get that. It's a memory that can't be erased with time."

"Or a brain that has a hard time locating all its files." Eyes suddenly suspiciously shiny, she knocked on the side of her own head. "Like mine."

Bailey met her gaze and felt her heart squeeze.

"And I think the people who ski at Cedar Ridge would love it," Carrie said. "A family-run resort like this one needs a centerpiece that people can talk about. Something other than the fact that the man who started the place was a deadbeat dad who mortgaged the resort to its eyeballs, couldn't keep it in his pants, and vanished on his kids."

Bailey felt her eyebrows raise. She hadn't heard this story.

Carrie reached for a small framed picture on her bed tray and handed it to Bailey.

It was of two boys, maybe eight years old. Identical twins. "My boys," Carrie said with clear adoration. "Hud just gave this to me for my birthday. You can't tell but they're actually mirror images of each other. Hud's right-handed and Jacob's left-handed. Hud's cowlick swirl on his head is clockwise, Jacob's counterclockwise. You ever hear of such a thing?"

Bailey shook her head. She knew next to nothing about being a mom, much less twins.

Carrie smiled but it faded quickly. "For all their similarities, my boys couldn't be more different. Hud always wanted to travel the world and experience new things. Jacob's a homebody. But they're two peas in a pod in so many ways. They never even had to use words with each other."

Past tense, Bailey thought.

"I know this painting isn't going to fix us," Carrie said softly, "or even put them back together. I'm not that far gone to believe in miracles. But I want to help. I need to help."

"And you think a mural will do that?" Bailey asked quietly.

"It will remind all of them of what once was," Carrie said. "That they are the most whole when they're together."

"That's a tall order for a mural," Bailey said.

"I know, but some of this is my fault," Carrie said. "Hud and Jacob fought and now Jacob's gone and Hud has all these regrets. And because of it, he pushes away the people he cares about most. He's good at it too. I'm their mom, Bailey. I have to do this for them. Please say you'll be the one to help me do this for them."

Bailey knew a little something about regrets. Or a lot. But this whole thing was way out of her wheelhouse.

"I promise I'm not crazy," Carrie said, and then grimaced. "Well, okay, so I'm a *little* crazy. But that has nothing to do with this. I saw your boards on Pinterest. You've done some beautiful work."

Maybe, but up until now Bailey's painting had been for herself, given to friends and family. None of her paintings was bigger than a bedroom wall, nothing commissioned, and nothing as big as the wall at the resort. She'd been painting by night in her grandma's memory for years because it brought her grandma, whom she missed with all her heart and soul, back to life in her mind. She'd been doing that while working as a graphic artist by day for her bread and butter. "You know that this would be my first mural," Bailey said. "Right?"

Carrie nodded. "Yes, but I figured it was just math, right?"

Bailey choked out a laugh. "Well, yeah, in theory..."

"That's good enough for me." Carrie reached for Bailey's hand. "The resort needs this. The kids need this. I need this, and I'm getting the sense that maybe you do too."

This woman had two young boys, one who'd possibly died and one locked in grief. Truly awful. She gently squeezed Carrie's fingers, having no doubt in her mind that Carrie and her young son Hud indeed needed this.

But did Bailey?

Given that for the last ten years, her sole focus had been on staying alive... Okay, yes, she wanted this, but that wasn't a reason to give in to the very nice but possibly very crazy lady. But Bailey liked the idea of helping people. Was this the right way to go about it, though? One thing she'd learned after all she'd been through—there were options, always. Her doctor had taught her that, offering her choices at every roadblock they'd hit. This was an option and an opportunity.

"Say yes," Carrie said, clasping her hands in front of her hopefully. "Say you'll do this to help my boys."

"Your boys don't need any help," a male voice said. A smooth yet gravelly voice, and Bailey froze before slowly turning to face...

Mountain Hottie.

Chapter 3

Hud had been surprised when he'd gotten to his mom's room to hear her talking about him and Jacob. Then he'd heard the actual words and he'd stopped short.

She felt that what had happened between him and Jacob was her fault.

Her sadness and regret pummeled at him and wrenched him back to a time he didn't want to think about. What had happened wasn't her fault, not by a long shot.

It was his.

The fight with Jacob had been the worst day of Hud's life, and that was saying something since there'd been a few doozies before and since. But that day Hud had said things to his brother, things that couldn't be taken back, and he knew he could never make it right between them again.

That was his cross to bear. Not his mom's. But apparently she didn't see it that way. Just as she didn't see him as a grown man. In her eyes, he was still a child. That wasn't her fault either. It was the dementia. Just the thought had his chest tightening. She'd been through so much, and apparently life wasn't done messing with her yet.

Nor him. Because the woman sitting at his mom's side was no other than the pretty cherry-red–capped skier from the resort. Bailey. Hud stepped into the room and looked at his mom. She was sitting up, dressed, wearing lip gloss and smiling. For a quick beat, he stared at her, so relieved he couldn't get a word out. She looked good today. Happy. Even playful—although that *never* boded well for him. "Mom," he murmured affectionately, and bent to kiss her cheek.

"Hey, baby," she murmured back, cupping his cheek. "Did you do your homework already?"

Ignoring that, he turned to Bailey and lifted a brow.

To her credit, she met his gaze head-on. "Hello again," she said with an easy smile.

"You two know each other?" his mom asked in delight.

"We met on the mountain earlier," Hud said.

"He rescued me," Bailey said, eyes smiling into Hud's. "Fixed my ski."

"Well that makes this even better," Carrie said. "She's an artist. I hired her to paint a mural. For you, Hud."

Because he hadn't taken his eyes off the woman in the chair, he watched her blink in surprise and her mouth fall open in shock.

"Wait," she said slowly, dividing a gaze between Hud and his mom. "You're her son? But you're not—"

He gave a small shake of his head and she broke off from finishing her sentence. *But you're not a little boy...*

Nope. "Mom, we've gone over this," he said quietly.

"You can't just hire people over the Internet, okay? They might not be what you think and you could get ripped off."

"Bailey's not going to rip me off," his mom said, frowning. "And you're being incredibly rude. Sit down. You're growing like a weed. You're so tall you're giving me a neck kink."

Hud didn't budge.

His mom sighed. "I don't know which of you is more stubborn, you or Jacob."

Hud knew. It was Jacob. By far.

"Well if you're not going to sit, at least stop looking like you're out for blood," his mom said. "*I* sought *her* out. *I* hired *her*."

"And now we un-hire her," he said. He looked at Bailey. "How much?"

She narrowed her eyes at him, sparks practically coming out her pretty ears. "I wouldn't take your money."

"I've seen her work on the Internet, Hud," his mom said. "She's decorated nurseries for babies. She did this magical forest in someone's nursery and it was…" She sighed in wonder. "Well, magical."

Hud turned to Bailey. Her smile was unguarded, easy. Contagious. And then there was her gaze, deep enough for a man to drown in. And in that single heartbeat, he felt the same urge he'd felt the first time he'd seen her. The urge to pull her in and stare into those eyes. They had something, he thought. An inexplicable chemistry. Sparks—and not coming out her ears this time but instead bouncing between them. "Mom, we're not in the market for a mural at the resort right now." Then he again turned to Bailey. "A word?"

"Sure." She got up and, at his gesture, went ahead of him. She was still in her snow gear, minus the red helmet and the sunshine-yellow ski jacket. Without the bulky parka, she was a tiny thing. Bailey was petite and, as he'd suspected, a little fragile looking. Her patterned ski pants were cargo-style with a lot of clear pockets that she'd filled. A packet of tissues. A baggie of nuts. A lip balm... He was still staring at the stuff and absolutely not at her sweet little ass when she turned to face him in the hallway and... arched a sassy brow.

He laughed low in his throat but it was at himself. "You can see why this can't happen."

"That's more than a word," she said.

Smartass. And hell, he loved a smartass, but he couldn't joke, not about this. "You can see she's not well," he said. "And even if she was, there's no budget for a mural."

"Yes, I get that she has problems." She hugged herself and looked away. "We all do. But don't worry, because if I do this, I won't accept payment for it. I've already got a paying job Monday through Friday, but I could be here on the weekends. All I'd need is room and board, like any of your other seasonal employees. It shouldn't take more than two months to get the mural done right."

The words *two* and *months* stuck in Hud's brain. That was a hell of a long time to have her around.

"Oh, that's a *wonderful* idea," his mom called out from her room.

Hud's stomach sank because, hell no, it wasn't a wonderful idea. Having to see this sexy adorable whirlwind for the next two months of weekends was the *opposite* of a wonderful idea. He leaned past Bailey—who still smelled so good he nearly pushed his face into her neck—and pulled his mom's door shut.

"Fine," she yelled from behind it. "But don't think you can sneak anything by me! No funny business, Hudson Kincaid. You still can't date until you're old enough to shave!"

Hud closed his eyes for a beat and then opened them to find Bailey's gaze on his, her own filled with concern.

Not pity.

He had to give it to her, he definitely appreciated that.

"She's pretty amazing," she said quietly. "And she loves you very much."

"Yeah." He scrubbed a hand down his face because, damn, she was just as sweet as she looked. "Look, I'll pay your expenses for today, okay? Just invoice me. I get that you've been through a tough time but—"

Her eyes narrowed slightly. "You get nothing."

He paused and considered his words carefully. "I meant because my mom dragged you up here."

"Oh." Looking slightly mollified, she nodded. "But the answer is still no."

"No?" he repeated.

"No, I'm not going to invoice you for my time," she said just as an orderly came down the hall pushing a cart filled with supplies. This forced Bailey to back up and give the guy room to get by, which was fine except she backed right into Hud, pressing him between the wall and her soft, warm, curvy body.

"Sorry," she whispered, stepping on his toe and bumping her sweet ass into his crotch. "Sorry—"

He stilled her with his hands on her hips, holding her there until the orderly had passed.

The sound of her sucking in air filled his ears, along with blood rushing through him at the full body contact.

When she could, she stepped clear and turned to face him, her eyes filled with awareness and shock.

Join my club, he thought.

"Okay, then," she finally said, looking more than a little dazed. "I'm just going to go. Please tell your mom it was lovely to meet her."

And then she was gone, leaving him to let out a low laugh. Clearly it hadn't been lovely to meet him. For some reason that little crystal clear snub kept him smiling to himself for the rest of the day.

Two days later Bailey was in her office—the living room of her apartment—staring at her two large computer screens and trying to finish up a job for a local health-food store. She'd been commissioned to create a new logo that would go on everything from T-shirts to menus to coasters. The job had been a huge coup and she'd been hugely excited when she'd landed it over several other, bigger graphic design companies.

But all she could think about was the resort, specifically one Hudson Kincaid, and how his lean, hard, hot body had been pressed up against hers. She could still feel his warmth and strength...

She'd ordered supplies for the mural, which she'd assured herself had nothing to do with Hudson.

And she'd meant it when she'd told him she wouldn't be invoicing him. In spite of the fact that she was—and would be for a long time to come—digging out of medical debt, she was doing this one pro bono. She was doing it for Carrie, the woman who maybe couldn't keep her mind straight but loved her boys so very much.

Because it absolutely was *not* for Mr. Tall, Dark, and Sexy Grumpy Ass.

Bailey glanced over at the small picture of her grandma on her desk and smiled. "And maybe it's also a little bit for you," she said, blowing a kiss to the woman she missed every single day.

Behind her, the front door opened. A heartbeat later, two hands settled on her shoulders and a mouth brushed a kiss into her hair. "You're tense." Fingers gently kneaded the knots. "You should take a break."

With a sigh she turned to face Aaron, and his handsome face creased into a smile.

"I don't need a break," she said. "And what are you doing here?"

"You usually nap in the afternoons," he said. "I just wanted to see if you needed anything."

She did her best to hold back the temper because he was right. For years she'd napped in the afternoons because she'd barely had the energy or stamina to make it through the day. "I haven't napped in months."

"You're pale, you're tense, and you've got shadows under your eyes," he said.

"Aw. You say the nicest things." She turned back to her computers, uncomfortable with her conflicting emotions, which had her torn between hugging him and strangling him.

"Bailey, honey, we both know you went back to work too soon. You're pushing yourself too hard—"

"Aaron, stop."

"Just because you dumped me doesn't mean we're no longer friends," he said.

He said this mildly. He said everything mildly. Just as he'd loved her mildly. She knew she owed him, that she should be grateful for all he'd done for her, and she truly was.

But she had so many emotions swirling through her at all times, wild uncontrolled emotions, and sometimes she resented that he didn't.

"Don't ask me to watch you run yourself into the ground," he said quietly.

"I'm not asking you to do anything." She took her hands off the keyboard, mostly to resist the urge to chuck it at his head—a terrible thought and a terrible instinct that she hated herself for—as she slowly turned to face the first and only man she'd ever loved.

She'd fallen for him on her first day of ninth grade. She'd just had her first chemo treatment for non-Hodgkin's lymphoma and had been feeling sick, but she'd refused to miss the first day of school. One hour into biology, staring at the slide on the big screen in front of the classroom showing a dissected frog, and she knew she wasn't going to make it out of there in time.

She tossed her lunch and what felt like her guts...right into Aaron's backpack as he held it open for her, somehow managing to hold her hair back as well.

He'd been holding her hair back ever since. Metaphorically. But God, how she wished that he'd show her an emotion, any emotion other than empathy and pity. She'd wasted a lot of time yearning for that.

Too much time.

Wanting him to stop treating her like a piece of fragile glass that might shatter, wanting him to be wildly passionate about...something, anything. Yearning to see him express a strong feeling, even temper.

Aching for him to grab her and take her against the wall . . .

"How about lunch?" he asked.

"Ex-fiancés don't do lunch."

"Maybe not, but you're not just my ex-fiancée," he pointed out.

Their eyes met, his revealing uncertainty. He wasn't sure if they were still friends, not after what she'd witnessed a month ago.

He'd tried to discuss it with her but she'd refused.

What he did, *who* he did, was no longer any of her business.

Then he caught sight of what was spread out on her second screen—a draft of the mural.

"What's that?" he asked.

"I've been commissioned to paint a mural up at Cedar Ridge," she said, and watched him calculate the two-hour travel distance from Denver to Cedar Ridge. Watched as he started to shake his head.

"Not your call," she said. "I plan to do this."

"Does your plan include running yourself into the ground then? Because that's what will happen if you work twenty-four-seven." He softened, his voice gentle. "Honey, you still have to take care of yourself."

"I know that," she said. God, did he think she didn't? "I realize I cheated death, Aaron. I get that. And because of it, I'm going to live like there's no tomorrow. The cancer isn't going to come back, because I won't let it. But if the worst happens and it manages to win in spite of everything, well then at least I'll have lived."

"Bailey—"

"I know what I'm doing," she said, and hoped that was true.

Maybe Aaron and her mom didn't, wouldn't, understand, but she knew this was the right thing. Yes, for Carrie and her sons, but also for herself.

She left before the crack of dawn on Saturday morning for Cedar Ridge and got lucky with good weather and clear roads. She parked in the ski lot and made her way to the lodge to take measurements of the wall.

It was a sunny and clear day, and according to her phone it was thirty-two degrees. But the early morning wind put a chill in the air, making it sharp and almost painful to draw into her lungs.

She loved it. Closing her eyes, she tilted her head back and let the high-altitude sun warm her face. From a distance she heard the *swish-swish* of skis on the snow.

The lifts were running but not open to the public for another fifteen minutes. She'd been watching ski patrol put up roped fencing lining the ski runs and around the lifts to manage lines, though she hadn't seen Hudson. The few skiers on the slopes were staff as well, and her eyes had caught on one in particular carving his way down the mountain like he was one with his skis.

Hudson.

She couldn't tell for sure, of course, but the set to his shoulders reminded her of him.

And then there was the way her heart started pounding.

She had no idea what this odd hyperawareness of him meant. She was hoping it was nothing but simple orgasm withdrawal.

Because orgasm withdrawal she could handle on her own.

Probably.

Maybe.

Okay, so the truth was she didn't know for sure. She had not exactly felt sexual in a very long time, but she'd like to think that would come back now that she had a new lease on life.

A life—period.

Chapter 4

The following weekend, Hud stuffed some food down and pushed himself back out on the mountain. It was a busy day and they needed to all stay alert and awake. Just yesterday, two hormone-driven twenty-year-olds had decided to have sex on one of the ski lifts. Because they were also idiots, they'd left the safety bar up and the lift operator hadn't noticed.

A gust of wind had come along and swept the poor pantsless girl off the lift, down thirty feet onto a— luckily—soft berm of snow. She'd lived, though she'd do so with a broken leg and frostbite in some pretty private places. Her boyfriend, of course, hadn't fallen, retained *his* pants, and reportedly broke up with her in the hospital due to the humiliation.

The story had made the news, but that wouldn't scare anyone off from trying out other ridiculous stunts. In fact, they could count on the opposite.

Now he was patrolling the mountain, skiing hard and

fast, pushing himself because it felt good to do so. He felt his phone vibrate from the depths of his pocket. Stopping on the edge of the run, he pulled out the phone and saw the ID. "You okay?" he asked his mom in lieu of a greeting.

"Of course, sweetheart. Just wanted to know if you cleaned your room yet."

He pinched the bridge of his nose. An hour earlier he'd taken a call from Max, an old friend who'd been in the army and was doing some snooping on Jacob for Hud. Not too long ago they'd gotten intel that Jacob's unit had taken enemy fire with injuries, but nothing more. No details. Max had reported that it appeared Jacob had been among the injured but had gone back to his tour of duty in Iraq, so all had to be well now.

Or relatively well.

Hud had been losing his collective shit worrying about his brother. The news that Jacob had to be okay enough to stay with his unit was good, but he didn't have the bandwidth for anything else to happen today.

"Well?" his mom asked. "Did you? Or did you just shove all your stuff under your bed again and call it good?" She laughed. "I'm onto you, you know."

"I know," he said, letting out a long breath and staring out into the early morning. A storm was moving in. Half the sky was a clear, crisp blue, and the other half dark and gray, the clouds churning like his gut. "Mom, I'm at work—"

"I don't mean to bother you. I just wanted to tell you that she's a good girl. I know you don't trust her, but I do. And you can. Or at least try."

He could usually keep up with the quick subject

changes, but she'd just lost him. She could be talking about anyone from his third-grade teacher to a random nurse at her home to an actress on TV. His mom mixed up days and years, and she mixed up reality with TV and books, so he waited for a hint.

"It seems like she's had a hard time," she went on. "I think she's just looking for something to give her some joy. So you see, having her paint the mural will give *all* of us joy."

Nope, not his third-grade teacher or an actress on TV. Bailey, the woman he'd given far too much thought to all week long. "Mom—"

"She's very special, Hudson. You need to treat her right. Now I know your daddy didn't show you how to do that but I certainly did."

He inhaled a deep breath. "I've got to go. I'll call you later—"

"You with Jacob working the lifts? I know you love it up there, that you're saving your money up to roam the world when you graduate, but don't forget, baby, school always comes first, before the resort."

"I know." Yeah, they wouldn't even have the resort if it hadn't been for their dad, but perversely they wouldn't be in danger of losing it now for the same reason.

Back in the day, Richard Kincaid, sole proprietor of the then very small Cedar Ridge Resort, had taken advantage of a sweet, innocent eighteen-year-old Carrie on a business trip to Jackson Hole. And when the stick had turned blue, he'd made himself scarce.

They'd later learned he'd had a good reason for that. The man already had a family. This hadn't stopped him from spawning a total of five children, though, to whom he'd left his Cedar Ridge Resort when he'd run off on all of them—but not before secretly mortgaging it to its eyeballs. He wasn't exactly a role model.

Hud and Jacob had been left to raise themselves *and* their mom—who'd started exhibiting erratic behavior early on, like forgetting to make sure the boys ate and went to school. Then things had fallen apart so completely that Carrie, Jacob, and he had come to Cedar Ridge for help from Char, Aidan and Gray's mom.

At twelve, Hud had thought he'd known everything he needed to know. And what he'd known was that he, Jacob, and Carrie were a tight unit of three that nothing could break. But Carrie had needed to go into a care facility and Char had gladly taken them in.

Suddenly Hud and Jacob hadn't had to worry about getting them or their mom fed. Or how they'd get to school. Char worried about all of that for them, mothering the hell out of them while she was at it.

It'd been... freeing. And Hud had immediately fallen in love with Colorado, with the mountain. With his half siblings. With Char. With everything. He'd loved it all, and even though he and Jacob had made a pact to get the hell out as soon as they turned eighteen, Hud had always known that he wouldn't want to leave.

That he'd never want to leave.

He and Jacob had taken jobs at the resort when they turned fifteen, starting out at the bottom as lift operators. Not a bad gig for two punk-ass kids who'd had a good time watching hot girls coming and going.

The best few years of Hud's life. But eighteen had come all too quickly, and then the fight of all fights with Jacob.

"Don't forget to get home in time for supper," his mom

said, bringing him back to the here and now. "I'm cooking up something special."

She'd never cooked. For as far back as Hud could remember, he and Jacob had put together whatever meals they'd eaten. Actually, he'd put together the meals and Jacob had taken care of the house the best he could.

And to make Carrie feel better about it, Hud had always promised her it was "something special," which usually meant he'd tossed together whatever shit he managed to scrape up. Hud remembered lots of ramen and even more apples and peanut butter.

Throat oddly tight, Hud squeezed his eyes shut and tried to dispel the images before they opened the door to more painful memories. "Gotta go, Mom."

"Love you, baby," she said, and disconnected.

Hud shoved his phone away and took a second to get his head together. It was the second Saturday in January, which meant high season. By noon they'd reach full capacity—great for the strained bank account of the resort, great for the shops and cafeteria, and all the other businesses in town.

It was great for everyone who didn't have to manage a mountain full to the brim with people in day-off mode, which meant a lot of them had short-circuited all good sense and were accidents waiting to happen.

It was the reason that ski patrol was the biggest division on the mountain, and the highest staffed. And that staff all had to be highly trained for . . . well, anything.

It was a high-stress job, but one Hud wouldn't trade for anything. Maybe once upon a time he'd dreamed of traveling the world but that hadn't happened. He was happy here. He got to be on the mountain, and between that and being a cop ten shifts a month, he made enough that he was able to help keep his mom in a place that was good to her and safe. He also got to be with his crazy-ass siblings.

All except for one, anyway.

He was thinking about that, about Jacob, when he caught the flash of a cherry-red knit cap at the bottom near the lodge. He tried to focus in but the sun slanted over the peaks and right into his eyes.

He shook his head. What was he thinking? Bailey wasn't here. She had no reason to be here. Clearly he was tired. He and his team were scattered across the mountain and had been since oh-dark-thirty o'clock. They'd been avalanche training, which was exhausting. He had a break coming at ten and he was looking forward to taking it stretched out on the floor of his office.

So naturally a call came in over his radio. A snowboarder had just crashed into a tree on White Chute. From where he stood halfway down Home Run, Hudson was closest, with fellow patroller Mitch right on his heels.

They cut through the trees due east, across the runs Stagecoach and Comstock, and came out on White Chute.

"If we made a YouTube video of someone hitting a tree in slo-mo, complete with the sound effects of the head going *splat*, we'd cut these incidents in half," Mitch said as the two of them navigated the rough terrain with the ease that years on this mountain had given them.

Mitch was a friend of the family. Like Aidan, he worked at the resort and was also a firefighter in the off season. He was also possibly the world's second-biggest smartass.

Right behind Hud himself. "Can't do that," Hud said,

ducking a low-lying branch and snorting when Mitch didn't duck fast enough and caught it across his helmet. "Our lawyer nixed it. Said it was bad promo."

They found the snowboarder sitting at the base of a tree halfway down White Chute, bookended by two buddies. Their guy was clutching his leg, not his head—a good sign. Another was that he'd remained conscious.

Hud dropped to his knees at the guy's side. Mitch was on the radio, directing the patrollers on their way with a sled to get the guy down the mountain if that was needed.

"I'm going to die," the guy said to Hud.

"You're not going to die," Hud said, visually assessing the situation. No visible injuries—which meant zip. "What's your name?"

"Sean."

"Okay, Sean, can you let go of your leg?"

"No." Sean shook his head, pale and waxy.

His friends looked the same so Hud didn't know if they were skiing on hangovers or if something was really wrong. "I'm going to open your boot," he said.

"Dude, no!" Sean shook his head vehemently. "If you take off my boot, my leg's going to fall off!"

Hud and Mitch exchanged a look. Sean and his buddies all had a certain scent to them that said they'd been smoking weed. Apparently they'd skipped the munchies and gone straight to paranoia. "I'll be very careful," Hud assured Sean.

"It's okay," Mitch told him. "Hud here hardly ever has legs fall off on his watch."

Hud had been very carefully loosening the guy's boot to get a look while Mitch spoke. And...shit. Sean had a compound fracture and it wasn't pretty. Blood had filled his boot.

"I'm going to die, right?" the guy asked, panicked, breathing erratically.

Hud met Mitch's gaze again and Mitch immediately reached for the radio. They were going to need more than just a sled. They needed a heli ride stat, straight to General Hospital Trauma Center.

"Oh, God, it's happening," Sean moaned.

"Listen to me," Hud said, leaning over him to make sure he had Sean's full attention. "You're not dying." As long as they got him to the hospital before shock set in or he bled out. Hud and Mitch went to work on that.

When the sled arrived and Sean was about to be loaded, he yelled, "Stop!"

Everyone stopped.

Sean slapped a set of keys into Hud's hand.

"What's this?" Hud asked.

"My car. It's a '68 Camaro, man. I want you to have it, so I bequeath it to you. It's in the lot."

Hud shook his head. "You're not dying."

"Just take the fuckin' keys, okay? Don't let these two assholes get their hands on my baby," Sean said, gesturing to his two cohorts, who were huddled together looking higher than kites. "The last time they did, they blew the engine and I had to rebuild her. So I'm begging you, keep her safe. You got me?"

Wanting to keep Sean calm so his heart rate didn't skyrocket more than it already had, pumping too much blood through his body, Hud nodded. "I got you," he said. "But you're still not dying."

They skied Sean down to the bottom, where the resort's

resident nurse and a trauma crew met them. In less than
twenty minutes from the original radio call, Sean was air-
borne, bound for the trauma center.

Now officially on break, Mitch headed for the cafeteria
for food. Hud stood amidst the lunchtime chaos outside
the lodge and found himself once again looking around
for that cherry-red hat.

But there was no sign of her. Telling himself he was
good with that, even if he'd given her way too much
thought over the past week, he pulled out his buzzing cell
phone.

"Cafeteria," Aidan said in his ear. "Family pow wow."

"Busy," Hud said. And by *busy,* he meant he had that
ten-minute nap on tap.

"Penny said to tell you *please.*"

Shit. Hud had no problem refusing his brothers Gray
and Aidan whatever they thought they needed, but Gray's
wife Penny was another thing entirely. She had big warm
eyes and was the sweetest tyrant he'd ever met. "Sure," he
said. *Sucker.*

He headed over to the lodge and stopped short at the
sight of a ladder against the north wall. A very bad feeling
came up from his gut and he strode inside. Gray, Penny,
Kenna, Aidan, and Aidan's fiancée Lily sat at a table having a late breakfast.

"Told you he'd come if there was food involved," Gray
said. "He thinks with his stomach. That's because he's
single."

"What part do you think with?" Penny asked him.

Gray waggled a brow suggestively.

Penny rolled her eyes. "And I put up with you
why again?"

"I'll remind you after breakfast," he told her, voice husky.

"*Eww*," Kenna said. "Old people shouldn't talk about sex."

"I'm thirty-two," Gray said.

"Old," the twenty-five-year-old said.

There was an empty seat waiting for Hud. A plate had been loaded with his favorites: bacon, eggs, hash browns, sourdough toast, and... a big, fat blueberry muffin, the top of it dusted with sugar.

His mouth watered. "Who died?"

Penny laughed. "No one, you big lug. Sit down and enjoy."

It was hot as hell inside. Making a mental note to have someone check the thermostat and make sure they weren't bleeding money with a heater cranked up too high, he dropped his jacket, hat, and gloves. He unzipped his sweatshirt and sat. Then he looked at Penny, aka the sweet tyrant.

"What?" she asked innocently.

Shit. He knew it. The plate had been a misdirect and he'd fallen for it. "Talk to me about the ladder against the wall."

Penny looked at Gray.

"Told you he was smarter than he looked," Gray said, stuffing his face.

"Your mom emailed us about the mural," Penny said as Hud picked up the muffin. "All of us. She said she thought of it as a family endeavor, a family picture, and you know what? I realized we don't have a single one of all of us. How sad is that? So she's right. We're taking a vote."

Well, hell. Hud put the muffin down. "I'm sorry," he

said. "She shouldn't have asked this of you. I know I should take away her phone but—"

"I like the idea of a mural," Gray said.

Hud stared at him. "What?"

"Yeah," Gray said. "Actually, we all like the idea."

Of course, because they were insane, each more than the next. "No," he said. "We don't *all* like the idea." He said this even though a small part of him was remembering his mom's joy at the thought of the mural. And her claim that Bailey was special, that she'd been through a hard time.

For all Hud knew, his mom had recycled a story she'd heard or seen on TV. Or hell, maybe Bailey had actually given her a sob story. He didn't know and didn't care. She wasn't his business.

The resort was his business. "We're not doing a mural simply because you all feel sorry for my mom."

"Well of course not," Gray said, stuffing his face with thick French toast. "That would be stupid. Hey, are you going to eat that food or what?"

Hud shoved his brother's hand away from his breakfast and pulled the plate in closer to protect it—necessary with this bunch. "A mural is impractical," he went on. "If you want a damn pic, we'll go to the mall and take one. But we're all busting our asses, and spending money on a mural would be a frivolous, stupid thing to do."

"Actually, no it wouldn't," Gray said. "You know the rumors going around town that the resort is in trouble. We put up a huge-ass mural like this and it shows folks we're staying right here. No matter what."

Aidan toasted Gray with his orange juice. Kenna, Penny, and Lily did the same.

Hud just stared at them. "No," he said again. *Why wasn't anyone listening?*

"And your exact objection is what again?" Aidan asked, snaking Lily's muffin.

In response, Lily scooted into Aidan's lap and nibbled on his ear.

Aidan's eyes closed and . . .

Lily snagged her muffin back and reclaimed her seat with a smug smile.

Aidan's look promised retribution. Lily just grinned at him.

"We're not doing the mural," Hud said out loud— again—to the crazy people. "For *lots* of reasons. One, our balloon payment on this place is barreling down on us, and last I checked, it was threatening to put us all out on our asses. Two, if we're going to spend money stupidly, then let's get Gray and Penny a damn room—"

Gray and Penny—who had been kissing—pulled apart, neither looking particularly sorry. "And three," Hud said, "the artist my mom hired to do the mural is already gone."

"No, she's not," Penny said, and waved at someone behind Hud.

Hud turned and . . . shit. There she was, along with her bright red ski cap. He stood up as she came to the table.

"Hey," Bailey said brightly.

"What are you doing here?" he asked.

"Rude," Kenna said, elbowing him in the gut. "Even for you, Hud." And since Hud had stood up, Kenna was able to kick his chair out and give it to the woman. "Sit," she said. "Hud was just holding the spot for you."

Hud gave her a long look, which she of course ignored.

Still avoiding Hud's gaze, Bailey sat. And then, unbelievably, she beamed down at *his* plate and picked up the blueberry muffin, slowly peeling back the paper and taking a bite like she was starving. "Thanks for the offer of breakfast *and* the ideas you all emailed me," she said around a bite. "Carrie had some wonderful ideas as well. She's incredibly artistic. I've got a sketch to show you."

Temper warred with something else within Hud, something he didn't want to acknowledge. He'd heard this woman talking to his mom before she'd known he was listening. She'd been patient with her. Patient, kind, and... sweet.

Dammit.

She was different if not special, and he felt an odd tug of affection for her, one he absolutely did not want to feel. "I'm sorry," he said to her. "But as I already told you, we're not commissioning a mural."

"I know," she said. "And as I told you, I'm doing it for free."

"What's the catch?"

"No catch," she said. "It's on my list." She fanned a hand in front of her face. "Whew. It's super hot in here, isn't it? I think it's the altitude. I'm not in sync with it yet." She reached up to shove off the hood on her jacket and her cap came off with it. While she twisted around to get the misbehaving cap out of the hood and slip it back on her head, Hud felt his heart hit his toes.

Clueless to his reaction, she picked up a fork and started in on his eggs.

The rest of them sat in startled silence for a beat before purposefully all turning back to their food as well.

Not only did he not have his food, Hud couldn't move.

He considered himself an unflappable, stoic, pragmatic sort of guy, not easily rattled.

But beneath her ski cap, she'd nothing but short blond peach fuzz. Not the kind of short you got from a new, cool style, but the kind of short you got from being sick.

Really sick.

Chapter 5

Like the others, Hud did his best not to react to the sight of Bailey's bare skull, but he was having a hard time with that. His heart felt lodged in his throat as things suddenly started to make some sense.

Why she'd felt so frail to him.

The list she'd referred to a couple of times. Jesus, he really hoped it wasn't a bucket list...

Beneath the table Gray kicked Hud—hard, dammit—and gave him a look that said, *Do something.*

And if Hud had known what, he would have.

"She's right," Penny said smoothly. "It's most definitely warm in here. And by the way," she said to Hud's breakfast thief, "we insist on paying for supplies." Her expression and tone were perfectly normal.

How the hell did she do that? How could she not want to cup Bailey's face and make her assure them that she was okay?

"That'd be great," Bailey said. "I do need scaffolding.

Carrie thought maybe you had some here somewhere. Does anyone know if that's true?"

Penny turned to Gray, who nodded. "It's in the storage container," he said.

Wasn't anyone paying any attention? Hud wondered wildly. Bailey was still fighting with her sweater, which she couldn't get unzipped because it'd gotten caught. He actually reached out to help but she swiveled and sent him a don't-even-think-about-it glance, so he shoved his hands in his pockets to keep them off her. Message received. She was fine and completely capable and wanted to ignore what she'd clearly been through, and he was to pretend to see no vulnerability. Got it. "You can't do this for free," he said.

She blinked those baby blues, leveling him, and he realized the problem. She thought he pitied her, which was actually the opposite of the truth. He admired her.

But he still didn't want a mural.

"Why can't I do this for free?" she asked.

Yeah, genius, why not? "Because..." Again he turned to Gray.

But Gray was very busy licking some butter off Penny's finger, the asshole.

"Because," Hud finally said, "it's not only crazy, it's not—" He broke off when his phone buzzed. "Excuse me," he said, and pulled out his phone, staring stupidly down at a text from...Gray. Lifting his head, he sent his brother a look across the table.

Gray jerked his chin to the phone.

Hud blew a sigh and accessed the text.

What the fuck, man? She's got a LIST. You can't call a dying woman crazy!

Hud quickly thumbed a response.

We don't know anything about her.

It was Gray's turn to work his thumbs, and a moment later his response came through.

Penny wants this, so don't fuck it up or I won't get sex for a month.

They already had sex more than bunnies. And the problem wasn't so much that Hud walked in on them doing it. It was that he *kept* walking in on them. Just last week he'd gone out to their building's private hot tub and there they'd been, steaming up the already steamy air, gasping and clinging to each other.

Hud had executed a one-eighty so fast a drill sergeant would've been impressed. But then two nights later he'd gone down to the kitchen for something to eat and found Penny sitting on the kitchen island with her hand down Gray's pants and her teeth on his throat. So Hud didn't give two shits about their sex life and he glared at Gray before responding with:

Jack off for all I care, we're not doing this.

Kenna raised a brow. "You boys going to share with the class?"

"*No*," Hud said, and poured her and Penny more orange juice. They both smiled at him but weren't distracted in the least, dammit.

Penny snatched her husband's phone.

"I'm in the middle of a game," Gray protested.

"Or texting Hudson like a three-year-old." She accessed the texts, read them, and rolled her eyes again. "Seriously?" she said to Hud.

"Hey," he said. "*Your husband* started it."

"I'm the youngest," Kenna told Bailey. "But as you can see, I'm most definitely the smartest."

Hud pinched the bridge of his nose, counted to five, and then looked at Bailey. She'd finished his entire plate. Either the food or the rest had put color back into her cheeks. Her eyes were shiny, bright with intelligence and warmth. She looked . . . happy.

Shit. "I thought you'd left Cedar Ridge," he said.

"No. Well, yes," she said. "I left for the week, but I'm back."

"But we discussed this," he said. "You said you weren't coming back."

"No, you said that, not me." She laughed, a soft, musical sound. "It takes more than some cranky-pants guy to get rid of me."

The kids in the playground were greatly amused at this. All except Hud because what the hell did that mean? He wasn't a . . . cranky pants. He simply worked hard to keep his life free of new complications because his entire life was one big complication. She was killing him here, just killing him because now he was torn between feeling handled—which he hated—and being distracted by needing to hear her say that she was okay.

He didn't like this, any of it. Because the truth was, he also felt outsmarted, which he liked even less than being handled. "You can't just start painting," he said.

"Well, of course not," she said demurely. "You all have

to approve the draft." She pulled out an iPad and showed them what she'd done.

Hud glanced at his family. Penny, Lily, and Kenna had scooted in close, looking at the screen raptly, "oohing" and "aahing" over what they saw.

In contrast, Gray was looking at Hud with a big, fat smirk. Ditto for Aidan. The assholes.

"It's a family tree," Bailey said, "since you guys are a family-run business. And I thought I'd do it as if it were an actual tapestry hung on the wall, the backdrop being the mountains, maybe the lake... highlighting the cameos of each of you on the family tree. I hear the Kincaid siblings are something of a legend, so I thought your visitors would love the little peek into your world."

No. *Hell no*, Hud thought.

"Yes," Penny and Kenna and Lily said in unison.

And given the looks on Aidan's and Gray's faces, neither of them were all that inclined to disagree with their better halves or their baby sister.

"Of course to draw each of you in your element, I'd need to interview you one-on-one. Just a few minutes of your time today, if that works."

Hud opened his mouth to say it didn't work at all, that none of it worked, nor did he have a few spare minutes today.

Or *any* day.

And that wouldn't be just bullshit, either, because he really didn't have a spare second, ever. His job took more hours than he had available in a day, and added to that were all the additional things that came with being one of the owners of the resort itself. Which didn't even begin to count his other responsibilities, like making sure his mother was taken care of, finding Jacob, and keeping Kenna on the straight and narrow—a full-time job in itself.

But before he could say any of that, his siblings all were nodding like bobbleheads. Even his brothers, who were clearly not thinking with their heads, at least not their big heads.

Their would-be artist beamed at them. "Great," she said.

"Not great," Hud said.

Everyone looked at him.

"Interviews?" he repeated. "We don't need to be interviewed for this. We're all too busy right now."

"You'll have to excuse him," Kenna said to Bailey. "He's got one of those busy-guy brains. You know, the kind that means they're not really listening when you talk."

"I listen," Hud said. "I just don't always agree."

"It's only going to take a few minutes of your time," Penny said. "I'm off today, so I'll cover for you if I need to. Anything to get our Harry Potter–like family tree up!" She was clearly thrilled. Which meant Gray looked thrilled too.

Bailey nodded, those slay-me eyes bright and excited. "Yes," she said. "It'll be very much like the Black family tree in Harry Potter. Except the heads aren't going to talk."

Everyone laughed.

Hud didn't see the funny, and Kenna looked his way and snorted. "He hasn't seen the movies if you can believe it," she told Bailey.

"*Everyone* should see the Harry Potter movies," Penny

said. She looked at her husband. "You loved them when we watched them, right?"

"Right," Gray said with a perfectly straight face and then when Penny turned away, he shook his head at Hud. He'd either slept through the movies or had been trying to have sex with Penny instead of watching them.

"No worries, we'll make time for the interviews," Penny assured Bailey. "Even my curmudgeonly brother-in-law."

"And if he doesn't," Kenna said, "you can just portray him any way that strikes you." She laughed the evil-baby-sister laugh.

Oh yeah, Hud thought. This just got better and better.

Chapter 6

Bailey spent the day individually interviewing the Kincaid family for the mural. Well, interviewing everyone but Hud, whom she'd saved until last.

Or more accurately, put off until last. She wasn't sure exactly what the problem was between them, but there was most definitely a problem. At least *he* had one.

She didn't. Well, other than being rendered stupid by his voice, his smile, and the way his ass looked in pants...

But it was more too. She'd seen the way he was with his mom. Genuine. Loyal. Fiercely protective.

Not muted.

She could tell he was the same way with his siblings—all half siblings, as she now knew—and his siblings' significant others as well. It appeared that when Hudson cared, he cared with his entire being, and damn that was attractive. In fact, several times he'd reacted instinctively to try to help her, a perfect stranger. First on the mountain and then at the table. And at first she'd assumed it was pity, exacerbated when she'd accidentally removed her cap and he'd seen her head. Knowledge had come into his gaze then.

And sympathy.

Which had made her grind her back teeth. Because it had only been after that when he'd accepted the idea of the mural really happening. And actually, not accepted so much as resigned himself to it.

And that made her mad. Furious, truthfully, because she didn't want him to feel bad for her.

But you do want his wall ...

And the truth was that she didn't feel pitied by him. She felt like maybe that was just who Hudson was to the very core—a guy who genuinely cared.

And as much as she didn't need him to, as much as she wanted to be independent and do things for herself, she couldn't help admitting that soaking up some more of his warmth and strength wouldn't be a hardship.

She sighed. She was sitting outside on a bench on the covered patio facing the wall. She'd just finished talking with Kenna when she caught sight of Gray and Penny in the throng of people moving about. They stood on the steps outside the lodge. Penny wore black leggings and fabulous high-heeled boots and a snug silver jacket that showed off an enviably curvy figure. Her long brown hair fell free to the middle of her back. She looked like a snow princess.

Bailey wasn't vain but she really did miss her hair. Three months since her last chemo treatment and she was lucky to have a few inches of new growth, but it wasn't thick or luscious. Nope, not even close. Instead it seemed like ostrich fuzz. Bedraggled baby-ostrich fuzz.

Gray grinned at Penny, a confident sexy grin, and for a beat he looked a lot like Hud as he leaned in close to his wife, putting his mouth to her ear. Penny laughed at whatever he whispered, probably a naughty little nothing, and wrapped her arms around him tight.

Gray lifted her up, one hand around her back and the other palming her butt, and kissed her. It looked like a really great kiss, and Bailey's heart gave an envious pitter-patter.

She wouldn't mind having a man look at her like that, like she was his entire world, and she really wouldn't mind being kissed like that either. Busy with that thought, she nearly jumped out of her skin when Hud slouched onto the bench next to her. He leaned back, stretched out his long legs, and tilted his face up to the low midmorning sun now slanting in beneath the patio roof.

He wore dark sunglasses and his ski patrol gear. Black cargo ski pants. Long-sleeved outdoor wear that fit him like a glove. At least a day of scruff on a square jaw. Dark short hair, wind tousled and standing up in a way that only made him seem sexier. Damn him.

So he was a brooding, silent type, so what? She had little to no experience with that because for far too long things like hot guys with 'tudes had been luxury items that she'd never had time for. She'd never had time for anything except survival.

But she'd done that, she reminded herself. She was alive and now planning on staying that way. So it was definitely time to treat herself to the things she'd missed out on.

Like painting a mural. Skiing in the Rockies. Learning to ballroom dance. Explore some castles in Europe.

See the Greek Islands. Skydive. Her list, basically. Which meant that the prickly Hudson Kincaid could bite her, sexiness and all. She took a quick glance and found him watching her, a look in his eyes that made her the prickly one. "We're not going to talk about *it*," she said. "Ever."

"Which?" he asked. "The fact that you can't read a map but you expect me to believe you can create a sixty-foot-long, thirty-foot-high mural? Or that you manipulated me into doing it anyway?"

She blew out a sigh. And then let out a low laugh. Dammit. He wasn't going to ask her to talk about *it* at all. She'd vastly underestimated him.

"Just tell me you know how to paint a mural," he said.

"Scared?" she asked.

"Terrified."

"Uh-huh." She arched a brow. "You don't seem the type to be afraid of much."

"You'd be surprised."

Maybe. She was certainly surprised at her unexpected attraction to him. She was also surprised at his phone and radio, both which were going off constantly. She could tell he was multitasking, monitoring the radio with one ear and concentrating on her with the other. His phone he simply pulled out, glanced at, and then ignored. She was fascinated by this, by him. He definitely hadn't shaved that morning. Probably not yesterday morning either. His hands were big and sexy, even with the ragged scars across his palms, and she wondered how he'd gotten them. "I can paint," she said. "I promise."

"Yeah?"

"Yeah." She smiled with what she hoped looked like

confidence and determination. "Trust me, Hudson, I can do this and it's going to be good."

His eyes darkened a little, whether at the use of his given name or the way she'd said it, which had been admittedly a little low and husky. Entirely unintentionally, of course, but the man made her feel things.

Such things...

He didn't say anything for a few moments, which should've been uncomfortable but in reality was the opposite. "Heard you interviewed everyone," he finally murmured.

"Except you," she agreed. And it'd been fun and fascinating. She'd learned a lot about the Kincaids from what they'd told her.

And even more from what they hadn't. "Are you ready to be interviewed?" she asked.

"Tell me what you think you already know."

She smiled. He didn't want to talk about himself. She got that loud and clear. Gray had been the first one up to speak with her and he'd told her there were five Kincaid siblings. They all had the same father, though no one had anything good to say about the man. The only other Kincaid missing from the mountain was Jacob, Hudson's twin. She'd heard that little bit from Carrie, although Bailey still wasn't clear whether Jacob was alive or dead.

Gray had been pretty close-mouthed about the subject, letting her know that it was Hudson's story to tell. Or not tell. Aidan had been even less forthcoming, saying only that Jacob had gone into the military at age eighteen and hadn't come back.

Kenna had been more frank. "Jacob's gone and Hud's

fucked up because of it," she'd said. "He misses his other half."

Bailey would eventually need the story if she wanted to represent the entire Kincaid clan, but she knew now it'd have to come from Hudson himself.

"What I know," she said carefully, "is that I love to draw caricatures of people, often times people I don't even know. I do it by observing and then assigning one word to them."

"And the words you assigned to us Kincaids?"

He was quick, she'd give him that. "Bossy, funny, adventurous, brave, original," she said.

He remained still, only the slightest of smiles curving his lips. "Gray, Penny, Aidan, Lily, and Kenna, in that order."

"I'm impressed," she said. "You know your family."

"Impressed and something else." He met her gaze, his shuttered from her by those glasses.

The way he read her with such ease was startling. "Nope," she denied. "That's it. Just impressed."

He cocked his head and studied her. "Liar," he chided. "And we both know you don't have to interview me for your one word. You already have it. What is it?"

She let out a low laugh. "I don't think—"

"Tell me."

"Know-it-all."

"That's three words," he said.

"I hyphenated."

His mouth twitched. "So you've got me all figured out. What else could you possibly need to know?"

"Lots, actually," she said.

He arched a brow, silently saying, *Such as?*

In for a penny, in for a pound… "Jacob," she said softly.

His expression shifted from mildly amused to absolutely stone blank. It was both fascinating and heartbreaking. "There are five of you Kincaid siblings," she said. "And going off what I've heard so far, everyone wants the mural to be a true reflection of the group. As a whole and individually."

No response from Hudson. Hell, she wasn't even sure he was breathing.

She let out a breath. "Maybe you could just give me enough to get started."

More nothing.

"I understand it's difficult to talk about," she said, and paused.

Nothing but crickets.

She remembered the time she'd designed a new logo for a local Denver clothing designer, family run. The patriarch had recently had a stroke, leaving his wife and children to run his two exclusive boutiques. They were in charge of everything top to bottom, including speaking for him. But the family was terrified of doing the wrong thing, such as taking the business in the wrong direction. So Bailey had gently steered them into discussing the man lying in a rehabilitation center, and in doing so, they'd been able to come up with exactly what he would have wanted. "Your siblings mentioned him," she said. "All fondly. They have good memories of him."

Hud continued to impersonate a statue, remaining quiet, so much so that she figured he had no intention of saying another word to her. Ever. She turned her head and looked at him.

His expression was still carefully blank, but she thought

maybe she could see something in there, a flash of something deep. Pain? Regret? She paused again. "Have you ever thought that talking about him might help?"

He turned his head toward the mountain run that led straight to the lodge, watching the skiers and boarders make their various ways down. Some were smooth and extremely talented. Some were clearly just doing their best to stay upright. And some were flat on their asses after a fall. Bailey had a feeling that Hudson was seeing none of that but something from his past.

"What do you think?" she asked quietly. "Talking about it, or...no?"

He snorted.

Okay so that was not only a no, it was also a big, fat no.

"Jacob's story isn't relevant here," he said. "Not for a mural."

"You've seen the draft," she said. "You know that—"

"Make something up. Hell, make the whole thing up. No one needs to know that much about us."

"Okay." She nodded and then had to ask. "So is it just me? Or are you always a little bit grumpy?"

He turned his head toward her but didn't speak.

She arched a brow in a question, wondering if he'd answer. He did, with a slow smile that actually stopped her heart for a second, *and* her ability to breathe. The smile was followed by a laugh, a full-bodied one that had his head tipping back. When he'd finished, he spread his arms out on the bench and grinned at her.

Nope. Still not able to breathe, she thought, a little dazed by him. Or a lot dazed. How long had it been since her lady bits had quivered?

Way too long.

But they were quivering now, coming to life with a tingle that she thought absolutely shouldn't be happening in broad daylight.

Or maybe it should.

It's okay to live, she reminded herself. Okay to be happy and excited.

And there was no doubt she was both, she thought, still staring at him.

When his smile slowly faded, she braced herself.

"Look," he said. "I don't mean to be an asshole. But the timing for this mural is bad, for reasons you don't understand."

"Because your mom mixes up the present and the past?" she asked. "Because the resort is in financial trouble?"

He gave her a long once-over, and when he spoke he sounded less than thrilled with her knowledge. "You've done your homework."

"I'm good at research," she allowed.

"So am I," he said, and lifted his phone, where he'd just plugged her into his browser. "You're a graphic artist and you work for yourself. You've created logos and brandings for a brewery, a local chain of two grocery stores, and for a few small towns. But you've never done an outdoor mural. You've never done any sort of public painting—period."

She held her breath, waiting for the rest, but apparently even Hudson Kincaid couldn't read at the speed of light.

"Tell me why you want this mural so bad," he said.

"Hey, you're the one being interviewed," she said playfully. "Hudson Edward Kincaid, also known as Hud, also known as head of ski patrol and a Cedar Ridge cop."

He smiled. "See, you have *plenty* of words for me. Looks like we're done here after all."

Smug bastard. But she returned his smile. "It's possible that if you gave me a few honest minutes, I'd come up with better words."

"I'm not really interested in how people see me."

Nope, he wouldn't be. She knew that much already. Maybe her word for him should've been stalwart. Or unfaltering.

Not to mention stubborn.

But one thing was certain, he wasn't going to open up and be honest about himself unless she made the first move to do so. "You have a great family," she said. "You're all..."

"Insane?"

She smiled. "Tight-knit."

He nodded. "Like a pack of feral wolf cubs. Which explains why we always want to beat the shit out of each other."

"You do not," she said on a shocked laugh.

He looked at her. "You have family, Bailey?"

Goodness, she liked the way he said her name. Slowly. In that voice as smooth as aged whiskey. "Just my mom," she said.

"Well, unless you've got a big family with too many siblings, you couldn't possibly understand the constant urge to beat the shit out of each other."

"That may be true," she admitted. "Although now that I've seen the Kincaids at the breakfast table and how you all interact, maybe I understand more than you think."

"We're usually worse. We were on our best behavior."

She laughed. Yes, they'd bickered, stolen food off one

another's plates, snarled, and insulted, but they'd had each other's backs. "Actually, I thought it was amazing," she said. "I was envious as hell."

He looked surprised. "Has it always been just you and your mom?"

She nodded.

"What happened to your dad?" he asked.

She shrugged. Her dad was around. He worked in steel and he actually didn't live too far from her. But they didn't see much of him, never had. She always hated to talk about this because it left her feeling like she was... pathetic. And she didn't feel pathetic. Mostly. "He's around. But not around, if you know what I mean."

"I do," he said with surprising understanding.

"He's not really a family guy," she said, "but I see him every once in a while."

He studied her for a long moment as the sun kept them warm. "Okay, so what do you need?"

The question astounded her. What did she need? Where did she start with that? She wished she could win the lotto to pay off some serious medical debts. She wished for her mother to understand that Bailey was really okay and didn't need to be babied through life anymore. She wished Aaron would give up on her without her having to further hurt him.

And after today, she realized she wished to get laid at some point in this decade before she jumped Hud's very sexy bones.

Options...

"I don't know," she said softly. "I'd be happy with the rest of the day going as well as the morning has."

He flashed that panty-melting grin and all her poor,

neglected womanly parts flamed to life and did the Macarena.

"I meant," he said, "what do you need to get this interview over with so you can get started on this damn mural?"

She felt her face heat. Right. One of these days she'd hopefully stop making a fool of herself in front of him... Maybe *that's* what she needed...

Chapter 7

Hud had been sitting with Bailey for the better part of an hour before he'd even realized it. He needed to go, needed to get back to work, but he didn't move.

"Tell me about your mom," Bailey said.

"Batshit crazy." He laughed softly. "But she's warm and kind and funny, and she's..." He shrugged. "Everything. She'd do anything for me."

"And you feel the same way," she said softly.

"Yes." His phone vibrated and he knew he could no longer ignore the work piling up as each second clicked by. This time it was a text from Aidan.

I've never seen you sit for more than five minutes ever.

He returned the text with a homemade emoji that Kenna had created for him—a closed fist with a middle finger sticking straight up.

"What?" Bailey asked. "Do you have an emergency?"

"Yeah. I need to go pummel Aidan."

She blinked. "You guys do that a lot? Fight?"

He laughed. "Depends on your definition of 'a lot.'" He stood and offered her a hand.

She slid her much smaller one into his and let him pull her upright. "Thanks for letting me keep you from whatever it is you do all day long," she said. "Rescue fair maidens, corral idiot thrill seekers, redirect people who can't read maps, et cetera."

When he snorted, she flashed him a smile and stuffed her notepad into one of her myriad of pockets. "I'll see you next weekend. I'll need access to the scaffolding at that time."

He walked her out to her car, and as before the silence between them felt oddly comfortable. He'd have to think about that later. For now he had something else on his mind.

Her car was a little piece of shit, emphasis on *piece of shit*, and he was glad for the day's decent weather. "You need winter tires," he said, nudging one with his boot. "Especially if you're planning on coming back and forth up the mountain. It's clear today but you're not going to stay that lucky."

"I don't know," she said with a mysterious smile. "I've been pretty lucky lately." She unlocked the driver's door and started to get in. He took a step forward, one hand on the door, ready to close it for her.

But then she straightened and turned back to him to say something at the same time he started to talk as well—and they ended up plastered together in that tight triangle between the car and the opened driver's door.

She laughed, that soft, contagious sound. "You go first," she said.

She hadn't moved back and neither had he, so they were nose to nose. Which wasn't exactly accurate. Her nose came up to maybe his shoulder. He could feel her soft breasts against his chest. She was a little chilled and he found his hands going to her arms. To steady her, he told himself as he swept them up and down. Keeping her warm.

She smiled.

He didn't. Couldn't.

"Did you forget what you were going to say?" she asked, teasing.

"No." Yes. *Jesus.* He let go of her and took a step back. "Drive safe."

"That's not what you were going to say," she chided.

Had he ever met a more endearingly/annoyingly up front woman in his life? Did she not have a coy bone in her body?

She was staring up into his eyes, her own knowing and warm. "You wanted to ask me a question," she said softly. "It's okay. Ask me anything, as long as it's not 'Are you okay?'"

But see, that's what he wanted to know, *badly.* "Are you?" he asked just as softly.

She dropped her head to his chest and let out a low laugh.

He ran his hand up her slim spine now and gently cupped the back of her head—still in the cherry-red cap— and tilted her face back up to his. "Tell me."

"I'm okay," she whispered.

He didn't move. Hell, he didn't breathe.

"Really," she said. "I'm more okay than I've been in ten years."

He stared into her eyes, caught the absolute joyous truth swimming there, and let out a breath and nodded in relief.

She was still smiling, looking pretty damn beautiful while she was at it, when her gaze dropped to his mouth and her breath caught.

"Bailey," he said, and her eyes met his and held. "Bay," he whispered, and she sort of melted against him as he brushed his hand down her cheek and then around to the nape of her neck.

The next move was hers, he told himself. Had to be.

She hesitated and he told himself he was good with that, but then her eyes dropped to his mouth again and held... And then after a heart-stopping pause during which they shared air, she leaned in and brushed her lips gently to his.

She tasted like warm sunshine and sweet woman, and when she whispered, "Really, really okay," against him, he groaned. He dragged her in closer with the hand he had on her neck and kissed her this time, deep and hot, until they were both breathless.

She drew back, just a fraction, and stared up at him with those eyes filled with a little surprise, like she couldn't believe the electricity between them.

He was not a little surprised.

He was stunned.

He could feel her warm breath on his face and the heat of her body just barely touching his, and he wanted her with an ache that couldn't be explained.

As if she could read that want, her mouth curved and then she kissed him again, sighing into his mouth, surrendering to the heat, the passion. His hands cupped her face as the two of them stayed locked together for an endless moment. She pressed herself against him like she needed even more, letting her hands drift over his shoulders, his chest, whatever she could reach. He absolutely returned the favor. Holding her head cupped in a palm, he caressed her breast, her nipple hard under his touch, her moan soft on his tongue.

When they finally broke apart it was to stare at each other. She licked her lips like she wanted to hold on to the taste of him, and he groaned.

She smiled a little shyly—like she hadn't just had her hands all over him—and without a single word slid into her car.

He was still standing there when her car vanished out of the parking lot.

What just happened?

The radio at his hip crackled and then his brother's voice came out of it. "What the hell just happened?"

Hud turned his head and found Aidan leaning out of his office window, so far that Hud kind of hoped he fell. "Nothing," he said.

"Nothing, my ass."

That's when Hud noticed the car that had been parked next to Bailey's.

A '68 Camaro.

Remembering the morning's rescue, which now seemed like a million years ago, he pulled the set of keys from his pocket and stared down at them. "Shit." He brought the radio back up to his mouth. "Can you find out about Sean, the compound fracture flown out earlier?"

"It'll cost you," Aidan said.

"Yeah, yeah, just do it."

A minute later Aidan was back on the radio, telling Hud that Sean was out of surgery and his prognosis was good.

Hud got Sean's address and called Gray to follow him and give Hud a ride back to the resort, but Gray showed up and slid into the shotgun position of the Camaro.

"What are you doing?" Hud asked. "I need you to follow me in your truck."

"A '68 Camaro," Gray said, lovingly caressing the dash.

Hud rolled his eyes and called Aidan. "Need you to come out to the lot with your car keys."

Aidan arrived, caught sight of the Camaro, and got in the backseat.

"You kidding me?" Hud asked him, eyeballing him in the rearview window.

"Man, do we have to take it back?"

Hud called Kenna. Thankfully she had a brain and followed them in her own car so that Hud could drive the Camaro home for Sean.

Back at the resort, they all scattered except for Gray, who stuck with Hud. "Tell me again why you returned your gift for rescuing some guy? And not just any gift, but a '68 Camaro?"

"He thought he was dying," Hud said.

"A '68 Camaro," Gray repeated.

Hud shook his head. "Next subject."

"Fine. You kissed our cutie-pie muralist."

Hell. "She kissed me."

Gray grinned.

"She did."

"You know what that makes you?" Gray asked.

"What?"

"Slow." Gray's smiled faded then. "Do we know her story?"

"You mean other than you guys decided we needed her to paint our wall?"

"You know what I'm asking," Gray said.

"Yeah," Hud said. "And she says she's okay." Which he really hoped was true.

"And you?" Gray asked. "You okay?"

"Why wouldn't I be?"

Gray blew out a breath. "Because ever since we heard that Jacob got himself injured, you've been..."

"*What?*"

Gray sighed again. "Intense."

Yeah, true story.

"And now with Bailey painting the mural about us, all of us including Jacob," Gray went on, "you're going to have to talk about it. You're going to have to see him on the wall every time you ski down the mountain."

"And whose fault is that?" Hud asked. "You wanted the damn mural, you've got the damn mural. I'll deal. I always do."

Gray hesitated. "Hud—"

"Stop. It's...Whatever," Hud managed. "Seeing the family tree on the wall with all of us? That's how it should be. Jacob's still a part of this family. If we have to have the mural, then he belongs on it."

"But?" Gray asked. "Because I sense a big, fat *but*."

But he had enough trouble dealing with what had happened between him and Jacob. The last thing he needed was for it to be illustrated for the world to see.

Gray took in his expression and shook his head. "You

do realize it is just a painting, right? And caricatures at that. It's not going to say anything personal."

"I know."

"Do you?" Gray asked.

"Christ. Yes. Back off."

"You're angry."

No shit. But it wasn't directed at Gray. Or even Bailey.

He was angry with himself because he could still remember everything about that day. It'd been June and he and Jacob had just graduated high school. They'd gotten into it right there at graduation, tearing off their stupid gowns and yelling stupid stuff at each other, a fact that haunted Hud every night.

Gray glanced over at him. "See, you really don't seem all right. You're not okay, are you?"

Hud was starting to get why Bailey hated that question. "I'm fine."

"I imagine the kiss helped," Gray said.

"Aidan has a big mouth."

Gray laughed. "He told Lily, who told Penny, who told me."

"You all need a life."

"We've got one and you're part of it," Gray said. "So . . . you going after that? After Bailey?"

"Are you insane?"

"Are *you*?" Gray volleyed back. "What the hell's wrong with you?"

"I don't know but I bet that you're about to tell me."

"You let Maggie walk."

Hud had been with Maggie for two years, but that had been five years ago. "She left me for being a workaholic," he said. "Old news."

"No, she left you because she wanted you to fight for

her. And then there's Quinn. She was in love with you and you walked away."

Hud shook his head. "Quinn wasn't in love with me. We were just messing around and then she decided she didn't want to anymore."

"More bullshit," Gray said. "You fight tooth and nail at work and you're the strongest person I know, so why are you such a pussy when it comes to this?"

"To what?"

Gray jabbed a finger into Hud's chest.

Okay, so maybe in some ways Gray was right. But he was still going to stay far, far back from whatever was happening between him and Bailey. Yeah, yeah, a shrink would have a field day with this. His dad had left him, and to some degree so had his mom, and then there was Jacob. Hud definitely had the whole abandonment issue down pat. Which he hated about himself.

Christ, he was tired. He rubbed the spot between his eyes where he had a headache coming. "I'm over this."

"Of course you are," Gray said. "You know, this reminds me of a conversation we had about six months ago about Aidan and Lily."

Aidan had resisted falling in love with Lily with a muleheaded obstinacy that none of the rest of the family had understood. "Lily was perfect for him," Hud said.

"Yeah," Gray agreed. "And she's it for him, just as Penny is it for me. There'll never be another woman for either of us and we're happy for the first time in far too long." He gave Hud a long, meaningful look.

"*What?*"

"You're the one who pushed Aidan to go for it," Gray said. "So now I'm going to do the same for you."

"Who told you I pushed Aidan to go for it?"

"Aidan told Lily, who told Penny, who told me." Gray grinned. "Sensing a pattern? We're all gunning for you to trip over your two left feet for a woman. It's your turn."

"Jesus," Hud muttered.

"What?"

"I just can't believe that you have yourself a hot wife and yet the two of you waste your time talking about this shit instead of—"

"Instead of nothing," Gray said. "Haven't you heard of pillow talk? Someday you'll have someone sharing your pillow, so after you get yourself some, you'll lie there with them and tell them all your funny shit."

Hud shook his head.

"No? You're really going to sit there and tell me that you're too busy to get laid every night?" Gray asked. "Too busy to roll over in the morning and find a woman waiting for you with a smile on her face?"

"Listen to you," Hud said. "You fell in love and got all stupid and mushy."

"You don't know what you're missing," Gray called out as Hud walked away from his brother's smug face.

He did know what he was missing. And that was part of the problem.

Halfway through the week Bailey had gotten an email from Cedar Ridge Resort and her tummy quivered. So did some other unmentionables because just the sight of the email brought her back to the weekend before.

She'd kissed Hudson Kincaid.

She had no idea what she'd been thinking. Nope, scratch that. She knew *exactly* what she'd been thinking—that she'd been so happy and excited and hopeful, and on top of that she'd been standing right there in front of a good-looking guy who'd been smiling at her like she was hot as hell.

He hadn't seen her as a cancer patient.

He hadn't seen her as someone to feel sorry for.

He hadn't seen her lying on the bathroom floor, sick as a dog, unable to lift even her head. He hadn't seen her throw up. He hadn't seen her stripped of her dignity, stuck on hospital death row in a gown with needles protruding from her everywhere.

He'd seen her as a woman, a sexy one given the light in his eyes. And it'd been the most empowering, wondrous feeling. She couldn't have contained herself if she'd tried.

So she hadn't tried.

She'd kissed him instead.

God, she'd really kissed him...

The email stated that her draft was family approved and she could start whenever she was ready.

So she'd rushed through the rest of the week and the following Saturday morning she hit the road before dawn. She was just pulling into the Cedar Ridge Resort parking lot when Aaron called.

"You're not home," he said. "I'm standing at your door with two McDonald's breakfasts and you're not home."

"Nope." She paused and bit her tongue so the automatic *I'm sorry* didn't pop out. She wasn't sorry. She was happy. She had an entire weekend of working on her mural in front of her. "I didn't know you were coming by. I told you what I'd be doing with my next two months of weekends."

"You're at Cedar Ridge," he said, none too happily.

"Yes."

"You had a long week at work," he said. "Scott said you were run ragged."

This was the problem with her biggest client being her ex's brother. She'd known that going in and she'd known that going out. The ties hadn't been fully severed and never would be. "I'm fine, Aaron," she said as gently as she could. And actually, she was so much more than fine. Excitement was thrumming through her and she couldn't wait to get to work.

"I'm tempted to come up and see that for myself," he said.

"No," she said. Not gently. Bailey forced herself to speak calmly for fear she'd set off his protective nature and he'd come up here no matter what she said. "I'm working. We're not together anymore, Aaron. You know this."

"What I know is that it was a mistake to let you go."

"My choice," she said quietly. Firmly.

"And my fault," he said just as quietly.

Unbidden came an image of Aaron locked in the arms of another woman, pressing her against the wall, his face a mask of savage pleasure—a side he'd never shown her, not once.

She'd wanted that kind of smokin' chemistry. She needed it and craved it like air.

But it was too late for that.

Another image came to her, a far better one. Hud pulling her in hard and kissing her like she'd *always* dreamed of being kissed, hard and hot and deep... "You're going to let me do this," she said.

No response.

"I'm going to repeat that," she said. "You're going to let me do this."

"As long as we stay friends," Aaron said. "You promised that, Bailey. And friends check on each other."

"Agreed," she said. "And I'll let you know when I need checking on." With that, she disconnected. She slid on her jacket and got out of her car, stretching her legs. The air was crisp and felt good. She felt good. Maybe she'd only been in Cedar Ridge twice before in her life, but somehow the place already felt like home.

Chapter 8

They'd had a big storm over the week, Bailey saw. The lot had been cleared but she could see several feet of new powder in the berms lining the walkways.

Kenna Kincaid greeted Bailey and shook her head when Bailey marveled at the new snow.

"Three feet," Kenna confirmed, sounding annoyed. "And people have come out of the woodwork to ski it this weekend too. Hud and his crew have been working twelve- and fourteen-hour days getting ready. It's going to be crazy today."

Bailey hadn't given much thought to the day-to-day life of those who actually lived here and had to run this place. But if Hud's phone and radio last weekend had been any indication, he was swamped twenty-four-seven.

Kenna took her to a large storage unit where they had scaffolding stored among other equipment such as a large snow-blower and a snowcat. "Help yourself in here," Kenna said, and then eyeballed Bailey's small frame. "You going to need help?"

In truth, Bailey had no idea. She'd never worked on scaffolding before, but she gave her standard statement. "I'll be fine."

When Kenna shrugged and left, Bailey went to work. She separated out the steel bars and wood planking and was banging with a hammer on two pieces of steel that were stuck together when the doubts slid into her brain.

What had she been thinking? How did she possibly think she could handle building the scaffolding on her own? Or for that matter, the mural itself? What did she know about painting on such a scale? Panic hit her then, right in the gut, and she sat on the floor and pressed her forehead to her knees.

Don't worry about staying inside the lines, darling… Bailey could still hear her grandma's voice, joyful and in high spirits, even though she had already been fighting the cancer that would slowly drain the life out of her. But she'd never lost her positive nature, never.

Don't worry about whether you can do it, Bailey-Bean. Just pretend you can. Pretend enough and it becomes real.

That was how her grandma had lived her life and it was how Bailey intended to live hers. Her grandma would want this for Bailey, and Bailey wanted it for herself. It was on her list. She wanted to paint a mural big and happy enough that her grandma could see it from whatever cloud she was sitting on, watching from above.

So she went back to hammering the shit out of the steel.

"What the hell?"

She whipped around and found Hud staring at her. He was in ski patrol gear today, looking official.

And officially hot.

She did her best to roll her tongue back into her mouth, and smiled. "Hey."

"My sister said you were about to be stupid and not admit you needed help."

"So you came by to get a front-row seat for the stupidity?" she asked.

He smiled. "You're going to drive people crazy with all the banging."

Pretend enough and it becomes real.

So Bailey lifted an eyebrow and pretended she was a sexy siren. "Now there's a complaint I've never had before," she said in her best Marilyn Monroe whisper.

He laughed.

Okay, so maybe she'd have to work on it. "So you, what, drew the short straw to go rescue the stupid chick?"

"No."

"No?" she asked, a little breathless because he'd come inside the storage unit and had stopped only when they were toe to toe.

"I won you," he said, his voice whiskey smooth.

Her good parts quivered. "What does that mean?"

"In our offices," he said, "everything that has to be done each week goes up on a scheduling wall, which inevitably starts a fight over who's going to do what, so we started a new thing this year. We throw darts for the chores. You were on the board this morning, or the scaffolding was. And you'll have to trust me on this, moving and building the scaffolding was the easiest thing on that entire wall, which meant we were all fighting for it." He smiled. "I won you."

The way he kept saying that had her heart doing a little squishy dance. And there were some other reactions, too, decidedly south of her heart. Had been ever since that kiss...

Was she the only one feeling it? Because that would be embarrassing. She looked down at herself and realized she was wearing approximately twenty layers of clothing to stay warm and that she was also now sweating thanks to the exertion and most likely also Hud's effortless hotness. She probably looked like the Pillsbury Doughboy.

A melting Pillsbury Doughboy. So much for being a sex siren.

"You sure you want to do this?" he asked.

"Yes, it's on my list."

Hud reached for his radio and put in a request for a few helping hands. He'd just put the radio back on his hip when it went off, something job related. He listened for a beat and then began barking orders. He'd no sooner slid the radio back into place than his cell phone rang. He grimaced and answered that too. He said something about how they needed at least three staff members in each of the outposts today and yes, he knew the fencing on the backside of the mountain needed to be replaced stat and that he was on it as soon as he checked the staff rosters to make sure everyone was able to take their required breaks.

There was more, a lot more. And it all boggled Bailey. His life boggled her. The reality of his job and the responsibilities of his day-to-day life here on the mountain were dizzying. "Do you ever get a day off?" she asked.

"No."

"That's...awful."

He reacted by not reacting. Shock.

His phone buzzed again and he shook his head. "I'm

sorry, I have to take this. It's my mom and I have no idea why she's FaceTiming me." He hit ANSWER and then there came a lot of white noise.

Hud blinked and held his phone farther away as if he couldn't quite process what he was seeing. "Mom."

Bailey peeked at the phone. It looked as if Carrie was holding it to show off her plain white ceiling.

"Mom," Hud said again.

"Well if that isn't the silliest thing," came Carrie's voice. "I don't know what I'm supposed to speak into."

Hud rubbed a hand over his eyes, like maybe he was getting a headache. "Mom, just hold the phone up in front of you."

There was a lot of movement and then there was a man. Older, bald, a little round. He wore wire-rimmed glasses, a button-down shirt, and...no pants. Just bright red boxers.

"Who the hell are you?" Hud stared at the phone. "What's going on?"

"Oh," Carrie said, and then the view of the man went upside down. They caught a quick flash of the ceiling again and then saw Carrie's smiling face. "There you are, baby. How are you?"

Hud was clearly not feeling friendly. "Why is there a man with no pants in your room?" he asked in a quiet but scary, badass voice.

Carrie laughed. "That's Terrance. I'm teaching him how to play cards."

Hud's jaw worked a moment. "Tell me you're not teaching him how to play strip poker."

"Well, of course not! Good Lord, Hud. I wouldn't do that."

Hud relaxed marginally.

"I mean, it's not even dark yet," Carrie said. "You can't play strip poker before dark."

Hud appeared to grind his back teeth together for a moment. "Then explain why he's not wearing pants."

"Well, baby, you're still a young one, but when a man gets older, he..." She tilted her head. "How should I put this?"

Terrance stuck his face next to Carrie's. "I don't like to crowd my bits," he said.

Carrie smiled at him. "Yes," she said. "That's a good way to put it."

Hud closed his eyes briefly. "I'm at work, Mom. I'll check in with you later."

"Okay, baby."

Hud looked Terrance in the eye. "Air out your bits in your own room, soldier, you hear me?"

Terrance sighed. "I hear you."

Hud disconnected and stared at the phone for a long beat. "Jesus," he finally muttered, looking tired.

"Your mom's quite a character," Bailey said.

"She's sure something," he agreed.

Bailey looked him over, wishing she could take a load off for him. "Hud?"

"Yeah?"

"When do you get to have any fun?"

He laughed humorlessly. "Let's put it this way, I don't have a list. I don't have time for a list."

"Fine, but what would be on it if you did?"

He shrugged.

She stared at him. "What does that mean?"

"It means I don't know."

"How could you not know?" she asked, stunned. "You don't have any hopes and dreams?"

"I already have my dream job," he said, which she couldn't help noticing didn't really answer her question.

"You have to have a list," she said.

A whisper of a smile curved his lips. "Who says?"

"Me." She pulled her little notepad from her saddlebag and thrust it at him. "Here, you can write it down as it occurs to you. It's small enough to fit into one of your cargo pockets."

He just kept looking at her, like maybe she was a species he'd never come across before.

She shook the notepad a little, and with a wry twist of his mouth he took the thing and stuck it into one of his myriad of pockets.

When his phone rang again, he looked at the screen and took the call with a terse "Kincaid."

She could hear a male voice, low and pissed off, barking something about a delivery of . . . obnoxious undies?

Hud listened for a few beats and then disconnected, all without a word.

"What was that?" she asked.

"Aidan."

She stared at him. "And?"

"Nosy much?" he asked.

"It was the mention of obnoxious undies," she admitted. "And yes, I'm nosy as hell."

His mouth twitched. "My brothers and I have an ongoing . . . thing. One of us sends another one of us a package. And whatever's in it has to be worn on the next day. Proof is required or there will be a dare. And trust me, no one wants to face a Kincaid dare."

"Package," she repeated. "As in the aforementioned obnoxious undies?"

"The more obnoxious the better." He smiled. "Aidan just got his delivery. Tomorrow he'll be wearing butterfly lace bikini panties with cutouts in some pretty strategic areas, and he's pissed because it's some kind of anniversary between him and Lily and he wants a pass."

"Which of course you're going to give him," she said. "Right?"

"Oh, so wrong." Hud grinned and it nearly melted the bones right out of her knees. He stepped closer. "Guess what?"

"What?" she asked, annoyingly breathless.

"It's my turn for a question now."

Oh boy. "Aren't you afraid that might express personal interest?"

His smile was a little naughty. "I've had my tongue down your throat. I'm pretty sure I've already expressed personal interest."

Good point. "So what do you want to know about me?"

"I want to know about your list." When their gazes met, her heart skipped a beat. Damn. She could stare at him staring at her all day long. He never looked at her all sad or worried, and he certainly never looked at her like he felt bad for her and all she'd been through.

It was so incredibly, amazingly attractive.

So she answered his question honestly. "I spent over a decade with an expiration date," she said.

"Cancer?"

"Non-Hodgkin's lymphoma. Got it just before I turned fifteen. I was handed a death sentence but somehow managed to wrestle the beast against all the odds." She shrugged. "I get that most people make a bucket list when something bad happens, but I never did. Ten years is a really long time and for most of it I wasn't normal. My life wasn't anything close to normal. I was really sick, way too sick to do much of anything." She shrugged. "Even so, my doctor always gave me options and she said one of those options needed to be a good spirit. So I secretly dreamed big. And when I got rid of the cancer and I started to feel... normal, I guess, I wrote down the list I'd been secretly dreaming of. A what-I-get-to-do-now-that-I-get-to-stay-alive list. Probably silly but there it is."

She waited for the usual platitudes, empty and meaningless and rather annoying, but again they didn't come.

What did come stunned her. "Not silly, not even close. I think you're incredibly brave," he said quietly.

She automatically started to shake her head *no* because she'd never thought of herself as brave before—the opposite actually. There'd been plenty of times when she hadn't been able to see the end of the line, hadn't been able to imagine herself getting to this point, had in fact wanted it just to be over.

So "brave"? Nope, but she sure could get used to seeing him look at her like she was and maybe she'd get brave by osmosis. "Thank you," she said just as quietly. It'd only been a week but she'd half convinced herself that she'd imagined the chemistry between them. She hadn't, and she was glad.

"So you're good," he said.

She nodded.

"Stay that way," he said, and took the hammer from her hand.

"Am I keeping you from anything important?" she

asked as he tossed the hammer aside and began to pull out long pieces of steel and planks of wood.

"Depends on your definition of 'important,'" he said, easily moving the long pieces of steel, the muscles of his shoulders and back moving enticingly beneath his shirt. "Been up since three a.m. on avalanche control and was about to grab breakfast."

Good Lord. He'd been working for six hours already. And now she had him loading steel and wood, carrying it around the side of the building, and putting it together so she could access the entire wall. "Listen, I can get someone else to help me—"

"Bailey?"

"Yeah?"

"Shh." Once he had all the material stacked near the wall they began to put it all together, and she had to admit she could never have managed on her own.

Not to mention that working in such close proximity as they were, there was a lot of accidental touching. A brushing of hands, bumping of shoulders . . . And every time he pulled back.

"What is that?" she finally asked when they stood on the second level of the scaffolding. She was hot, insulted, and dammit, also annoyingly turned on.

"What's what?" he asked.

"You know what. You're acting like you're afraid to touch me."

"We both know that's not true," he said, eyes hot, making her remember when he'd pushed her back against her car and touched her plenty. In fact, if he'd touched her for another minute or two, she'd have had an orgasm right there in the parking lot.

"I'm not afraid to touch you," he said.

"Then you feel sorry for me because I was sick," she said, hating that idea.

He winced with guilt but not pity, which was good. Pity would have brought out her homicidal tendencies.

"I told you I'm not sick now," she said.

Hudson looked her right in the eyes. "And I heard you."

Her heart skipped a little beat. "So if you're not afraid of me and you don't feel sorry for me, what's the problem?"

He didn't answer. Instead, his gaze swept over her, from her eyes to her mouth, and locked in.

Stepping into him, she poked him in the chest. "Well?"

He scrubbed a hand over his face. "Don't push me on this, Bailey."

She pushed him.

He gave her a long, hard look that didn't scare her off. Nor did he budge.

She glanced up at him, hands on hips.

He shook his head and muttered "fuck it" and then hauled her up against him and covered her mouth with his.

The kiss was hot and wet and deep and amazing, and by the time he lifted his head from hers, she could hardly remember her point, much less her name.

Holy.

Cow.

A couple of wolf whistles had her jerking back from him. Some of Hud's crew had arrived to help with the scaffolding.

Good timing, too, because God knew she wouldn't have found the strength to stop what had probably been the hottest kiss of her life. "That's not a problem," she whispered, deciding to play it light. "That was fun." She turned away before he could get the truth in her eyes, but he grabbed her. "Careful."

Right. They were on the second tier of the scaffolding, fourteen feet up from the ground. Given the look in his eyes, she hadn't been the only one feeling the heat. "I'm okay."

That got a half smile out of him. "Glad someone is."

So he was just as affected as she. Something to think about. Later. When her mind cleared of the sensual daze he'd put her in.

The guys went to work building the scaffolding and she went back to standing there as if nothing had happened. As if her world hadn't just been completely rocked to the very foundation.

The entire structure was in place by eleven.

And then she was alone with her wall. She had the iPad and her rough draft, and with that she went to work dividing the wall into equal sections to begin sketching.

That night Bailey stayed in a one-room efficiency apartment on-site. She stayed up late filling in more details for the mural and got up early to get back to the wall. When she walked up to it and took in the sheer size of it, the doubts crept back in.

Hard.

As she stared at it and the reality of what she planned to do, her heart started pounding, and in spite of the thirty-two degrees and the windchill factor, she began to sweat.

It's just math, she reminded herself. It was just a management of size, and as a graphic artist, she knew this. She was good at this.

But standing there with an impending anxiety attack barreling down on her, she panicked. What made her think she could pull this off? The mural, the list...hell, everything. What did she know about living life?

"Problem?"

At the sound of Hudson's voice behind her, she jumped and shoved her iPad back into her cross-body saddlebag at her feet. "No."

"Then why are you talking to yourself?"

"I always talk to myself," she said.

"You always tell yourself you're an idiot?"

She sighed and turned to face him. He was in his gear, and given the tenseness of his shoulders it appeared to have been an extremely long morning already. Or maybe it was her. "Remember how you didn't want me to do this?"

"Yeah."

"Well you win."

"Tell me it's a six-pack of beer and a pizza."

Not able to find the funny, she shook her head. "I'm going to get white paint to cover the grid I made and put it back to the way it was and make your day."

He stared at her for a long beat. "Did I leave and come back to an alternate universe?"

"Yes. And the Bailey in this universe is messed up." With that, she scooped up her bag, threw the strap over her head, and stalked off. The effect was less dramatic than she'd have liked since she caught the bag on the scaffolding and was jerked around and brought up short. Which meant she had to untangle herself with an audience, and that of course took way too long.

Hud actually had to come help her, his big hands and dexterous fingers pushing hers aside and easily freeing her.

"I was trying to walk off in a snit," she said.

"I have a sister, so I majored in snit," he said. "Talk to me."

She sighed. "I think I just need to go home and clear my head."

"Understandable," Hud said. "But tell me you're coming back next weekend."

She met his gaze and realized her mistake because his eyes drew her right in. "You didn't even want this," she said quietly.

"Things change," he said back just as quietly. "Go home. Regroup. I'll see you next weekend."

"How can you be so sure of that?"

He studied her for a long moment. "Because I know what it's like to doubt yourself. But I also know what it's like to want something bad. And you want this. The mural."

And you… "Maybe things change," she said.

"Maybe," he agreed. "But my money is still on you."

Chapter 9

Hud lived in a 1950s ski lodge about a half mile up the fire road from the parking lot. The resort had abandoned it in the '80s for a new lodge, so the Kincaids had taken it over and now called it home.

The three-story log building was drafty in the winter, leaked in the spring, and couldn't be efficiently cooled in the summer. But to Hud and his siblings, the place was the only true family home they'd ever known.

The Kincaid siblings had divided the lodge into four living quarters. Aidan and Lily, and also Hud, were on the bottom floor in two separate suites. Kenna had taken half the second floor, the other half being full of all the crap they'd accumulated over the years. The third story was for the marrieds Gray and Penny, and the rest of them tried real hard to ignore the occasional fighting match—and then the squeaking bedsprings that always followed said fighting match.

The weekend had ended and the crowds left Cedar

Ridge en masse. Including Bailey, who hadn't painted over her markings on the wall. Hud was going to take that as a sign that she would be back. He hoped so, which surprised him. There was something about her, something that made him smile, made him think, made him... yearn.

Monday night he and his siblings ate pizza in the open living room. *Annihilated* might have been a better word. It'd been a Ski for Schools day, meaning that Cedar Ridge cut the price of the ticket by fifty percent and then split the proceeds with the local schools. It was their way of giving back to the schools, and it brought a ton of traffic in. People loved to ski for half off. And the resort more than made up for the lost income in rentals and food. The full house actually gave them a huge boost for the day—and gave them extra income to go toward their debt.

It seemed that just about everyone within five hundred miles had turned out to ski that day.

"Met with the bank today," Gray said quietly when they'd eaten everything but the cardboard boxes the pizzas had come in.

Penny sighed and slipped her arm around him, setting her head on his shoulder.

"We've got nine months before the balloon payment is due," Gray said. "No extension."

Kenna opened her mouth.

Gray pointed at her. "Don't. Don't say it."

"But I have buckets of money locked away," she said. "Because *you* made me lock it away. It's worthless to me, dammit. I want you to use it. Why won't you let me give it to you for this, to save us?"

"I said no," Gray said firmly, voice flat.

Kenna stared at him. "What-the-fuck-ever," she finally said, and stormed out, probably to hole up in her room like the hermit she'd become.

"Gray," Penny said softly.

"No, Pen," Gray said tightly. "She earned that money with her own blood, sweat, and tears. She's not using it to bail us out of the mess our asshole dad left us in."

"But he's her dad, too, and she wants to be one of you."

"She is one of us," Gray said. "She's our baby sister and we protect her, not use her." He looked at Aidan and Hud. "Agreed?"

"Agreed," Aidan said, and reached out for Lily's hand. She smiled at him and nodded.

"Agreed," Hud said just as easily.

Kenna had been a professional snowboarder from the age of fifteen to last year, when she'd crashed and burned, both physically and metaphorically.

She still wasn't on the people train and had been hiding out here at Cedar Ridge, pouting, playing Candy Crush on her tablet, refusing to answer her phone to any of her old contacts.

When she'd first come home again, Gray had talked her into locking up her winnings and sponsorship loot. He'd deposited it for her—long-term investments—so that she wouldn't be further weighed down by her own ruthless, self-destructive streak.

It'd been nearly a year now and she was no longer walking around like she might kill the first person to look at her wrong, but she was far from back on track. None of them could stomach the idea of using her money to save their hides when the day could very well come when she might need it.

Gray got a text, something about a computer problem. Shortly after that, Aidan got a search and rescue call. And then Hud got his own call as well, someone on duty at the police station had gotten sick and Hud was needed for the graveyard shift.

And so, on went the week.

By the time Friday came around, he was done in. But that night he worked another cop shift and no sooner had he started than an alarm came in for a burglary call. An eighty-year-old man had called 9-1-1 claiming someone was in his kitchen eating his brand-new raspberry tarts. And he'd been right. There'd been someone in his kitchen eating his raspberry tarts—a three-hundred-and-fifty-pound bear roughly the size of a VW Bug, sitting at the guy's kitchen island, calm as you please.

Bears were more common than traffic accidents in Cedar Ridge.

The next call was from the local drug store. Three reportedly armed suspects had gotten into the ceiling vents, working their way toward the safe. Unfortunately for them, they'd fallen through the ceiling tiles. Hud and two other units arrived just as the suspects were stirring, writhing on the ground, moaning in pain.

They were teenagers, not armed—although they were drunk—and dressed as superheroes. One of them had gotten the brilliant idea to rob the store. Not for cash.

Nope, the geniuses had wanted candy.

It was three in the morning before Hud got home. Assuming no one else needed him, he had two whole hours of sleep ahead of him. He fell into his bed, and as often happened when he was exhausted, he dreamed badly.

"What did you just say to me?" Hud asked Jacob, standing nose-to-nose with him immediately after high school graduation.

"You heard me."

"I couldn't have heard you correctly," Hud said to his identical twin, the one person on the face of the planet who knew him inside and out. *"I couldn't have heard that you're out of here. I couldn't have heard that you're already packed and we leave tonight."*

"And what's wrong with that?" Jacob asked. *"It was always our plan. Go see the world."*

" 'What's wrong with that?' " Hud repeated, shocked. *"Are you kidding me? What isn't wrong with that? What about Mom? Or the fact that for the past six years since we first came here—with nothing!—we actually have a roof over our heads and food when we need it, food we didn't have to beg, borrow, or steal. We have family now, Jacob. People who care about us. There's no reason to go."*

Jacob shook his head, frustrated, pissed. "I get all that. And they've been really good to us but, Hud, staying was never the plan. Leaving was. Always. Travel the world, see shit... Have you forgotten? Maybe with life being so easy here, you like being fat and lazy."

Hud managed a laugh at that. They were still both so lanky and thin that people were always

*trying to shove food down their throats. And as for
lazy, neither of them would know what to do with a
day off. "Mom's here," he said again. "She can't
go. And we can't just leave her. We're all she has."*

*Jacob closed his eyes and then opened them, and
when he did they were full of pain. "We'll send all
our money back to her, everything we earn. But listen to me, Hud, and know that this kills me every bit
as much as it does you—she knows, she's always
known, that we wanted to leave. She doesn't expect
us to stay. She loves it here. And hell, man, half the
time she doesn't even know whether we're with her
or not." He stopped and in a move that was identical to the one Hud made when he was the most frustrated or unsettled, Jacob scrubbed a hand down
his face. "She'll be okay here," he said. "Here more
than anywhere else."*

*Hud knew that. He did. And he'd absolutely
made plans with Jacob to do this, but that had been
before. Before they'd met Gray and Aidan, and
Char, and then Kenna. Before they'd all become
true family in a way they'd never had before. They'd
had their mom, yes, but the mother/son bond had
always been tenuous, dependent on the day of the
week and whether Carrie had her feet based in reality or in the clouds. The fact was that they'd raised
her, not the other way around, and here in Cedar
Ridge, for the first time in their lives, they truly had
someone, several someones, at their backs.*

No matter what.

*At least that's how Hud felt. But Jacob had never
really settled in here, had never allowed himself to*

get to know the rest of their family. He'd kept himself apart and that had driven a wedge between
the twins that Hud had never imagined happening.
"We have family here," he repeated, wanting Jacob
to get it. Needing him to. "Jacob, we don't have to
leave like we thought we would."

"We've had family before," Jacob said stubbornly. "Never made any difference to us."

"If you're referring to Dad," Hud said, "be careful cuz he's not the best example. But hey, if you
want to be like him and split, fine. Do it."

Jacob narrowed his eyes, temper lit. "What does
that mean?"

Hud's temper matched. "You want out? Then go,
man." He shoved Jacob back a step. "Get the hell
out. Just like he did. Who needs you?"

Jacob stared at him for a long beat. "Apparently
not you. And if that's how you feel, preferring them
over me, your own flesh and blood, then fuck you,
I'm gone."

"Fine!"

"Fine!" Jacob echoed.

And then, sick to his stomach, had come the
words Hud didn't even know could be strung
together in a sentence, words born of frustration
and a stupid teenage bad 'tude. "If you go," he
said, "we're no longer brothers."

Jacob stared at him for a long beat and then
without another word, walked away. He didn't look
back.

When he realized his phone was vibrating with an

incoming call, he sat straight up in bed, heart aching. But it was nearly a decade later, time to get over that shit. Besides, it was four in the morning on Saturday and the job needed his attention, which made him groan. Two hours of sleep wasn't going to cut it, but what choice did he have? He scrubbed a hand down his face, still feeling the loss of his twin as if no time had gone by at all.

Dammit, Jacob.

Back then, on that long-ago day, Hud had nearly gone after him, but in the end he hadn't. He couldn't leave his mom and he wouldn't leave the rest of the family either.

True to his word, through an online bank, Jacob had set up an automatic payment that dropped into their mom's account every single month since he'd been gone.

Which at times had been Hud's only indication that Jacob was still alive.

At first, hurting at missing out on the adventure with Jacob, Hud had gone for the closest thing—the police academy. He'd become a cop and had also worked his way up through the resort to run ski patrol.

And it was ski patrol calling him.

Mother Nature had dumped another six inches of snow since he'd fallen into bed, which meant he needed to get with his avalanche patrol crew and check the mountain.

By dawn they'd deemed the place safe to open for the day. Hud sent his guys off to breakfast before they had to be back out there setting lines and patrolling when the resort opened.

"You're not coming with?" Mitch asked inside the cafeteria, surprised when Hud didn't head toward the food with them.

"Got something to take care of," he said.

Mitch's easy smile faded. "News on Jacob?"

"No." Nothing new to report on that front was better than bad news given that Jacob was still completely incommunicado, something that both frustrated and scared him. "Nothing new," he said to Mitch. "I'll meet up with you."

He headed into the cafeteria kitchen. It was hustling and bustling, people cooking and preparing food to support the resort for the day. His nose was assaulted with the scent of coffee, bacon, cinnamon rolls... all of it making his mouth water.

"Hudson," a female voice purred.

He turned to find Quinn, one of the chefs and the ex Gray had mentioned the week before. She smiled warmly. "You've been avoiding me," she said with her usual frankness. Like it didn't even matter that the last time he'd seen her, she'd chucked his own phone at his head. Her smile and teasing tone promised all was forgiven.

"Just busy," he said. The utter truth. She was beautiful and fun and he told himself if he'd had a spare second, he might have taken her up on the promise in her eyes, even if it'd lead to another blowout. But as of two weeks ago and one blue-eyed muralist, he hadn't given another woman a single thought.

Quinn shook her head and called him on his bullshit. "You're such a liar, Hud. No one's that busy."

And that was an argument they'd had a million times and the reason he couldn't go there again with her. "I just need to get some stuff to go," he said, gesturing to the food.

"Want me to take a quick break and eat with you? It's been a while." She smiled. "I'll even resist throwing your phone at your head when it goes off the whole time."

"Quinn, I'm on the run. I'm sorry."

"Sorrier than you know," she murmured, and shrugged. "You're the one missing out, Hud."

This he knew firsthand. He selected what he wanted, put it all in a bag, and swiped his card. He didn't really know why he was doing this. It would let Bailey in on a little secret, tell her something that he didn't particularly want her to know.

That he'd been thinking of her. That he'd hoped she'd show up and not give up—although he knew she'd at least indeed shown up, as he'd checked the employee housing log.

Insanity, really, all of it. He'd kissed her last week half hoping that it would burn out the embers. Instead it'd done the opposite.

Yes, he'd wanted her gone. But now he just wanted her.

"So who is she?" Quinn asked.

No one he wanted to discuss.

Quinn shook her head, annoyed now. "What is it with you Kincaids? You're all wild and crazy and fun, and then one day a woman captures your heart and it's game over in a damn blink."

Was that true? It sure had been for Gray and Aidan.

But not him. It didn't happen that fast, couldn't happen that fast. He wasn't going to allow *it* to happen at all. He didn't have the time in his life for this.

You could make time, a little voice said. A voice he steadfastly ignored.

                              *   *   *

Bailey awoke with a start, completely discombobulated.
She sat straight up in a bed that wasn't hers, a gasp on her
lips.

She'd been dreaming again, the recurring nightmare
where she was back in the hospital hearing the results of
her tests, only they weren't good.

> *"The treatment didn't work," her doctor said solemnly,
> so unlike last time when the woman had practically
> danced a jig in her excitement to impart the good news
> to Bailey. "It's time to make sure your affairs are in
> order…"*

A knock on the door made her jump. She got the feeling
it was the second or third time, which solved the mystery
of what had woken her up.

She was in her efficiency apartment on the resort property. A place she'd been given for the weekends over the
next two months as she worked on the mural.

Which of course was no longer going to happen since
she'd come up here to tear down the scaffolding, apologize to Carrie, and paint the wall white again, hiding her
grid.

Or… get over herself and her doubts and paint the
mural.

Another knock on the door—whoever was out there
had clearly lost patience with waiting.

She sighed and slid out of the bed. She went up on tiptoe and peered through the peephole. Damn. She sank
back onto her bare feet and stared at the wood, heart
pounding.

"I can hear you breathing," Hudson said.

An entire week and still just the sound of his voice made her nipples happy. "You cannot." *Dammit.* She bit her tongue to keep herself silent.

"Come on, Bailey. Open up and let me have it. You know you want to."

Yeah, far too much.

"I have coffee, donuts, and bacon," he cajoled. "I wasn't sure what your poison was so I tried to cover all the basic food groups: caffeine, sugar, and trans fats. If none of those work, I'll..."

"What?" she asked.

"I'll tell you about Jacob."

She stilled and then whipped open the door. "You will?"

He strode in and kicked the door shut behind him, slouching onto the couch, making himself comfortable. "No."

"So you lied?" she asked, shocked.

He looked amused at her disbelief. "I needed to see you." He handed over the coffee.

Eyes still narrowed, she greedily took the coffee and sipped because the caffeine was calling her name.

Huh. Sugar and a shot of vanilla cream, just the way she liked it.

She supposed that was all the apology she was going to get. She stared at him, telling herself she was not moved in the slightest by the sight of him. Even if the sight of him was incredibly sexy, all clad in a skintight black Under Armour shirt and black cargo ski pants loaded with gear coming out of every pocket.

And then there was his smile as he waggled the bag,

wafting the scent of bacon and donuts, damn him, like he knew very well she couldn't possibly resist. She blew out a breath and sat next to him.

He opened the bag. "Donuts or bacon?"

She gave him a look like he was an amateur, making him laugh.

"Both it is," he said. He handed the whole bag over and she wasn't mad enough at him not to dive in.

"Crispy," she said on a moan around a bite of bacon. Just the way she loved it. And there were two donuts. She grabbed the old-fashioned chocolate glaze and offered him the other. "It must be Christmas." The first bite of the donut yanked another moan right out of her. She had to close her eyes to savor it.

"Need a moment alone?" he asked, sounding amused again.

"Yes." But when she opened her eyes, he was still there.

In fact, he hadn't taken his gaze off her. "I'm glad you're here. Glad you didn't give up," he said.

She was glad too. "I'm not equipped to have a deep conversation until all the sugar and fat and caffeine sinks into my system." She licked the sugar off her thumb and dove back into the bag.

He patiently waited until she'd finished every last bite.

She looked at him, his fathomless eyes holding everything close to the vest, his square jaw suggesting equal parts strength and stubbornness. Emphasis on the *stubbornness*, she was beginning to learn. His broad-as-the-mountains shoulders that held the weight of his world.

He both drew her in and terrified her. "I regrouped," she said.

He smiled. "Glad to hear it."

"But I still don't have all the information I need to do the full Kincaid family tree," she reminded him.

Jacob. His name hovered between them a moment.

"Fair enough," he said. "One question, whatever you want."

"Where is he?"

"Missing."

She waited for more but true to form, nothing came. "I want to ask what that means," she said. "But the truth is, I can leave Jacob out or I can fake it. I'm a damn good faker," she said. "I'm also insanely nosy. I'm trying to curb it out of respect for you, but I've never been very good at curbing myself."

"No kidding." He paused. "We were eighteen when he left."

"Left? But you said he was missing."

"Missing from my life." He took her empty coffee cup and shoved it into the now-empty bag and wadded it all up. Then he executed a perfect three-pointer into the trash in the kitchenette on the other side of the room.

It hadn't occurred to her that Jacob had walked away from his family and never returned. Bailey had been upset with her mom plenty over the years, but she'd never once considered going away and breaking off all contact, every last tie.

"I meant it about quitting, Bailey," Hud said, stretching out an arm along the back of the couch where his fingers settled just behind her neck. "Don't quit. Not because of me. Don't let me win. I don't deserve it."

"It's not because of you."

"Then what?" he asked. "You're not the quitting type."

"You don't know that," she said.

"I think I do."

She met his gaze. His mouth was still curved slightly but his eyes were serious. Serious and she found herself wanting to fall into them and drown. "I let my doubts take over," she admitted.

"You can do this."

The words fueled her and filled a hole she hadn't realized was inside her, much less that it needed filling. Before she even realized what she was doing, she leaned toward him.

He cupped her jaw, his thumb rasping over her lower lip. Then he sucked the pad of that thumb into his mouth. "Mmm," he said, voice low and gravelly. "Chocolate."

That's when she remembered she was in her pajamas—a pair of sweat bottoms cut off to indecent heights and a thin, tight tank top that wasn't going to hide the fact that certain parts of her were happier to see him than other parts. She was embarrassed but she could tell by the heat in Hud's eyes that embarrassment wasn't what he felt... Far from it.

"Oh boy," she whispered as he cupped the back of her head and drew her mouth to his—

His radio went off.

He stilled for a beat, their mouths a fraction of an inch apart, the anticipation so high she nearly cried before slowly pulling back. "Duty calls?" she asked.

"Yeah." Blowing out a sigh, he rose to his feet.

Bailey did the same, a hand to her chest, trying to calm her heart rate.

Impossible.

Especially when he looked at her for a long moment and then pulled her in again for one quick kiss. Just the appetizer on his menu, but no less potent for it. It left her dumbstruck—*kiss*-struck, she corrected.

He flashed her a crooked smile. "Kick ass today, Bailey," he said.

And then he was gone.

Chapter 10

Hud left Bailey's knowing he'd be deeply distracted by the memories of her, soft and warm from sleep, in those teeny-tiny PJs that spurned even more fantasies—all of them down and dirty—for the entire day.

Not two minutes after leaving her, his body still thrumming with want, ski patrol was called to the top of lift eight.

Two young twentysomethings, brothers, had been seen fighting on the lift as it neared the top. Apparently one brother had started out with angry words that degenerated into fists. Somewhere along the way, one of the brothers slipped off the lift and fell about twenty feet. Wearing a helmet had definitely saved his noggin, but he'd broken his arm and possibly his clavicle as well.

Which hadn't slowed down the fight much. Reportedly, the other brother had climbed down the lift to join his brother.

When Hudson and Mitch and a bunch of other ski

patrollers arrived on scene, the pair were still rolling around on the snow, fists flying, directly beneath the lift, which the lift operator had stopped.

This meant that there was a long line of people hanging over the mountain, skis and boards dangling as they waited for the lift to get moving again, watching in rapt fascination as the idiot brothers wrestled and yelled at each other.

"I didn't say you could sleep with her!" one yelled.

"She dumped you!" the other yelled back. "You said she was a crazy bitch!"

"Yeah, so why did you screw her?"

"Because she's a *hot* crazy bitch!"

"I'm going to kill you!"

Hud dragged one free while his team grabbed the other.

They looked so much alike that they were clearly brothers. And they continued to fight, though now they were united in that fight as they tussled with the ski patrollers instead of each other. But Hud and his team quickly got them under control and restrained.

One of the brothers, the one who'd slept with the "crazy bitch," was cradling his clearly broken arm.

"Shit," the other said, staring at the arm. "You broke it again."

"*You* broke it!"

They argued about that the entire time Hud and Mitch were strapping the injured brother to a sled, preparing to take him down the mountain.

As they began the descent, the uninjured brother stayed alongside so that the two of them could continue to yell at each other.

"And don't think I've forgotten that you owe me fifty bucks," the injured one yelled from flat on his back. "I won our last two bets and you've never paid up! *Cheapskate!*"

"I don't owe you shit! You stole my bike and crashed it!"

"That piece of shit was no good anyway!"

And so it went on.

When they got to the bottom, they loaded the injured brother directly into an ambulance. Yet another fight broke out when the uninjured one wanted to make the ride with his brother and the EMTs refused to take him because he kept stirring up their patient.

The ambulance drove off and the uninjured brother stared after it, suddenly silent and looking deflated. He lifted his head to Hud, eyes shiny and miserable. "They'll take care of him, right? They won't let him die?"

"They won't let him die," Hud promised, and turned away to get back to work.

But the guy grabbed Hud's arm. "You swear it?"

Hud looked into his devastated face and was propelled back to another time, another fight, with his own brother. Ten years ago this had been them. Young. Cocky. Hot-headed idiots. "I swear it," Hud said.

"I can't be without him," the guy said quietly, the fight gone, the adrenaline draining.

Yeah, Hud got that too. Once, he and Jacob had been like a pair of porcupine siblings, constantly needling each other but unable to be apart either.

How quickly they'd gotten okay with that. Except Hud had *never* gotten okay with it, not really. Every single fucking day he missed Jacob, like he'd miss a damn limb.

"I need a ride to the hospital," the guy suddenly said.

"How did you get here?" Hud asked.

"My brother drove his new truck. I crashed his last one, so I'm not supposed to drive this one. He said he'd kill me if I did."

Hud shook his head and pointed to the shuttle's pickup spot. "Every twenty minutes a bus comes by and drives into town."

"Twenty minutes is a long time." The guy looked thoughtful. "Maybe I should hot wire his truck...you know, since it's an emergency situation and all."

Normally Hud was excellent at compartmentalizing his life. All the Kincaids were. Family was family. Play was play. Work was work. And while he was most definitely affected by what he did on the job, and occasionally also moved by the people he helped, for the most part he didn't allow any of it to stick to him. Couldn't, or he wouldn't have anything left to give the next day.

But these guys were brothers. They'd fought, and one had gotten hurt.

There were too many similarities between them and himself and Jacob for him not to be moved. "Listen," he said to the guy. "You can do what you want, but I'm telling you to think about this long and hard. One of these days you're going to pull a stunt that he can't get over or forgive, and he'll leave you. Do you understand me? So do yourself a favor and take the damn bus."

The guy blinked. "Okay, jeez."

When he'd stalked off, Mitch came up beside Hud. "That was a little harsh."

"It was the cold, hard truth," Hud said, and walked away. He headed for his office but then decided fuck it, he needed to take a ski run to clear his head. Ten minutes later, he was flying down Devil's Face, the wind in his face, his thighs burning, his lungs taxed, and feeling much better.

When the lodge came into view, he slowed and then stopped.

From here he could see the wall, which for as long as he could remember had been blank.

No longer.

It was crisscrossed with the scaffolding and he could see a small figure on the third tier. From here he couldn't see much else since she was just sketching things in, but he knew that over the next few weeks that would change. Soon enough he'd be able to see himself and his family portrayed on that wall.

For better or worse.

He wanted to stay stoic about it, but there was something about the free-spirited Bailey Moore that grabbed him by the heart he'd thought long dead.

He liked her. There was no denying that. But he didn't like the feelings she invoked from deep inside him. He could feel himself being drawn into her more each day.

But that didn't—couldn't—matter. His head was too full. He needed to help get the resort out of their dad's debt before they lost it. His mom was getting worse and that weighed on him. And then there was Jacob. The guilt and regret were killing Hud. He simply didn't feel like he deserved to be happy until he had Jacob home where he belonged.

Even if that meant missing out on what he suspected was the best woman to ever happen to him.

The following week was both painstakingly slow and whipping by. Hud visited his mom on the only night he could get away from the mountain and took her for her favorite—pizza at the local brewery, the Slippery Slope. He had a few of her friends there, including Char—Aidan and Gray's mom.

At the end of the meal Char had the waitresses bring in a cake and they all sang "Happy Birthday."

It wasn't Carrie's birthday but she liked to celebrate birthdays. If they didn't do hers, then they had to celebrate his—which he hadn't done since Jacob left.

Char had brought a roll of quarters and they loaded up the jukebox with '80s hair-band songs, and then they sang each and every one word for word. Char had them using spoons for microphones and she even got up on a table to dance—until her boyfriend and Cedar Ridge equipment manager, Marcus, got her down.

"Enough beer for you," he said.

Char beamed at him. She and Carrie were a huge hit and it took another hour to get them out of there.

"Best birthday ever," Carrie said on the way home. She always said that.

When Hud got her tucked in, she smiled hopefully.

Hud dropped a wrapped present in front of her and she clapped in delight. "Oh, baby! You shouldn't have!"

She always said that, too, every single week. The presents he gave her ranged from her favorite candy bar to movie tickets to a preloaded Visa that she could use online, though right now she had his credit card—which he needed to get back from her. They were going with preloaded from now on.

She squealed and nearly pierced his eardrums. She'd opened the iPod that he'd filled with her favorite music because she refused to listen to music on her phone. She saved her phone battery for "talking and shopping."

"Oh, Hud!" she cried. "You shouldn't have, but I'm so happy you did!" She shook the thing and he realized she had no idea what it was.

"It's an iPod, Mom. For your music."

"Well, I know that!" She stopped shaking it and held it up to her ear.

He found a smile. "Want me to turn it on for you?"

"No, I've got it. I love it, Hud." As she always did, she carefully folded the wrapping paper into a square and untangled the ribbon, both of which he'd stolen from Kenna's desk drawer.

He stood to leave, watching while his mom turned the iPod over and over. "The power button's on the side," he said, and tried to show her but she clutched it to her chest.

"I've got it!"

He had to laugh. He and Jacob were both stubborn to the end. The apples hadn't fallen far from the tree. But this part of the visit with his mom always made him feel awkward. They hadn't done presents when they were little. She'd never been able to keep dates straight. So that had meant no birthday celebrations, no Easter. No Christmas. At least not on the correct dates. He and Jacob had done their best to keep some semblance of normalcy, but they'd had their hands full with things like making sure bills had been paid and that they had food and a roof over their heads. Holidays and birthdays had been a luxury they'd never given themselves.

Which reminded him what he'd seen on his Visa bill. "Mom, did you order water balloons from Amazon?"

She pretended to be vastly interested in something on the iPod. He was pretty sure she still hadn't gotten it turned on but there was no way she'd admit it. "Mom?"

She lifted a shoulder. "I don't think so. Why would I do that? You're a grown man."

Okay so she was with it tonight. Or at least at the moment. And if she was, then he had another question for her. "And cigars?"

"Of course not," she said, now shaking the iPod like it was an Etch A Sketch. "You can't smoke at your age."

And there went the blink-and-you'll-miss-it reality portion of the evening...

Bailey got out of Denver on Friday heading toward Cedar Ridge only to get stuck in mountain traffic, all of them slowed down by unexpected icy conditions. It stressed her out making the drive at night on the windy mountain roads, and she white-knuckled it the whole way. By the time she got to Cedar Ridge, she literally fell out of her car and into her unit.

And slept straight through until her phone beeped an incoming text from Aaron the next morning.

> *You never texted me that you'd arrived in C.R. last night. Let us know you're safe or I'm coming up to find you.*

I'm fine, she quickly texted him back, hating the royal use of the "us"—which in this case meant Aaron and her mom.

They were quite the pair.

It drove her nuts in the worst way. She felt like such a jerk, but she hated that Aaron was still close to her mom. He'd friended her on Facebook and she kept him up to date on all things Bailey.

She got that there'd been a time when the two of them had needed each other, when they'd been each other's support system, when they'd taken turns going to the doctor with Bailey and compared notes on everything from her mood to her temperature to her numbers to her damn bodily functions.

But these things weren't necessary anymore.

She was fine.

She was more than fine. She was alive and planning on staying that way.

And yet they still maintained that unhealthy link, even now when she and Aaron were no longer seeing each other.

It didn't work for her on any level. She was tired of trying to convince them both separately and as a team that she was not working herself into an early grave, that she was loving her choices. They both meant a lot to her, a whole lot, but she and Aaron had broken up for a reason.

He was a saver.

And she didn't need saving.

Since the Breakfast God didn't knock this morning, she showered and dressed and hit the cafeteria herself. She grabbed a coffee to go and a quick breakfast burrito, which she ate on the walk to her car.

Once there, it took her three trips to unload the supplies she'd brought and another half an hour to get herself situated on the scaffolding.

She'd finished penciling in her grand plan, using a big carpenter pencil that she loved working with. The Kincaid family tree had started to come to life, complete with drawings of each of the Kincaids in such a way as to present their unique personalities on the mountain.

Now it was time to start painting.

Challenging as it was, some of it was easy. The background and the tree itself were fun and the actual people would be even more so. She knew exactly what she wanted for each of the siblings. Well, except for Jacob, who she still didn't have a handle on.

And Hudson...but that wasn't because she didn't have a handle on him. That was more thanks to the fact that just thinking about him turned her upside down and sideways.

After she had started with the tree and got it situated the way she wanted, she took a moment to just sit there high up off the ground, cradling her coffee, staring at the mountain in front of her.

The day was...glorious. A painfully blue sky streaked with a few long tendril-like clouds. The rugged peak dotted with the dark green pines, whose tips were frosted in the morning sun. There were people on the mountain, traversing their way down.

It was all so perfect it could have been a painting, and she sat there momentarily overcome by gratitude that she was here to experience it. She tipped her head back and let the sun warm it, let the fresh pine-scented mountain air fill her lungs, and let herself just enjoy and appreciate that she was even here to have the moment.

"Working hard?" asked the now unbearably familiar masculine voice that never failed to send the most delicious kind of shiver right through her body. The sensation pinged off some parts more than others, leaving her both warm from the inside out and also a little dazed. It was a lot of reaction to get from just a voice, but he was also a lot of man.

Chapter 11

It'd been a whole damn week since Bailey had heard that voice, an entire week to replay the feel of his mouth on hers, his body warm and hard against hers. She'd told herself she'd exaggerated his effect on her.

Turned out nope.

She forced herself to remain still, cool, calm, and collected as he leaned his skis against the scaffolding and climbed his way up to her with an effortless ease that had her mouth going completely dry.

There were other reactions, too, reactions she planned on firmly ignoring. Even when he crouched down at her side, balanced on the balls of his feet, and looked over the wall.

She realized she was holding her breath, waiting for his reaction.

It was an endless minute as he absorbed it all, slowly, taking his time to see everything before he turned back to her.

"Okay," he said. "So you know how to paint."

She let out the breath in a *whoosh* and made him smile.

"Like you care what I think," he said.

If he only knew. She blithely ignored this and offered him her coffee.

He took it with a heartfelt gratitude that had her taking a second look at him. "How long have you been up?"

"Since two thirty this morning," he said. "Got called in. The conditions were ripe for an avalanche."

She must have paled because he smiled. "We got it handled."

"How do you handle it?" she asked.

"Explosives."

She blinked.

"Don't worry," he said. "We're good at it."

She let out a breath. That easy confidence was incredibly attractive. Or maybe it was the element of danger she found exciting, though she wasn't sure she liked what that said about her.

Still, the fact remained that she couldn't even begin to imagine all the responsibilities he faced on a daily basis. "The most dangerous thing I face on my job is a paper cut," she said.

He shrugged. "You could fall off this platform. You ever think of that?"

She eyed the drop and felt her stomach quiver. "Not until now, thanks."

He flashed a grin and she stared at his mouth.

His eyes heated. "You're going to need to change the subject now," he said, voice sexy and low, "or we're going to risk the both of us falling off when I haul you over here and—"

"Your list," she said quickly. "You make it yet?"

He pulled her small notebook from one of his cargo pockets, giving her a small smile. He'd kept it on him. That gave her more than a small thrill.

But the notebook was empty of new writing.

"Didn't have time," he said.

"How about now?"

He looked around. "Here?"

"Sure. Unless you're the sort to get stage fright..." Which she knew damn well he was not... "How about I go up a level and give you some privacy."

She'd been up there for five minutes before he spoke again, saying just her name. She was sitting facing the wall working on the tree, and had to twist and bend low to look beneath her.

He was sprawled out on his back, knees up, using a thigh as a surface for steadying the notepad. He looked extremely comfortable. Kind of like a big, lethal wildcat taking a rest before pouncing... He smiled up at her and her pulse kicked. "I'm ready," he said.

Good God. So was she. She cleared her throat. "Let's hear it."

"Number one," he read. "Have sex on scaffolding."

She choked and nearly fell off.

He flashed that devastatingly sexy grin. "I was watching you work above me. I didn't know that painting was so sensual. You move as you paint, your whole body moves, did you know that?"

And he'd had quite the view from below her... She suddenly felt like amending her own list to also include having sex on scaffolding...

"Number two," he read. "Encourage our new muralist to wear a dress when she paints."

Her legs actually quivered. "You're awful."

"Awful sexy, right?"

He was teasing her, and she rolled her eyes and went back to her work. "Since you're not taking this seriously..." she trailed off, and vowed to forget he was there.

"Oh, I'm taking this very seriously."

"Get a room," someone yelled up to them.

They both peered over the edge and found Kenna below, hands on hips and looking irritated. "You're making me remember how long it's been since I got laid," she snapped, and strode off.

"Number three," Hud went on as if Kenna hadn't just called them out on their sexual tension. "Experiment with paints."

"I can teach you how to paint," she said. "But not on my wall."

"*Your* wall?"

She blushed. "Yes. For the duration."

"No worries." His bad-boy smile, naughty to the core, reappeared. "I wasn't talking about painting on your wall."

"On paper?"

"Nope," he said.

She blinked. "You can't mean...body painting?"

"I can't?"

Her entire being trembled at the thought of him, paintbrush in hand, working it across her body.

Maybe they did need a room.

"Oh boy," she whispered, and had to sit again, which she did with a *thunk* that made him laugh.

"Okay," she said. "I get it. The list is silly."

There was a beat of silence and then he climbed up to her level on the scaffolding. Crouching at her side, he put a hand on her belly to steady her but didn't speak until she opened her eyes.

"The list isn't silly," he said. "Far from it. I didn't mean to trivialize it. But any list I'd make would have to be fluid. It'd change all the time as I change. Some things would become not as important as they were and other things would take precedence as I went through life. And that's the point of the list, right? To make sure you're living your life?"

She stared up at him, shocked to the core that he'd taken her from sheer lust to deep thought in a single heartbeat. "Yes," she said. "You're right."

And he was. She *wasn't* the list and she was cheating herself out of exactly what she'd been trying to do—live her life—by limiting herself to the things she'd written. "I need the notebook back."

He pulled it from his pocket and handed it to her. She flipped to the back page, where she had her own list, and added:

Be flexible.

He read it upside down and smiled his approval.

Their gazes met and Bailey realized that once this mural was done she wouldn't have this with him. She'd be gone. Back to Denver. But one thing facing death up close and personal had done for her was teach her to live in the here and now.

And her here and now still had at least a month on the clock, and she was determined to enjoy every single moment of it, even knowing that eventually she would be walking away.

When she shivered, Hudson zipped her jacket up to her neck and pulled her hood up over her ski cap, making sure she was covered. "You wearing sunscreen?" he asked. "We're at altitude and your skin is fair."

"Pale."

"Fair," he repeated. "And beautiful."

He didn't see her as pale and sickly and she could've thrown herself at him for that alone. But there was the whole on-a-scaffolding thing, so throwing herself anywhere would be dangerous.

Still not nearly as dangerous as melting under his touch...

At the look on her face, he grinned, and she couldn't stop the question that fell from her lips. "Are you reading my mind?"

"Don't have to. Everything you think crosses your face for the whole world to see."

"Dammit." She put her hands on her cheeks and sighed. "So now we both know what I want to do."

"Do we?"

He asked this with such faux innocence that she laughed and shook her head. "You need me to paint you a picture?" she asked.

He grinned. "Would you? I'm confused, very confused, so make sure it's real clear. Best add instructions."

She laughed.

"Oh, I'm not kidding," he said. "And I want those instructions, Bailey. In great detail."

"Uh-huh," she said dryly. "Because you have no idea what you're doing, right?"

He was still smiling but his eyes were suddenly very

serious. "When it comes to you? Hell no," he said. "With you, I'm so far out of my league I can't even see the league."

She stared at him, her body suddenly very still, like it couldn't quite take this in. Her brain also struggled to keep up. "Are we still playing?" she whispered. "Cuz I'm not very good at games."

"I'm not playing with you at all."

She blinked, trying to process what this meant. "Then what are we doing?"

His gaze touched over her features and then came back to her eyes. "You need to put a label on it?"

"You don't?"

He gave a slow negative shake of his head.

She was still taking that in when he reached out and ran a finger along her temple and then her jaw. "It's no secret that I want you, and I want you bad," he said with a small wry smile. "But the truth is that probably isn't smart, for either of us. I work twenty-four-seven and am emotionally unavailable, and you . . ."

She'd sucked in a breath at the emotionally unavailable part. That was indeed a huge doorstop. "I what?"

"You live two hours away."

She blinked. "That's it?" she asked. "That's the worst thing you can think of about me?"

He smiled. "Nope, but here's the problem. The fact that you're a smartass and even more stubborn than I am? It totally works in your favor."

"Oh," she breathed, having no idea why that was so . . . well, arousing. He was attracted to her biggest flaws. *How do you not fall for a guy who likes your flaws?* "And I'm supposed to resist?"

"It's your call," he said.

"Great." She blew out a breath. "You should know that I'm not real good at resisting."

He flashed another smile, but she never got to hear what he might have said to that because his radio went off. She was torn between thinking, *Dammit,* and *Oh, thank God,* because he had to go. There was going to be no time to do anything stupid, like keep talking and forcing them to put a name on this…thing between them. Her heart was ever so much safer just as things were. No complications. Just a few admittedly hot stolen moments. No real intimacy.

But he didn't rush off. He stood there and looked at her very seriously. "What's it going to be, Bailey? We going for this?"

Oh boy. So he wasn't the sort to put off a decision. She should have known that about him.

I'm not emotionally available…

Those words haunted her. She wanted him, but she wanted more than just his body—didn't she? Or at least she wanted the *chance* at more. Holding his gaze, she gave a slow shake of her head. She wasn't exactly looking for The One right this minute, but if she was going to get intimate with someone, she wanted him to at least have potential to be that person. She would need to protect herself against Hud since he'd taken himself out of the race. "You aren't The One," she whispered.

Hud held himself still for a heartbeat before letting out a low breath and nodding. "Smart choice." That said, he hauled her up to her toes and kissed her with a whole lot of tongue and frustration, and by the time he pulled back she had his shirt in two tight fists.

Good Lord. Forcing herself to let go of him, she smoothed the wrinkles she'd left. "What was that?" she whispered.

His mouth curved slightly. "That was one part damn-I'm-an-idiot-for-letting-you-go and one part good-bye."

And then he turned, leaving her standing there dazed as he lithely climbed down and vanished.

Chapter 12

That night Hud was actually alone in the old lodge, something that almost never happened because Kenna rarely went anywhere off the premises. But Lily and Penny had dragged her out for girls' night, something about dinner and an indie theater viewing of *Fifty Shades*—which they'd already all seen a dozen times.

Hud didn't understand going to that particular flick without someone to get laid with, but Penny had told him that since he was a penis-carrying human he couldn't possibly understand. He was going to trust her on that one.

Aidan and Gray were both still at work. Hud would've been, too, except he'd been on the graveyard shift the past two nights in town and could hardly keep his eyes open.

He'd ordered a pizza, which would arrive any second. He intended to inhale that, snag a few of Aidan's beers from the fridge, and crawl into bed for no less than eight straight hours of sleep.

When the knock came, he'd just gotten out of the

shower. Wrapping a towel around his hips, he grabbed the money he'd left on the foyer entry table and pulled open the front door.

But it wasn't the pizza guy.

Instead, Bailey stood there. She'd been looking at her clasped hands in front of her, but she lifted her head, slowly, her gaze taking in his body as she did.

Her mouth fell open.

Gratifying, he had to admit. "Not that I'm not enjoying the way you're looking at me like I intend to look at my pizza when it arrives," he said, "but what are you doing here?"

Her eyes were still locked on his torso, her teeth sinking into her lower lip.

"Bay," he said.

Her eyes heated at the shortening of her name, and he let out a rough laugh and gripped the doorjamb at either side of him rather than reach for her. "You can't look at me like that and tell me nothing's happening."

"Yeah, and while we're on the subject..." She lifted her gaze to his and blushed. "I might have been...hasty in some of the things I said last time I saw you. That's why I'm here. I came to retract part of it."

He stilled. Or most of him did. One particular appendage did the opposite of being still. "Which part?"

She swallowed hard and stepped into him, setting her hands on his stomach. Head bent, she stared at her fingers on his bare skin, her brow furrowed in concentration.

Up or down, babe. Either way works, but I pick down...

She drew in a shaky breath. "The whole point of me even being here in Cedar Ridge was to gain experiences I couldn't have before." Her fingers shifted slightly, driving him crazy. "Things I thought I'd never get to do because my only focus was surviving."

Aw, hell. "Bailey—"

"No, please, let me finish," she rushed on. "I'm twenty-four and I've lived so damn sheltered that I didn't even know some of what I was missing. But when I'm with you…" She smiled and bit her lip again. "I feel things. *You* make me feel things."

"Like irritated? Annoyed?"

"Yes," she agreed, and laughed. "But also warm. And…" Her fingers flexed and so did his libido. "Fuzzy."

"Warm and fuzzy?" he repeated, running the unexpected adjectives through his brain. "I'm not a pair of slippers, Bailey."

"No—I know that," she said, and seemed to get flustered, lifting her hands from him and waving them around like that might help her find the words she was looking for.

Feeling his chest constrict, he caught her hands in his. "You're trying to tell me something."

"Yes!" She sucked in a breath. "I've never had a… fling." She grimaced. "I bet people don't even use that word anymore. But whatever they call it, hot, up-against-the-wall sex, or gorilla sex, or—" She broke off and stared up at him when he choked on his own breath of air. "What?"

He shook his head, not wanting to interrupt her, but God, she was the sweetest, sexiest thing he'd ever seen and she had no idea. Not a single one. "Are you a virgin, Bailey?"

She sighed. "No, but I can see why you'd ask me that. I don't know how to say this, that's all."

"Just say it," he said quietly. "You can say anything to me, anything at all."

"Okay," she said. "I'm having trouble finding words because I've never done this before. A one-night thing. I've been with someone. I was in a relationship with him for a long time. But this...me vocalizing it, that's new to me." She drew in a deep breath. "What I'm trying to say is that I want a one-night stand." She met his gaze, clearly waiting for his reaction.

He opened his mouth and then closed it again. She'd been in a long-term relationship. That wasn't what she wanted from him. What she wanted from him was just a fuck. He was trying to figure out why that bugged the shit out of him when she went on.

"With you," she said. "In case I wasn't clear. I want you."

"For tonight," he clarified.

"Yes."

Ignoring the unmistakable flash of disappointment— *What the hell is that about?*—he pulled her inside, kicked his door shut, and gently pushed her up against the wood and cupped her face. "You need to be sure."

"I am." She blinked. "Are you? Because it's okay if you're not. I can find someone else. I can make a list."

This stopped him. She could make a list? Of who? *Not important*, he told himself. *Shake it off.* "You're not going to need a list for this, Bailey."

She stared at him. "No?"

Hell no. "I already told you that I want you. Now I'm going to show you." He gave her a few beats to absorb that before he leaned in and kissed her, putting every ounce of his want and need into it. In answer, she moaned and wound her arms around him.

Without breaking the kiss, he straightened and cupped

the backs of her thighs, encouraging her to wrap her legs around his waist.

And then he carried her to his suite.

Bailey was already completely lost in Hudson by the time he carried her through the place. So lost that she didn't even look around to appease her curiosity. She couldn't and she didn't want to break off from kissing him. And, oh Lord, his kisses… She loved the way he kissed. Lots of lip movement, lots of tongue. It made her wild. No one had ever kissed her like Hud did, like he couldn't get enough of her.

She really hoped no one else was around, not that she would've noticed. She was very busy as he carried her, silently flirting with her hands, running them over his shoulders and arms, pressing in as close as she could get.

Hud was much more up-front. His hands teased, stroking over her back and hips, squeezing a butt cheek in each hand, his lips hot on her throat. From what seemed like far away she felt and heard him kick a door closed, and then they were alone in a large, open-style suite.

He shifted, holding her with one hand under her ass, using his other to slide the lock into place.

She lifted her head and stared at him as, with her arms and legs still wrapped around him like a monkey, he climbed onto a huge bed and lay all that luscious male weight on top of her. Wearing only a towel… "Hud," she whispered.

He rubbed his jaw to hers like a big cat. Only this big cat had just the right amount of stubble to make her weak kneed. Good thing she wasn't standing because God, he was just so big and hard—everywhere. And gloriously male.

That's when her nerves set in. Maybe she should've set her sights lower, maybe on someone who *also* hadn't done this in a long time. Yeah, that would've been smarter. A little practice never hurt anyone. She gulped. "Maybe we should have a drink first—" She broke off with a helpless moan when Hud found the spot where her neck met her shoulder and nibbled on it, melting her bones.

"After," he murmured.

She made a noise that was half a laugh, half panic.

Lifting his head, he studied her. "You're nervous."

"No." She swallowed. "Okay, yes."

He smiled. "Good."

"How is that good?" she demanded.

"It puts us on even ground."

She stared up at him, her fingers somehow tangled in his hair. When had she done that? Oh, right, when she'd been holding his face to hers so that he couldn't take his mouth away. "You expect me to believe *you're* nervous?" she asked, heavy on the disbelief. "Hello, have you *seen* you?"

He smiled. "Maybe you won't like my moves."

She snorted. He was teasing her. He knew damn well she liked him and his moves. Way too much, in fact.

"Maybe I'm nervous that I won't do it for you," he said, and at that, she outright laughed. As if!

Having suitably distracted her, he went to lift off her sweater, but she put her hands over his. She had a scar above her right breast two inches long and red and angry from the port where she'd received chemo treatments. She wasn't ashamed of it, actually the contrary. The scar represented her treatment—her successful treatment. But she understood that it wasn't pretty and that it certainly wasn't conducive to a sensual mood. "Um," she said brilliantly.

His gaze met hers. "We stopping?"

She squirmed a little bit, knowing men were visual creatures. She didn't want to talk about it nor did she want to watch him pretend to ignore it. "I'm...It's just that—" She sucked on her bottom lip a moment. "No. I don't want to stop. I really, really don't."

He smiled warmly. "I'm with you on that."

She nodded but didn't lift her hands from his. Hud didn't push, just waited with a patience that made it easier for her to speak. "It's just that I have this scar..." she started.

"Do you? Me too." He lifted up a little, pointing to a slash on his left side from his highest rib to his lowest. It was an old scar, faded and white, but she could only imagine what pain it'd caused. "What happened?" she asked, running a finger along the tender spot, fascinated by the way his ab muscles bunched under her touch.

He cleared his throat but when he spoke, his voice still sounded rough. "Jacob and I tried to fly from the top of our storage shed when we were ten." He lifted a shoulder. "Turns out we weren't related to Superman."

She laughed and then bit her lip. "Mine's my port scar. From treatment."

"I could kiss it all better."

This sounded like a really, really great idea.

"Trust me," he said softly.

She stared up at him. She'd known him for all of what, three weeks? So the idea should have been ludicrous. But the fact was that she did trust him. Way more than she was comfortable with, in fact. She nodded, probably like a bobblehead.

With a smile, he kissed her and again reached for her sweater. He pulled it over her head and they both looked down at the pale peach cami she wore beneath—which was when she remembered something else. No bra today. "I didn't have a chance to do laundry before I left Denver," she said quickly. "And—"

He let out a low, very male sound of approval at the sight of her thin, washed-a-million-times cami, apparently liking the way her nipples were trying to poke their way free to get to him. Then he encouraged the straps of the cami to slip, allowing his big hands to dip into the gaping front and cup her breasts.

"Oh," she breathed on a shuddering exhale, her head falling back. She'd forgotten how good it felt to have hands on her for reasons that had nothing to do with saving her life and everything to do with sheer pleasure.

"Okay?" he murmured.

"Very," she whispered, eyes closed. "More please."

He laughed softly, his warm breath caressing her throat as he did. "So polite."

"I t-t-try," she managed, stuttering as he lifted the cami up and over her head.

When he didn't make a sound or move, she covered her scar and sighed. "I told you," she said, and opened her eyes.

He bent and kissed her fingers. Then he pried them away from her body and kissed the scar itself. "You're beautiful," he said against her skin. "Every inch of you, in and out. Don't apologize for the scar. It's a part of you, a really important part."

She smiled, the words warming her. "I wasn't worried for me," she said softly. "I just didn't want to wreck your mood with it."

He let out a low laugh, shook his head, and leaned in. "You're amazing," he said, and brushed his mouth over hers. "Don't ever worry about my mood. My mood is not your problem or your responsibility. Ever. And in any case, you elevate my mood." He stroked his hands down her torso and went straight for the button on her jeans.

"Hudson?"

He lifted his head from his task and looked at her, his eyes so dark they appeared nearly black, heavy lidded with all sorts of thoughts that seemed entirely about her and entirely erotic.

And she promptly forgot what she wanted to say.

Leaning up, he cupped her face and kissed her, soft, sweet. "Bailey, if you're not ready—"

"No." She put her fingers over his mouth and shook her head. "I'm ready," she promised. She kissed his jaw and then rubbed her cheek against it, letting out a low hum of arousal at the feel of his stubble on her skin. He had a scent that every single one of her senses responded to. The texture of his skin, the taste of his tongue, the latent strength in his hands—everything about him did it for her. "I want this," she said. "I want you." She moved her hands down his sides, trying to absorb the feel of him. Her fingers found the edge of his towel and she reached to unknot it.

Catching her hands in his, he slowly slid them up to either side of her head. He looked at her for a long moment, and the intensity with which she wanted him actually hurt. "I was thinking now," she murmured.

He laughed low and sexy in his throat and kissed her then—long, languid kisses that brought a slow build. Rocking up into him, she tugged her hands free, gliding them over his silky smooth shoulders and back, then lower to explore over his towel.

And then beneath.

With a growl, he sucked on her lower lip, then slid away from her mouth to kiss and nip along her jaw and down her throat. When he found the sweet spot at the curve of her shoulder she involuntarily squeezed her thighs against his sides, trying to arch up into him and ease the pressure building inside her.

He rewarded her desperation by rocking that amazing body against hers. She'd been this far before with a man she knew far better and for much longer. She'd been further before.

But this time, with Hudson, felt different. Aaron had always been in careful control and very, very gentle, as if she'd been a fragile flower. So gentle it'd kept her from letting go.

Here, with Hud, there was nothing holding her back. "Hudson," she whispered, moaning when he bent his head to her bared breasts, using his warm hands and then his even warmer mouth.

Need rolled over her in waves. Desperate, clawing need, and his name tumbled from her lips again, a cry this time. She could feel herself oscillating her hips to his, rubbing his erection against her center. Mindless, she'd twined herself around him, gasping when he slid his hands to her ass.

Her bare ass.

He'd slid off her jeans without her even knowing. The

little bikini panties she wore matched her cami, the one now on the floor somewhere. "Pretty," he said. And then he dragged them slowly down her legs, sending them flying to land near the cami.

His towel followed.

And then he was back, continuing on with his teasing as her body temperature rose alarmingly. He stretched out beside her, stroking her with his big, warm hands, his fingers dancing over her entire body. When he finally nudged open her thighs, he growled in pleasure as he found a few more places to tease.

But one knowing stroke with those callused fingers and she lost her mind.

Completely. Lost. Her. Mind.

He held her through the shattering orgasm and when she could breathe again, she let out a breathless laugh and stared up at the ceiling.

"Bay? You still with me?"

She blinked. This had already been the best sex she'd ever had and all he'd done was touch her.

He came up on his elbow to look into her eyes. "Yeah," he said, sounding quite full of himself. "You're still with me."

"Show-off," she managed to say, and quivered again when he bent his head and nibbled her hipbone. She felt his lips curl into a smile as he shifted and sucked a patch of skin into his mouth, making her gasp. When he made as if to move again she dug her fingers into his hair, not wanting him to go.

He merely flashed a grin up at her and easily resisted her. The next thing she felt were his wide shoulders making themselves at home between her thighs and then his tongue, warm and strong and incredibly dexterous.

She cried out and nearly rocked them both off the bed.

He tightened his grip on her and went on with his merry torture, his lips creating a sucking, drawing sensation that left her panting and whimpering in seconds.

But every time her body tightened up, he moved away from her center and rubbed his shadowed jaw against her inner thighs until she swore at him, making him laugh again.

When he wanted her to, she came as shamefully easily as she had the first time. Not that she spent even a nano-second feeling shameful...

He climbed up her body, staying close, close enough that they were touching from their kissing mouths to their entangled feet, though he carefully held most of his weight off of her. She rubbed against him, touching every inch she could reach.

And then some of those really great inches were covered with a condom and inside her, and her thoughts scattered like the wind, replaced by a feeling that nothing had ever felt as good as this, as him.

Nothing.

Her legs wrapped around his waist—just in case he had some notion about getting away. The world was a better place with him buried deep inside her.

Much better.

Hud nudged her face up, meeting her gaze with his hot one for a beat before he kissed her again, serious now, very serious, as he began to move within her. Slowly at first, letting her adjust, carefully fueling her hunger, her need. But her favorite part was when he let go of his own control and forgot himself, thrusting hard. She gasped and rocked up into him as her name was ripped from his lips in a tight, strained voice that flung her right over the edge into a free fall. And this time, she took him along with her.

When they finally staggered out of his room several hours later, loose, sated, starving, there was a cold pizza waiting on the porch for them.

Chapter 13

Midweek found Hud replaying the night wrapped up in Bailey's hot bod while simultaneously running a training session an hour after the mountain had shut down. He was a most excellent multitasker. It was already dark out and snowing like a mother, and everyone just wanted to get through the damn training, which was made all the more difficult by the weather.

Which, as Hud knew as head of ski patrol, made perfect conditions to practice in. They had to be prepared for anything, always. The winds kicked up even more with the snow coming in sideways now, blowing right in their faces. Hud had the entire rescue team with him on Devil's Face practicing extractions when he got a call from his mom.

Another FaceTime call. Damn, he should never have taught her how to use that app, but at least she'd figured out how to look into the camera. Her bright, cheery face filled his phone screen. She lifted a Star Wars lunch box. "Honey, you forgot your lunch."

He managed to conclude the call, though for the rest of the night his team took turns FaceTiming him to ask if he'd cleaned his room and done his homework. He finally deleted the app.

Things were blessedly quiet for a few days and on Friday, his first night off, he brought his mom dinner.

"Missed you this week," she said, kissing him hello and then looking around him for someone else. "Where's Jacob? Don't tell me he's in detention again. That kid is going to be the death of me. Maybe I should call the principal and tell him that I need him here. Our fence is down again, so I'll put him on that. It'll use up some of his energy."

Guess it'd been a bad week for both of them.

He opened the bag he'd brought with two cupcakes— one with a candle—and hoped that would do.

As for Jacob, he'd heard zip. Nada. Nothing. And although he should be used to this by now, he wasn't. Through Max, he'd been following Jacob's unit the best he could, which wasn't all that well.

There'd been no word. Even worse, all his attempts at communication had been ignored.

Which wasn't the only thing on his mind. Bailey. He had Bailey on his mind.

All the damn time.

Their night had been...amazing. And seeing as she'd been pretty clear about it also being their only night, it was also messing him up since it'd been the best one he'd had in a long time.

Or ever.

Which meant he was going to have to get over it.

"Hud?" his mom asked. "What's wrong?"

"Nothing. Don't worry about Jacob, Mom. I'll take care of him."

She smiled and patted his hand. "You're such a good boy. You take so much on your shoulders. I know it's not fair how much I've leaned on you. How much we all have."

He lifted his head and met her eyes. Clear. He stilled. "Mom?" he asked quietly. *Is that you in there?*

Her eyes shined brilliantly, with so much sadness. "It's not your fault, honey."

"What's not?"

"That he left."

He tried to swallow the sudden lump in his throat but couldn't. She was lucid. Really lucid.

"You're both so stubborn," she said. "But sometimes it's okay to just let go of the past, to wipe the slate clean and start over." She gave a small smile. "That saying is so outdated now, isn't it? No one uses a slate chalkboard anymore. I bet kids these days don't even know what chalk is. They just..." She made a swiping gesture with her finger, like she was swiping a touch pad. "Goodness, how different our lives are today than they used to be."

Hud slowly set down his sandwich and even more slowly reached for her hand, as if his movement might scare her brain into retreating again. "Mom—"

"And don't even get me started on this whole texting thing," she said. "Do you realize that we have now raised an entire generation of people who don't know how to talk to each other face-to-face? Even you have never known the terror of calling a girl you like and having to ask her dad if she can come to the phone. You probably never even call the girls you like. You probably just text or Snapchat."

She narrowed her eyes. "You do go to their door to pick them up though, right? You don't just honk for them? And tell me you open their doors and buy dinner when you take them out. None of this Dutch thing. I'm telling you, romance is dead, but that's no excuse for bad manners—"

"*Mom.*"

She smiled. "What, baby?"

He didn't take his eyes off of her. "Stay. Stay right here, right now, okay? Stay with me."

"Well of course I will. Where else would I be? You going to eat your pickle?"

Stunned, speechless, throat burning, Hud handed over his pickle.

Carrie munched on it, and then they ate their birthday cupcakes. She smiled at him.

He smiled back, feeling his heart lighten and a load come off. "It's a nice night," he said. "Do you want to take a walk outside?"

She eyed the clock. "Nice try but it's past your curfew. Off to bed with you. Go on now."

Hud let out a long, slow breath and nodded, the pain back in his chest. He got up and leaned over her to kiss her on the cheek. "Sweet dreams."

She smiled sweetly up at him. "Right back atcha, baby."

Hud walked out of her room and shut the door. Leaning against the wall, he pulled out his cell phone, called Jacob's, and left a voicemail. "I don't know where the fuck you are or what the fuck you're doing," he said, "but you're a complete asshole." He paused. "And I'm fucking sorry. Okay? I suck as a brother and I'm sorry. Now get over it and get your ass home."

He shoved his phone in his pocket and walked out of the building. The night was dark and stormy. Winds had died down. The skies were trying to decide between a very light snow and clearing up.

He found a tall, broad shadow leaning against his truck, hood up, head down.

"How is she?" Gray asked.

Hud shook his head.

Gray studied him for a moment and then turned and looked into the night. "Good conditions."

"Yeah."

"You thinking what I'm thinking?"

"Yeah."

Half an hour later they were at the top of the mountain, skis on. Night skiing was their secret thrill, and they gave in to it in times of high stress. "How did you know where I was?" Hud asked when they stopped to catch their breath.

"Penny." Gray shrugged. "Like I told you, it's good to have a woman at your six, man. And not just any woman, but *your* woman."

Hud looked out into the black night lit by a sliver of a moon. They each wore headlamps so they didn't do something stupid, like ski into a tree. If Penny discovered where they were now and what they were doing, she'd kill them.

But much as Gray loved her—and Hud had no doubt that Gray would die for her without hesitation—Penny didn't know about this. But she knew about everything else as it pertained to Gray, *everything*—the good, the bad, the ugly.

"How do you know when it's time?" Hud asked.

"To let someone in?"

"Yeah."

When his brother didn't answer, Hud turned his head and looked at him.

"You'll know," Gray said.

"How?"

"Trust me. You'll just know. Clear?"

Yeah, clear as mud.

Late on Friday night, Bailey drove just ahead of a storm, which followed her up the mountain. It was a little stressful but she liked the idea of being able to wake up and go right to work.

Plus it meant more time in Cedar Ridge.

It's not Cedar Ridge you rushed up here for . . .

Laughing at herself, she dropped off her bag at the efficiency apartment and walked in the dark to the village. Past the tiny coffee hut, closed now, but she could still smell the faint scent of the caffeine and sugar that were mainlined there every morning. The rental shop was shut up tight as well, for once utterly devoid of the hundreds of skiers and boarders that passed through the place every morning seeking equipment. The beauty salon was closed, too, but there was a light on and within she caught sight of Aidan's girlfriend Lily hunched over a laptop. She waved.

Other than that, there was no one else around. The mountain had closed to skiers and boarders several hours ago. The only thing open now was the cafeteria, and that was getting ready to close too.

The path had been cleared and rock salt laid down to keep it from icing up. They'd had a bunch of snow this week, she thought, a little surprised at the berms built high on either side of the trail. The wind had died a little bit and the snow fell silently in thick lines, each snowflake the size of a big white dinner plate.

It never failed to awe her as she stopped and just took it all in: the glorious view of the mountain backdropped against the black night, the eerie, calm quiet echoing around her.

She stared up at the mural—protected from the elements by two walls of the lodge and the huge overhanging patio roof. The beautiful tree was the centerpiece, stretched across the top and bottom of the wall, framing in the highlights on the family tree as they moved in chronological order from left to right. She'd started with Gray, since he was the oldest. The leader. The glue.

Well actually, Penny was the glue, Bailey corrected with a smile. She loved them both already, adored their relationship, and knew that the others did as well.

In any case, she could now see what the entire tapestry would look like and for a moment she felt an overwhelming surge of emotion.

Pride.

Because she was really doing it. Surviving and living and doing something with her life, something she'd never expected to get to do.

From the corner of her eye, she caught a profile of a man in the shadows. Hudson. Her heart skipped a beat and she smiled at him.

He smiled back, much more muted than she expected. Then he stepped closer and she realized her mistake. Not Hudson at all.

Aidan.

He looked up at the mural and smiled. "So it turns out that you *can* paint."

She went brows up. "Lucky for you."

He laughed. "I had a feeling."

She stared at him. "You hired me on a feeling?"

He lifted a shoulder. "Well you did come at a good price." He flashed her a smile that was so close to Hud's her heart skipped another beat. "And as a bonus—you get Hud."

"That's a bonus?" she asked.

He laughed. "Hell yeah."

She cocked her head at the echo of what sounded like a couple of guys whooping it up. Turning to the mountain, lit only by the glow of the night, she saw them.

Two skiers, careening down the run at breakneck speed. "Ohmigod," she whispered. "Is that—"

"Yeah." Aidan let out a low laugh as he acknowledged two of his brothers doing the unthinkable—skiing in the dark, in a storm. "It's how they let off steam."

She couldn't take her eyes off the two figures attacking the mountain with that incredible speed, and yet each movement they made was sheer, unchoreographed grace. "Isn't it dangerous?"

"Living is dangerous," Aidan said.

"I'm serious! They can't have very good depth perception."

"Actually," he said, "with the lighting the way it is right now with the snow and the reflection from the clouds, it's pretty awesome. It's not too cold, the wind died down, and they have the entire mountain to themselves. It's not dangerous for two guys who know this mountain inside and out as they do."

"So why aren't you up there then?" she asked.

The smile widened. "I kicked Gray out of his office because he works too hard. And I don't think Hud's taken a day off in...I have no idea. Between running all of ski patrol and working shifts at the cop shop several times a week, I don't even know how he's still on his feet. With all he's got on his plate, I'm glad he's taking a break."

The moment was interrupted by low voices carrying across the night air.

The skiers returning.

Gray waved. Hud met Bailey's eyes but didn't wave. They vanished into the thick woods.

"They're climbing back to the top for round three," Aidan said. "Or maybe it's four."

"That's as crazy as skiing in the dark!"

"It's part of the adventure," Aidan said on a low laugh. "It's what we Kincaids do."

"And what's that? Dare death at every turn?"

He smiled. "Live. Live *hard*. Confront life at every turn. We're tough, and that's because we've had to be."

Okay, she was starting to get that. If there was a problem, Hud faced it head-on, dangerous or not. He faced everything that way, without flinching.

He thought *she* was the tough one, but she wasn't. All her life she'd just gone along with the tide, letting the ride take her where it would.

That wasn't Hudson's style. In fact, given all that she knew about him—how he'd grown up and the way he watched out for his family at any cost—*he* was one of the toughest people she'd ever met. She said so out loud.

Aidan nodded at that, his eyes solemn now. "Yeah, he is." His warm hand touched her cold face, a brief caress. "So the question is, are you tough enough to take him on? How brave are you feeling, Bailey?"

"I'm not—" She swallowed at Aidan's steady gaze.

Hud thought she was brave and she'd loved knowing that. Maybe it was time she owned it. "It's not what you think."

"What I think is that my brother is one of the best guys I know, and he deserves a hell of a lot more than the hand he's been dealt. If you're not willing to push hard to get to the finish line with him, then you should think about dropping out of the race now before anyone gets hurt."

"We're not... There's no race." But she was talking to the night air because Aidan was gone.

Chapter 14

It was past midnight when Hud and Gray had had enough of night skiing. Exhausted, Gray left Hud so that he could crawl into bed with Penny.

Hud knew he should get into bed too. The night before he'd been called in to sub for a graveyard shift in town where he'd gone on one idiotic call after another. The first one had set the tone for the night. It'd started as a domestic disturbance. A couple had gotten in a fight at their home, where they'd each—from separate rooms in the house—thrown the other's shit out the windows.

Their mistake had been when one of them had somehow come to the conclusion that lighting their spouse's belongings on fire would be a good idea. They were instantly copied by the other—of course neither would cop to starting it—and they'd accidentally set their yard on fire as well. Consequently, while they were yelling and screaming at each other, their house had gone up in flames.

This had brought the wife to tears and the husband had caved at the sight, promising her another house, better clothes, and the whole world if she'd only stop crying.

Instead, they'd both gone to jail.

After that had come a bar fight at the Slippery Slope. Two fifty-something-year-old men had come to blows over who was going to pay the bar tab. No one could say who'd thrown the first punch, but in less than five minutes the entire bar was one big brawl.

When Hud and his fellow officers had broken up the fight, everyone had pointed their fingers at the two men who'd started it.

Turned out that they worked together and one had slept with the other's ex-wife.

Hud had been handcuffing one when the other had jumped him. "Get the fuck off him, you asshole!" the idiot screamed in Hud's ear.

Hud flipped him over his shoulder and held him to the ground, with the sole of one of his work boots to the small of the guy's back. The two other cops who raced to Hud's side gave disbelieving headshakes at the insanity of the night, and then they handcuffed both of them.

Seated elbow-to-elbow on the curb, they were suddenly united as one and cursing the police as assholes.

It was the theme of the night. Now here Hud was after another long day and some very satisfying night skiing with Gray, sitting in his office at the resort. Too keyed up to go home to bed, he'd come here to catch up and work through days of unread email.

He had one from Max, and Hud froze as he read it. Jacob's unit had taken enemy fire—no word on injuries.

Or fatalities.

The email was dated two days ago. Nothing since, which only meant there'd been no new info.

Two days. Fuck. Anything could have happened, and there in the dark of his office Hud stood and sent his phone flying across the room. He heard rather than saw it bounce off the wall and hit the floor.

Along with a shocked gasp.

Pulling his gun in one swift move as he turned to the door-way, he aimed it at the shadow's face— "Jesus," he muttered, and immediately lowered it again. Shoving the gun into the back of his jeans, he hit the light. "How did you find me?"

Bailey blinked up at him, eyes huge. "I went to your place and then tried here next. Hudson, I'm sorry, I just—" She shook her head, her eyes glassy.

He grabbed her arm, kicked his chair out from his desk, and lowered her into it. "Not your fault." He ran a hand over his eyes and mentally kicked his own ass. "I'm sorry," he said, and turned away, staring out past the window into the dark sky beyond. "It's been one of those nights." Weeks. Months...

Most everyone he knew would have left him alone, retreated in the face of his obvious bad mood, leaving him to lick his own wounds.

Not Bailey apparently. She rose out of the chair he'd put her in and came up behind him. He could feel her, her worry, her anxiety.

He was such an asshole. Hud knew it but he couldn't turn to her. He couldn't do anything right then but obsess about Max's email and Jacob. For all their growing-up years, they'd been connected. It seemed at times oddly so. They could always tell what the other had been thinking or when one of them got hurt.

For a while after Jacob had left that ability had lingered, but over the years it'd faded away, leaving Hud nothing of Jacob. Staring out into the night, he should've been able to feel his twin.

He couldn't.

And that scared him to the bone.

"You took a night off. That's rare," she said. "The world still spinning?"

He let out a low laugh. Shockingly, the world was still spinning, going on without him. Something to think about.

"Are you okay?" Bailey asked quietly.

This had him closing his eyes. He'd put a gun in her face. He should be comforting her and yet she stood behind him, hovering, wanting to comfort him. He forced out a low laugh. "You hate that question, remember?"

"I do," she said. "Let me reword. What's wrong, Hud?"

He felt her hand on his back and instead of pulling away like he would have if it'd been anyone else, he wanted to turn and yank her in tight. To make sure he didn't, he shoved his hands into his pockets. "Just a long night. Go to bed, Bailey."

Go to bed? Oh no, thank you very much. Bailey knew he was probably well used to dismissing people with that authoritative tone, but she wasn't one of his employees and couldn't be dismissed so easily.

Growing up, her teachers had always commented about her stubbornness in her report cards. Fact was, she had it in spades, which she believed had helped save her life. She was too obstinate to die.

The office was silent except for her breathing. If Hud

was breathing, she couldn't tell. When he finally turned to face her, he arched a brow—and not in an amused way either. More in a frustrated, you're-being-a-PITA kind of way.

"I don't know about the other people in your life," she said, "but I don't usually do as I'm told. It's a known problem."

He gave a small smile but it faded quickly enough as he focused in on her. "You're shaking."

"No."

"Yes, you are." He pulled her in.

She happily snuggled in, wrapping her arms around him. "It's not me, Hud," she whispered, trying to wrap her entire body around him. "It's you. *You're* shaking."

"Shit." He dropped his forehead to her shoulder, running his hands up and down her arms as if soothing her would soothe him. "I'm sorry I scared you," he whispered against her jaw.

"No," she said. "I should've knocked when I first got to your doorway, but you were staring at your phone so intently I didn't want to interrupt you, and then—"

"It's okay," he said. "My fault, not yours." He kept his mouth against her so every word ghosted over her skin.

She shivered but didn't want to let him distract her. "Will you tell me what's wrong?" Knowing it was the last thing he wanted to do, she put her hand on his chest. "I can tell you've had a rough night—"

He snorted.

"Okay, a rough week maybe," she said. "I've had a few of those myself and I know that sometimes it helps to say what's bothering you."

He was quiet for so long she thought, Okay, I guess he's

not going to say a word. But then he quietly said, "I got an email about Jacob's unit."

She pulled free to search his face for a hint, but he was damn good at giving away nothing when he wanted. "What happened?" she asked.

"They took enemy fire. No word on if there were injuries." He paused. "Or fatalities."

Her heart broke at all he didn't say. "And you've had no contact from him?" she asked.

"No."

"I'm sure he'll get in touch with you as soon as he can."

Hud slowly shook his head and scrubbed a hand down his face, which she knew now to be one of his rare tells. He had to be exhausted to let it slip. "No," he said. "Jacob won't be in contact."

"But he's got to know how you and the others will be worrying about him."

"Trust me," he said grimly. "You couldn't understand."

She stared up at him. "You think because I don't have any siblings I can't understand an obviously difficult relationship?"

"We're dropping this," he said. "It's not up for discussion. Or for public consumption in the mural."

She absorbed the unexpected hurt of that and turned away, getting as far as the door before she stopped and stared at her hand on the doorknob, remembering what Carrie told her.

Hud pushes away the people he cares about most. He's good at it.

Bailey let out a breath and turned, walking back to him until she was toe-to-toe with him. "I almost let you do it," she said.

"Do what?"

"Push me away. It's apparently your MO when it comes to the people you care most about. Like Jacob."

Still as the night behind him, only his eyes tracked to her. "You don't know what you're talking about," he said.

"I think I do. So if that's what you're doing now, Hud? Pushing me away because you care too much? You should know that I won't go. I can't be pushed." To prove it, she moved back to the door and hit the lock.

"What the hell are you doing?" he asked.

She dropped her sweater on the floor on her way over to him. "If you don't know, I'm not doing it very well."

"Bailey—"

"No," she said, and pointed at him. "You don't feel like talking, remember?"

"You said last week that this thing was one night," he said.

Was he worried that she'd try and cling to him? "I said one night?" she asked innocently, purposefully misunderstanding him. "My mistake. I meant two." She gave him a little push until his desk hit the backs of his thighs.

"Bailey—"

"Shh." She unzipped his sweatshirt and shoved it off his shoulders.

His hands went to her hips. "Bay." His voice came out a low, barely there rasp. "This is a bad idea."

"Well of course it is," she said. "All week I'm thinking about you while pretending I'm not. And you're here doing your best to keep me at arm's length, which I know damn well means that you think about me too." She smiled. "Really, we're quite the pair."

"Fucking pathetic." But he returned her smile with

a small one of his own and then he was tugging at her clothes and then his, exposing the necessary parts—and God, she loved his necessary parts—so that they could make good use of his desk.

And after that, the loveseat against the wall.

"I sit on this thing and work sometimes," Hud murmured much later when Bailey was sweaty and still panting in his arms. "I'm never going to look at it the same way again." She felt him smile against her damp skin. "In fact, I think I'll have it bronzed."

Chapter 15

Hud worked his ass off on Saturday afternoon, but that night he did something he couldn't remember ever doing— he took himself off the roster at both the resort and the station. He also turned off his phone.

And then he knocked at Bailey's employee apartment.

She opened the door and stared at him.

"Hey," he said.

"Hey." She wore his favorite outfit—her skimpy PJs.

"Did you say two nights?" he asked, holding up a bottle of wine and a bag of Chinese takeout. "Or three?

Holding his gaze, she took the bag, dropping eye contact to peer in at the food. She smiled. "Oh, most definitely three."

The following week was as crazy as all the others in ski season. On Thursday night Hud took his mom out for her "birthday." On Friday he, Aidan, and Gray went out to dinner. They shared a pitcher of beer and recapped their week. This was usually a weekly thing. Sometimes Penny and Lily joined them, but tonight it was just the boys plus Kenna. She had blessed them with her presence even though she did spend most of the time on her phone.

Aidan gave Hud a worried look, but Hud knew she was simply playing Words With Friends and probably at this very moment kicking his ass.

"Our insurance company called to let us know we had three serious injuries this week," Gray announced.

"Actually it was four," Kenna said with head down and still concentrating on her phone. "Don't forget that stupid snow bunny who sat too close to the fire pit in the lodge. She was striking poses on the bench in front of it, trying to get a good selfie, and fell on her ass. And since she was wearing ridiculously high-heeled boots, she couldn't get up quickly and singed her hair extensions. Our mountain had nothing to do with it."

"Yeah, well," Gray said, annoyed. "However it happened, they're sending a rep out next week to discuss better safety precautions. I don't care if we have to put a sign by the fire pit that says women with hair extensions have to sit twenty feet back, we have to make sure it doesn't happen again."

Gray took any affront on the resort personally.

Kenna rolled her eyes. "You can't put out a sign like that. You'll have feminists the world over hating on you."

"Fine, make the sign say that *anyone* wearing hair extensions needs to stay twenty feet from the fire."

"We've upped our training from every other day to every day," Hud chimed in, hoping to avoid a fight. "We're fully staffed. Unlike most of the other resorts, we didn't make big cuts on either staffing or safety. They're not going to find any reason to mess with you."

"Yeah, well, see that they don't." Gray thumbed his way down a list on his iPad. "We were asked to sponsor the high school's ski team again this year." He lifted his head and looked at Hud. "They're down a coach and asked for you. You got any time available?"

Shit. No he didn't. And yet he could remember when all he'd wanted was to be on that ski team. There'd never been enough money for it. No way did he want a single kid to miss out on a dream because of money. "I'd find time if they let us give out scholarships for kids who have the skills but not the money. If I'm the coach, no one misses getting on the team for lack of funds."

Gray eyed him over the iPad, amused. "And you're going to pull the money for the scholarships from where exactly, your ass?"

"We'll find the money."

Aidan refilled Gray's beer. "I'm with Hud. We'll find the money."

"Christ," Gray grumbled, and made some notes. " 'Find the money,' " he muttered. "Sure, we'll just find the goddamn money."

"I have the money," Kenna said, actually looking up from her phone.

When Gray started to open his mouth, she set down the phone—something rarely seen out in the wild—and stood up. And then, making a face at how short she still was, she let out a pissy noise and stood on her chair, snatching the pitcher of beer to her chest as she did. "You won't let me help the resort," she said to the table. "You won't let me do shit because you think I'm fragile. Well fragile this, I'm not giving the beer back until someone says I can sponsor the goddamn high school ski team with my own goddamn money!"

"You have my vote," Aidan said.

Kenna eyed him. "You just want more beer."

"Yes," he said seriously. "But I also want to see you smile."

"I vote for you too," Hud told her. "On one condition. I'm going to need a co-coach for the ski team."

Kenna turned to him. "Me?"

"Well, I didn't mean the Easter Bunny."

Kenna stared down at him very solemnly. Heartbreakingly earnest. "You want me to co-coach with you."

"God yes," he said. "Have you met any high school girls?" He shuddered. "They're terrifying."

She blinked and then gave him a smile that seemed more than a little rusty.

"Cool?" he asked.

"Cool," she whispered. She carefully climbed down off her chair and filled up his beer to the tippy top.

"Hey," Aidan said. "What about me? I voted for you first, *chica*."

She filled up Aidan's glass too.

Gray raised a brow.

"First you have to say you would've voted for me if I'd asked," she said.

"Whatever you want," Gray said.

She laughed in delight. "*Whatever* I want?"

"Yes," Gray said. "Because you are to me what high school girls are to Hud. Terrifying."

She laughed again. "Really?"

"*Always*," Gray said fervently. "And another always? Me backing you. In anything and everything, Kenna. All of us," he said. "You have our vote no matter what. You hear me?"

She stared at him for a long beat, her eyes suspiciously shiny. She hated crying, rarely if ever did it. The last time Hud saw her cry was ten years ago when her cat had gotten out and been stolen.

Except it hadn't really been stolen. The truth was, a coyote had killed it. He and Jacob had stayed up all night burying the thing so Kenna would never know.

Kenna let out a long breath, nodded at Gray, and dipped her head so that they couldn't see her face. She then tipped up the pitcher and drank the last of the beer right out of it.

"Seriously?" Gray asked.

She swiped her mouth and smiled. "That's 'seriously, *coach*' to you." She flashed a grin none of them had seen in far too long. "Next round's on me," she said, and headed to the bar.

Aidan gave Gray a punch to the shoulder.

"Ow," Gray said. "And what the fuck?"

"I've been telling you all she needs is something to do, to feel self-worth again. Stop babying her. You should know by now she hates it."

Gray snatched Aidan's beer and flipped him off while downing it.

Aidan turned to Hud, tossing him a brown bag he pulled from his backpack.

"What's this?" Hud asked distrustfully. He had good reason not to trust a damn thing Aidan handed him in a bag.

Aidan smirked. "Worried?"

"Fuck yeah."

"Jeez, give a guy a snake one time…"

Gray grinned. "That was a lot of fun."

Asshole brothers. Hud took the bag with two fingers. "If this is a snake, you'd better say your last prayers."

Aidan laughed. "That was ten years ago and it was a fucking garter snake, man. Harmless."

"Harmless my ass. It bit me!"

"It did not," Aidan said. "You just told everyone that because you screamed like a banshee."

"I repeat," Hud said stiffly, "you tossed a snake into my lap."

"You nearly shit your pants."

That he hadn't was solely due to the fact that he'd been sitting next to Trina Anderson, at the time the hottest thing he'd ever seen. He'd been working his way up to getting in her pants when Aidan had ever so helpfully screwed him over. "So I have one fear," he said now. "So what? Everyone's afraid of something."

"You're afraid of *two* things," Aidan said. "Open the bag."

Hud shook it. Nothing hissed or even moved. Considering it safe, he peered into the bag. "*Shit.*"

Aidan grinned as Hud pulled out the pair of siren-red male bikini briefs from Big Dog. On the fly it read:

CHOKING HAZARD!

Hud stared down at them while Aidan laughed his fool ass off. The ongoing gag, of course. Now he had to wear these tomorrow or suffer the consequences. Way back, they'd started out with obnoxious ties. Hud missed those days, but Penny had vehemently objected after Gray had been forced to wear a tie with a large penis on it to a bank meeting.

So far Gray had managed to keep this new trend from her, but it was only a matter of time.

Aidan was still grinning, clearly quite proud of himself because he knew Hud wore boxers and hated briefs with the same intensity he reserved for snakes and spinach.

"Notice the timing," Aidan pointed out helpfully. "You have to wear them tomorrow—Bailey will be up tomorrow," he added, cackling like he was bent over his cauldron.

"Be afraid," Hud said. "Because you're next."

Aidan didn't look too worried.

Hud shoved the briefs back into the brown bag, flipped Aidan off, and finished his beer.

Bailey didn't get out of Denver Friday night as planned. She'd had a late-afternoon doctor's appointment—a big visit. Three months had passed since her first all clear—six months total since she'd last shown cancer the door. She desperately wanted to hear that the second three-month check confirmed the same but she knew the drill. It was a hurry-up-and-wait thing. It'd be Monday or Tuesday of next week before she got the results.

Still, as always, her oncologist had given her a list of options of what could happen and how they'd deal with it. Mostly, and most importantly, the doctor felt optimistic that Bailey was still in the clear.

Bailey liked that option best herself and decided to take a page from her grandma's book.

Worrying about something is like wishing for it to happen. Just pretend it's all good. Pretend enough and it becomes real.

So she set her alarm for four in the morning and at the asscrack of dawn on Saturday, she hit the road, arriving at Cedar Ridge with the first hint of the sun.

She parked and went to stand in front of her wall. Her breath crystalized in front of her face and she was glad the day was supposed to get up near fifty degrees. She didn't want her paints to freeze.

She tilted her head back and took in the mural. The tree was finished, its roots stretching across the bottom of the wall, the branches and leaves looking alive as they took over the top. Along the way there were spots for the five Kincaid siblings to appear. Gray sat on a throne—his ski helmet his crown and his staff a ski pole. Penny sat in his lap with one arm around his neck and the other on a ski pole as well. Skis adorned all four of their feet.

When Bailey shifted slightly, so did the image—as planned. Depending on how you looked at them, they were either sitting looking at each other or sharing poles as they skied as one.

Aidan was in search and rescue gear, hanging off a branch of the tree like Tarzan. Lily was tucked under one arm, and the two of them were looking at each other and laughing.

Everything to the right of that was still only penciled in and even then only up to Hud. She'd drawn him in ski patrol gear complete with his backpack right in the middle of a crazy jump off the top of the tree—which she'd covered in snow so that it also looked like a mountain cliff. He was in great form with knees bent and skis high enough to see the bottoms. Which read: I'VE GOT YOUR BACK.

She still had to draw Jacob and Kenna, but she knew she'd done a good job and had never felt so excited about her work before.

"Bailey?"

At the voice she hadn't expected to hear, she whirled around and yep, there was Aaron. He stood at the base of her scaffolding, although she hardly recognized him without his usual suit. He was in jeans and a down jacket, and she was so surprised to see him that she nearly slipped off the scaffolding as she climbed down.

His arms came out to steady her but she stepped back as soon as she could. This wasn't one of those happy surprises. More like the opposite. Cedar Ridge was hers. This was her little secret, her happy spot.

Wrong as it might be, she didn't want to share it. "Aaron, what are you doing here?"

"I wanted to see what you were up to."

Still staring at him, she lifted a hand and pointed upward to the mural.

Instead of even looking at it, he gripped her arms and pulled her in and kissed her with a desperation she could taste. For a beat she allowed it, holding still, trying to feel it.

But she didn't. She didn't feel anything except his admittedly very nice mouth pressing against hers and his equally nice body doing the same. It was . . . nice.

No fireworks. No shortness of breath. No quivery belly, and the bones in her knees didn't dissolve. Shaking her head, she pulled free.

"You didn't feel anything," he said, sounding unhappy. "Not even a little bit."

She grimaced. "Aaron—"

"No, I get it. I didn't either. Christ." He pressed his forehead to hers. "I'm sorry. I knew it. I knew things changed for you after I screwed up and hooked up with Donna, but I had to give it one last try." He cupped her face, and with eyes soft gave her one last kiss. Light this time. Friendly. Warm. "I'll always be here for you," he said.

"I know." She ran her hands up his arms and hugged him. "And thank you."

"For?"

She smiled. "For hooking up with Donna."

He smiled back. "One day you're going to miss me."

"I know."

He winked at her and slipped his arm in hers. "Breakfast? Come on, I'll buy while you wait for the temps to come up a little."

Why not. "Okay," she said, but then—drawn by a force she didn't understand—Bailey turned her head. And found Hudson standing about twenty-five feet away. He wore his dark sunglasses, but she didn't need to see his eyes to know he'd witnessed the kiss. Nope, that was in every tense line of his tall, leanly muscled bod.

Chapter 16

Hud's morning had started at oh-dark-thirty with a ski patrol training session and then an incident report meeting, which had been interrupted just now by a call. A bunch of teenagers had gone up to Devil's Face and dared each other to race down. Problem was, Devil's Face was a double diamond and these teens were at best intermediate skiers. The math didn't add up.

Not that this had stopped them.

One of the teens had apparently crashed and burned on the moguls, but no one had actually seen him go down. His buddies had all skied by, leaving him up there knocked out by his own snowboard.

The teen's dad blamed one of the other dads, and then the moms had gotten into it, too, and also a grandma. The ensuing fight belonged on a trashy TV show and not on Hud's mountain.

It was nine in the morning and he was already burned out for the day.

So things weren't overly improved when he'd caught sight of some guy sucking on Bailey's face.

It turned out that his day *could* get more shitty. Good to know.

"Hudson," Bailey said when she stopped kissing the guy and the two of them walked his way. "Hey."

"Hey." He looked at the man at her side.

"Oh," she said, putting a hand on the guy's arm—her *free* hand because the other arm was already linked in his. "This is Aaron," she said. "Aaron, this is Hudson Kincaid, one of the brothers who owns this place."

So now Aaron knew who Hud was. But Hud still had no idea who Aaron was.

The guy offered a hand, and Hud spent a nanosecond trying to decide between shaking it and shoving his fist in the guy's face.

Except that made no sense. None at all. Bailey wasn't his, and even if she hadn't made it crystal clear the week before that she wasn't in the market for a relationship with him, he didn't want one.

So he had no idea what his problem was.

None. Zero. Except...he did. He knew exactly what his problem was and his name was Aaron.

"I just needed to see that she's in good hands when she's up here," Aaron said. "She's important to me."

Yeah, Hud was getting that loud and clear.

"As her fiancé," Aaron went on, "I worry."

Hud stopped breathing. His lungs just refused to accept air.

"Ex," he heard Bailey say firmly. "*Ex*-fiancé." She smacked Aaron in the chest. "You always forget that part."

"Whoops," Aaron said. "Sorry." Except he didn't look all that sorry.

And he didn't look like an *ex* either.

Hud pulled his radio off his belt and stared at it wondering why it went off twenty-four-seven except for when he needed it to. "I've got to go," he said, still staring at the radio.

"But it didn't make any noise for once," Bailey said.

"Got a meeting," Hud managed, and spun on a heel and took off toward the offices.

Marcus, their equipment manager, intercepted him halfway. "Hey, there's a problem with the quad chair on the backside. My guys'll have it under control in a few minutes but I just wanted you to know—"

"I'll check it out," Hud said.

"I got it, I didn't mean for you to—"

"I've got it," Hud repeated.

Ten minutes later he was at the quad chair, which indeed had jammed. But Marcus had been right, because maintenance had the problem solved before he even got there. Which left him at the top of the mountain and, for the first time in too long, with nowhere else to be.

Which meant his mind was free to go ninety miles an hour and it did so, flashing images across the back of his eyelids at warp speed.

Bailey sitting at the top tier of the scaffolding with brush in hand, holding a look of fierce concentration on her face as she painted the Kincaid family tree in supersize.

Bailey sitting with his mom, listening to her babble on with sweet patience and not an ounce of condescension.

Bailey laying on his bed, flushed, eyes hot, body soft as she showed him her port scar, a visceral reminder of her fucking bravery.

Bailey meeting his gaze head-on and saying she didn't want a relationship...

Bailey kissing her ex-fiancé...

His radio went off. Thank God. An emergency, which would take his head out of his own ass and put him back in the game.

A kid and an adult had reportedly collided on the bunny hill down at the bottom, near the parking lot. From where he stood it was a seven-minute hard ski. There were at least five team members who were closer than Hud, and who could and would get there first.

But he still headed that way. Three minutes into the trip, he was able to take in the lodge as it came into view and he nearly wobbled off his skis. He'd been skiing since he could walk and it'd been a damn long time since anything had shaken him into a near tumble, but this did it.

Apparently just as momentarily stunned by the sight, Aidan pulled up next to him and stopped short, sending snow flying into the air with his edges.

"Wow," Aidan said.

Yeah. It was a big holy shit moment for Hud too. Not only was Bailey an artist—a hell of one, too—but she'd captured the Kincaid spirit. Her mural was the embodiment of what the mountain meant to them, depicting the love of the entire place in a simple tapestry-like painting of the family tree.

"*Really* amazing," Aidan said softly. Reverently.

Speechless, Hud could only nod.

What had once been just a wall that no one had even looked at was now a nearly half-painted mural. It was a gorgeous, epic rendering with vibrant colors that popped.

Gray and Penny were...amazingly 3-D. As was the half
of Aidan she'd filled in.

This morning he'd been close enough to see some
of what she'd planned for him. The bare outline of
Hud depicted him in the middle of the sort of ski jump
only a superhero could have made, but it had made him
smile.

She was having fun with it and fun with them, portray-
ing the family in a way that included their patrons in the
joke.

"So what happens when she's done?" Aidan asked.

The question didn't help the burning in Hud's chest.
The mural was both a tangible thing and a ticking clock,
and the time was already winding down. "She leaves."

Aidan tore his gaze off the mural and met Hud's eyes,
his own lit with surprising understanding. "Have you told
her you don't want her to?"

Hud looked at him.

"Don't even try to deny it, man."

Hud sighed. "I can't."

"Can't?" Aidan asked. "Or won't?"

"No, I mean *can't*." Hud shook his head. "She just
came through what should've been a death sentence.
Do you get that? She's lived the past decade of her life
thinking that tomorrow wasn't going to come at all. Ever.
Those days and weeks and months and *years* were spent
inside doctors' offices and hospitals, in cold, white rooms
with no sense of joy or hope or anything real." He stared
at the mural. "And then when it was miraculously over,
she made a list. A list of things she'd never been allowed
to do, things she could only dream about—like painting a
mural—and she's working her way down that list."

"Cool," Aidan said. "But what does that have to do with not telling her how you feel?"

"How are you not getting this?" Hud asked. "The mural's the first thing she's done from that list. What in the hell kind of guy would I be if I selfishly tell her my feelings and then maybe she ends up staying with me instead of going off and sailing the Greek Islands or learning how to ballroom dance in Rome?"

"The kind of guy who fell in love," Aidan said. "The kind of guy who could do the list *with* her because he's been just as locked up for the past decade as she, making sure everyone in his life gets taken care of except himself."

Hud stared at him. "Bullshit."

"No," Aidan said, taking a step into him now and getting right in his face. Angry. "What's bullshit is that you think it's okay for her to go get the life she deserves but you don't think it for yourself."

"My life doesn't lend itself to relationships."

"Look at that—even more bullshit," Aidan said, not impressed. "I mean, yeah, you've got a lot going on. And more responsibilities than you know what to do with. But your family's standing right here at your six, man, willing and able to take more on to ease some of it. All you have to do is let go."

Hud thought of his mom. How was he supposed to pass off the burden of her care? She was his *mom*. And then there was Jacob. Wherever the hell he was, Hud was going to find him, but that was on him. Just as he was Carrie's son, he was Jacob's twin. And as for Gray and Aidan, he already was more indebted to them than he could ever pay back for taking in his little family of three when they'd had nothing. Plus, they all had their own shit to deal with. Shit Hud could and would help with because they'd done so much for him. But no way in hell would he add to their burdens. "It's not that easy to let go," he said.

"Yes, it is," Aidan insisted. "The people in your life, the very people that you're counting now in your head as responsibilities, they don't have to be a burden to you. We don't *want* to be a burden to you."

"You're not," Hud said.

"Yeah? Then prove it. You're standing right here telling me Bailey can't love you because she has too much to do, but we both know you're the one who feels that way. You won't let yourself love."

"Will you stop with the love shit?" Hud asked. "I've got more important stuff than to worry about that right now."

"Jacob, right?" Aidan asked. "But Jacob's gone, man. He'll come back when he's good and ready, and not a second before. That's not on you, Hud. You don't have to put your life on hold just because he's gone."

Hud closed his eyes. "Yes, I do."

"Why?" Aidan demanded.

"Because it's my fault he's gone." Hud swallowed hard and shook his head at the memory of his harsh words. He was still able to perfectly see, even after all this time, the look of shock and hurt on Jacob's face.

"Hud," Aidan said with shocking gentleness. "No one blames you."

"*I* blame me," Hud said tightly. He opened his eyes and met Aidan's confused ones. "There's no one else to blame."

"What the hell are you talking about?"

"The last words I said to him were 'we're no longer brothers.'"

Aidan stared at him for a beat and then sighed. "You were angry—"

"No excuse."

"You were hurt—"

"So was he," Hud said.

Aidan put his hand on Hud's shoulder. "Listen to me very carefully because I'm only going to say this once so you need to really hear me." He paused. "What happened was every bit as much Jacob's fault as yours. *It was*," he reiterated when Hud opened his mouth to speak. "You've got to stop beating the shit out of yourself over it. More than that, you have to forgive yourself."

"Yeah? And why is that?" Hud asked.

"Because wherever Jacob is right now? He's forgiven you."

Hud stared at him, wanting to believe that was true. "How do you know?"

"I know," Aidan said in a voice of steel. "I ever tell you about the time I crashed Gray's truck?"

"You never crashed Gray's truck."

Aidan laughed mirthlessly. "Wrong. I was fourteen and a real punk-ass, too, just like you. No doubt it's in the Kincaid genes. Just one more thing to thank our dad for, right?" He shook his head. "Anyway, Gray had just gotten a truck. He'd saved for a couple of years, from even before he could drive. And he loved it more than he did girls, if that tells you anything. He was fixing it up every night after school and work. I wanted to help, but he wouldn't let me. He told me to keep my grimy hands off it."

"Let me guess," Hud said. "You didn't."

"Nope. One night after he'd gone to bed, I stole his keys and took it for a joyride. It was snowing."

Hud grimaced. Gray was notoriously, ridiculously attached to his vehicles. "You had a death wish?"

Aidan grinned. "Yeah, pretty much. The driveway out of the apartment complex we lived in—you remember it from when you came a few years later."

"That driveway was a sheet of ice in the winter," Hud said.

"Yep. I slid all the way down the thing and hit the mailboxes at the other end. Which of course saved my life because it meant I didn't slide into the street and oncoming traffic." Aidan let out a breath. "Which didn't save me from Gray's wrath, by the way."

"A little pissed, was he?"

Aidan laughed. "*Beyond* pissed. I'd never seen him so furious before, or since, actually. Luckily, I had a concussion and had to go to the hospital. I fully expected to be arrested for grand theft auto when I was released, but instead Gray was waiting for me." Aidan shook his head. "I saw him and thought, well, it was a good run, I'd managed to keep myself alive for fourteen years, and had a good time while I was at it."

Hud laughed. "He kill you fast, or torturously slow?"

"I was just hoping for fast," Aidan said. "But he shocked me. He hauled me in for a hard hug and said we were blood. He said that we'd never stop being blood and blood didn't kill blood—much as it might want to. Gray also informed me that until further notice when he asked me to jump, I was only to ask how high." Aidan shook his head. "I was his bitch for months."

Hud laughed even as the humor was replaced by a hard

knot of something in his chest. Grief. Regret. Frustration. "Jacob isn't Gray."

"No," Aidan said. "But he is blood. You might have some hoops to jump, but nothing can change that one fact—blood is blood."

Chapter 17

It was several hours later before Hud got any kind of break and headed back to the lodge, starving. He ran into Gray on the steps and they entered the cafeteria together.

At a corner table sat Penny, Lily, and...Bailey. The three of them were clearly enjoying a late lunch together, laughing over something.

Gray grinned. "I just found what I want for lunch."

Hud rolled his eyes and followed Gray to the table.

"And then, hand to heaven," Penny was saying, "I heard Hud say to Gray, 'Touch that remote, even think about switching the channel from *Say Yes to the Dress*, and I promise to act appropriately grief stricken at your funeral.'"

Lily snorted tea out of her nose.

Bailey laughed so hard she slid out of her chair and hit the floor.

The story was complete bullshit with not a lick of truth to it.

Okay, fine, so maybe he'd watched the show *one* time, but only because Penny had been really sick with pneumonia and they'd all taken turns sitting with her—babysitting her. When it'd been Hud's turn, she insisted on that show. And yeah, maybe they'd spent the entire afternoon critiquing the dresses and soaking up the family drama on-screen. Hud looked at Gray, who went palms up like, *Hey, don't look at me, I can't control her.*

Shaking his head, Hud walked over to Bailey and scooped her up, setting her back into her chair. He knew better than to ask her if she was okay. Besides, she was still laughing so hard he had to keep his hands on her shoulders to hold her into the chair so that she wouldn't slide to the floor again.

She got herself together enough to say to him, "I like that show too."

Christ. He slid Penny a you're-going-to-die-slowly look, which she, predictably, ignored.

Lily was trying to clean herself up after snorting her tea. "Damn," she said to Penny. "I know better than to drink when you're telling a story."

Penny innocently dabbed her mouth with a napkin, smiling up at her husband. "Hey there, big guy. Want to buy me dessert?"

Gray grinned at her. "I've already got your dessert, babe."

She gave him a saucy look before reaching for her purse, stopping to glance at Lily. "You gotta go, too, right?"

"In a few," Lily said, and then suddenly jumped with an "ow" and a dirty look in Penny's direction.

"Thought you had to get back to work too," Penny said

meaningfully, jerking her head in Hud's direction. Either she was having a seizure or she wanted them all to leave Bailey and Hud alone.

Subtle. *Not.* But Lily wasn't getting it. "I've got another ten minutes—" She started, only to jump like she'd been kicked again. "Dammit, would you stop doing that—"

"You said you had an appointment," Penny said slowly, once again going with the head jerk in Bailey's direction.

"Oh!" Lily said, the lightbulb going off. She too grabbed her bag and stood. "Right. You're so right. I've got an appointment."

"Uh-huh," Hud said, smelling a rat. A matchmaking rat named Penny. "And what's this appointment for?"

"Dentist," Lily said.

"Client," Penny said at the same time.

The two of them looked at each other.

"I've got a salon client," Lily corrected. "A cut and color—"

"She has a dentist appointment," Penny said at the same time.

Disgusted, Hud looked at Gray.

Gray was hiding his smile behind his hand as he rubbed it over his mouth. He hauled his woman into his arms. "Dessert?" Gray was a one-track-mind sort of guy.

"Mm-hmm," Penny said, and kissed him.

And then they were gone, heading straight for the staff entrance, which led to the offices.

Which meant that they'd be in Gray's office with the door locked and no one would see either of them for at least an hour.

"I'm off too," Lily said.

"To your dentist appointment," Hud said with narrowed eyes.

"Um, yes. Right."

Hud shook his head at her but she just smiled, went up on tiptoe to kiss his cheek, winked at Bailey, and then was gone too.

When Bailey stood, Hud grabbed her hand and reeled her in a little bit. "Where you going?"

"Back to work."

"You really going to run off after they worked so hard to get us alone together?"

She met his gaze, studying him a moment. He studied her right back. Her knit cap was sunshine yellow today, suiting her rosy complexion, which was a lot less pale than it had been her first week up here. She'd gotten a little color from being outside on the weekends, giving her a healthy glow that made him happy to see.

She'd shed her jacket and was in just a stark white, long-sleeved V-neck T-shirt that fit her like a second skin and pretty much took his breath away. She also wore skinny-cut ski pants today that hung low on her hips and were tucked into boots that made her legs look a mile long.

She had a streak of pale blue paint on her yellow cap, some purple over her jaw, and forest green across one breast.

She'd never looked better to him. "Tell me about the fiancé," he heard himself say.

"You mean the ex-fiancé."

"He was kissing you," Hud pointed out.

"Right," she said. "*He* was kissing *me*. I was not kissing him."

He just looked at her.

She blew out a breath and looked around. "Listen, I'd like to tell you the whole, sordid story but I can't go on until I get some chocolate. And I promised myself that I'd take a few ski runs during my lunch break today. I really want to be a better skier."

He took her hand and tugged her toward the front of the cafeteria. The lines were long today. Too long. So he steered her past them, grabbing a handful of candy bars on the way.

At the front he waved at the checkout clerk. He'd known Sydney since tenth-grade algebra. He'd done her math homework and she'd written his English papers for him. And sometimes, when he'd gotten very lucky, they'd done other stuff for each other in the back of her daddy's truck. For each other. *To* each other...

She winked at him and nodded that she'd put the candy bars on his account, waving him off at the same time. Fifteen minutes later he'd gotten Bailey skis and boots from rentals and had her on a lift with him.

"What are we doing?" she asked, breathless, and it was no wonder. She made getting on a lift a dangerous sport, knocking out an entire line of people. Hud had shown her the right way to get on, which didn't involve injuring any of his paying guests. "You're telling me a story," he said. "And I'm going to make you a better skier."

At least a non-dangerous one...

"Cocky much?" she asked.

"Nope. Just good." He dumped four different candy bars into her lap. "Wasn't sure which one you'd like."

"You didn't ask."

"Didn't need to, because I covered all the options available," he said. "Pick your poison."

"And if I said I wanted all of them...?"

He laughed. "I'd probably try to sweet-talk you out of the Snickers."

She didn't look impressed. "She winked at you."

"She?" he asked.

"The cute blond clerk at the checkout."

"She did," Hud agreed. "Sydney."

"*Sydney* the cute blond clerk winked at you."

"Jealous?"

"Of course not. Why did she wink at you?"

"Because I'm cute too?" he asked.

She narrowed her eyes. "You're something," she agreed. "But not cute. A mountain cat isn't cute. Smart, sleek, beautiful, and *deadly*, maybe. But not cute."

He laughed again. He was doing that a lot around her. "You think I'm smart, sleek, and beautiful?"

"And deadly," she pointed out. "And most definitely *not* cute."

The lift slowed and then stopped entirely. Someone had undoubtedly fallen off of it either at the top or the bottom. But for once Hud was happy to be stuck on a lift. "Tell me more," he said.

"About...?"

"Eric."

"Aaron." She narrowed her eyes. "And you knew that."

He shrugged. Yeah, he'd known that.

"He was my first boyfriend," she said. "For a lot of years. And he's my only ex."

"Only?" he asked, not sure he could have heard right. She was sweet and cute and sexy and smart and talented... Why in the world would she have had only one boyfriend?

Because, you idiot, she fought cancer for most of her life.

"I got sick when I was fifteen," she said softly, confirming his thought as she stared out at the scenic view of the Rockies for as far as the eye could see.

Reaching over, he covered her hand with his. "You don't have to—"

"No," she said. "I want you to understand. It wasn't pretty, Hudson. I ended up out of school more than I was in it. Aaron lived next door and he would bring me my homework and help me."

Well, hell. He'd been working up a good and instant dislike of the guy and as it turned out, Aaron deserved more than that from him.

The lift still didn't budge. He could hear the conversation on his radio, turned to low. A beginner had fallen getting off the lift. She was six and was apparently in the middle of a full-blown temper tantrum.

Hud had never been more grateful for a spoiled little kid in his life.

A low cloud had moved in and blanketed most of the landscape, leaving them in their own little world. Bailey looked lost in her memories, and unhappy.

He squeezed her gloved hand with his. "You were sick for a long time," he said quietly, wanting her to keep talking.

"More accurately, I was a dead girl walking."

He made a completely involuntary sound from deep in his throat. It could only be described as sheer grief at the thought of her no longer being in this world. She turned her hand over to grip his fingers in hers.

Comforting him.

Yep. Most amazing woman he'd ever met.

"I'm sorry," she said. "I always forget. I had a lot of years to get used to it, but I shouldn't blurt it out like that."

"Yes," he said. "You should. Don't ever sugarcoat things, Bailey, not for me. I want to hear it, all of it."

She nodded. "I wasn't supposed to live. We all knew it. Aaron stayed by my side, even when..." She grimaced. "Even when I knew we didn't love each other in the right way. I dreamed of passion, and I craved it, but I didn't feel that with him. And yet he was a rock for me, always. Even when, as it turned out, he also needed...more. So yes, he's still in my life. Sometimes more than I want him to be," she said wryly. "But I've already broken his heart. I won't push him away as a friend too. I can't."

"I get that," Hud said. He also loved that about her. Loyalty meant everything to him, and she was the definition of the word.

"We're not together, Aaron and me," she said, turning her head to meet his gaze as she revealed her own, open and honest. "Not like that. And haven't been for a long, long time."

All Hud could manage was a nod because for a while now he'd had a fist around his heart. Part of it was worrying about his mom and her condition. Another part of it belonged overseas, wherever Jacob was fighting for his country and probably his damn life—he'd had no word from Max.

But some of that grip on his heart was Baily and it had just loosened.

Which was bad. Very bad.

The lift started again and then stopped with another jerk. The radio squawked to life. The newbie skier two chairs behind the little girl had been inexplicably wearing jeans—which had gotten frozen to the seat of the lift—and as she'd tried to get off, she'd ended up dangling upside down.

"Do you think she's literally hanging by the seat of her pants?" Bailey asked, horrified.

He shrugged. "It happens."

"Not to me," she said. "Even I know better than to wear jeans to ski."

"Yeah?" He smiled at her. "What else do you know?"

She gave him a slow smile. "That I want another night with you."

Chapter 18

When Hudson smiled, Bailey promptly lost her train of thought. They were fifty feet in the air, and their feet were dangling over nothing but snow and trees. She should've been her usual anxious.

Instead she wanted to crawl into his lap, wrap herself around him like a monkey, and get some more of his mind-blowing kisses.

Not going to happen up here with people both in front of and behind them. So instead, she opened the Snickers and offered it to him.

He flashed another smile, leaned in, and took a bite, and then nudged it back to her.

Something fluttered low in her belly at his smile, and she took a big bite of her own and let out an entirely involuntary, heartfelt moan.

"You okay over there?"

"Oh, my God," she said, licking her lips. "You have no idea."

Hudson's eyes darkened and she quickly searched her brain for a diversion. "So...you were a juvenile delinquent?"

His gaze lifted from her mouth to her eyes. "Yes."

"Did you find the trouble or did it find you?"

"Both."

She smiled. "A real badass, huh?" she asked.

"Still am."

"Okay, let's make a deal," she said on a laugh. "How about you answer my questions with more than two words and I don't push you off this lift? Sound like a good plan?"

He grinned. She couldn't push him anywhere and they both knew it. A good wind could blow her away.

"Jacob and I came to Cedar Ridge when we were twelve," he said. "We were just about as feral as they come."

She blinked. "Wow, a whole sentence. Keep going."

He glanced around them as if looking for his own distraction and she laughed. "Oh, no you don't," she said. "For once the radio on your hip is silent. There's a lull on the mountain, probably because most of the skiers and boarders are at the lodge filling their empty bellies and warming their extremities. Talk."

He studied her for a long beat and then let out a slow smile. "Maybe *you're* the badass."

"Uh-huh," she said, "and don't ever forget it. Talk."

He smiled at her. She was pushing him but they both knew that he wasn't going to say a single word until he was damn well good and ready.

"Jacob and I didn't grow up here," he said, surprising her. "We grew up near Jackson Hole. My dad came into town on some business, during which he took advantage of a very young, sweet girl working as a hostess at a dive bar and grill."

"Your mom," she breathed.

"Yeah. She got pregnant, kept us, and did so with minimal help from Richard Kincaid. She did the best she could with what she had."

"She's pretty amazing."

"Yes," he agreed. "But there were plenty of problems. You've seen her fade in and out of reality. It made holding down a job difficult for her. It all kind of collapsed around the time we hit middle school."

"That must have been awful," she said. "What happened?"

He lifted a broad shoulder. "Jacob and I took over for her. We got jobs."

"In middle school."

"I didn't say they were legit jobs. Which they weren't, by the way. But we were already dodging child protective services and didn't want to get taken away from her. She needed us. And we needed money to keep our heads above water."

Bailey's stomach sank thinking of him at that age, doing whatever he had to do to keep his family together.

He took in her expression and gave her a small smile and a shake of his head. "You don't want pity, so don't you dare give it to me."

"Not pity," she said, and forced herself to swallow the lump of empathy in her throat. "Admiration. What happened?"

He shrugged again. "We did what we had to do. Jacob worked at a local vet's office at night cleaning up all the cages and walking the dogs for cash. He'd then take that cash and go play cards with the older kids in someone's garage. Jacob had a thing for numbers and could count cards."

She blinked. "And you?"

"I cooked at the old folks' home. The breakfast shift. That's where I learned to get up at four in the morning."

She tried to imagine him as a kid cooking breakfast for an entire old folks' home. "Seems slightly safer than what Jacob was doing."

"Hell if it was," he said. "I got my ass pinched every single morning by all the old ladies taking too many hormones. All these years later and my ass still hurts."

She covered her mouth but the laugh came out anyway.

His eyes lit at her humor. "Would you still feel sorry for me if I told you at night I'd go play pool at some guy's house down the street, conning him and his buddies out of their hard-earned cash to double my own cash flow?"

"You didn't."

"I did," he said. "The rent had to be paid and my mom's meds weren't cheap."

And then there were food and other necessities, she thought, aching for the twin boys who'd never really had a childhood. "But then you came here?"

"And inherited three half siblings," he said. "Aidan and Gray's mom took us in as her own so my mom could get the help she needed."

"Wow," Bailey breathed. "That's a good woman right there, considering you were the offspring of the woman her husband had cheated with."

"Char had dumped Richard Kincaid's sorry ass by then," Hud said. "And she has a heart of gold. She not only took us in, she took us *on*, loving us the same as she loved Gray and Aidan."

"So things got better?" she asked.

He paused and she found herself holding her breath. She wanted that for him and wanted that badly. And she'd seen how much Gray and Aidan and Kenna adored him.

"It was better for a while," he said quietly. "But before we got here, before we knew what we'd find, Jacob and I made a pact. We swore to each other that we'd leave the second we turned eighteen. We'd strike out on our own and stick together, just him and me."

Her heart kicked hard because she knew she was finally going to get the story on what had happened to Jacob and why the twins weren't together.

"But then we settled in here and I took to this place, hard and fast," Hudson said. "It instantly became home for me. But not for Jacob. He wanted to leave before we ever even got here, and he never lost sight of that goal. Unlike me. I actually forgot all about it until high school graduation."

"What happened?" she asked.

"Jacob said it was time for us to go. He'd been biding his time, counting down, and he wanted to leave as soon as possible. I didn't. We fought about it."

"But what about your mom and your siblings?" she asked.

"Jacob never got attached here like I did. And because of it, he held himself back. He didn't get close to the others. And though he always paid for half of my mom's care—and still does—he was bound and determined to leave no matter what. He needed adventure. He needed to live the way he'd always wanted—untethered."

"And so he just left?" she asked in disbelief.

"Not before we had the big blowup. But yeah, he left and has never been back."

"Oh, Hudson," she said softly. "I'm sorry he left you like that, after all you'd been through together."

"No, you don't understand," he said. "It was my fault. I said..." He closed his eyes. "I said shit to him that I can't take back. That's still between us, and I know it always will be. I did this. Not Jacob."

She stared up at him. "What could you possibly say to him that couldn't be taken back?"

He turned forward, his jaw tight. "I told him if he went, we weren't brothers anymore."

She took that in. "Well surely he knew those were just angry words spoken in the heat of the moment."

"Yeah well, I also said that if he wanted to be like our dad, then he should just get the fuck out."

"Oh, Hud," she whispered, and set her hand on his arm. "I'm sure he knew that was just the anger talking. If not then, then surely later when he thought about it. My God, you were just eighteen-year-old kids. No one says what they mean when they're eighteen."

"I don't know what Jacob thought," he said. "I've spent a lot of time wishing I could take it all back, but I can't. Fact is, you see, I pushed him away. And as you've already noted, I'm pretty damn good at it too." He straightened. "Face forward. Feet up."

"What?" she asked, still lost in his story, aching for his regrets. She looked up just in time to gasp.

They were at the top of the mountain.

She barely got her feet and ski tips up before she was making the transition from chair to snow. She wobbled, squealed, and was one hundred percent going down—

But a hand fisted in the back of her jacket and lifted her

enough that she got her skis beneath her. When Hud set her down, he gave her a push.

She gasped and clutched her poles and wavered.

"Bend your knees," he directed, all calm and perfect on his skis, the ratfink bastard.

But she bent her knees and...didn't crash. When she drifted to a stop off to the side, she turned her head and glared at him.

"Problem?" he asked.

"You pushed me!"

"Yes, because you stopped right in the lane and were about to get run over by the people getting off the lift behind us."

She stared at him, but her pride was not sure if it was ready to forgive.

He smiled. "You're welcome."

"I'm not thanking you until I live to the bottom of this run."

He flashed that badass smile. "How will you thank me?"

Instead of stabbing him with one of her poles, she pushed off and headed down the hill, which from here looked to be about one hundred miles of ski run but actually was probably only two. As it always did, the sensation of gliding over the snow, combined with the utter lack of control she had over that snow, gave her heart a hard kick. But...she was doing it. She was skiing! She laughed out loud with the sheer joy of it. "Look at me," she yelled back to Hud, smiling wide. "I'm doing it!"

That's when her ski caught an edge. For about three seconds she fought the valiant fight, no doubt looking like a cat trying to scramble across linoleum, unable to catch her grip. She heard Hud behind her, voice calm. "Find your center. Bend your knees. Lean forward, not to the side—"

Too late. She leaned.

And she fell.

Right on her face. And for extra shits and giggles, she slid on her face down the hill another twenty feet or so. Sprawled out, she pushed up and spit out some snow.

She was hauled to her feet. Hud, of course. He dusted off the front of her and then turned her to get her backside. He slapped her there more than a few times until she twisted free and glared at him.

"Excuse me," she said. "Are you sure you were thorough enough?"

He smiled. "Can never be too thorough."

She narrowed her eyes. "You didn't ask me if I was okay."

"You hate that question."

And just like that, her annoyance drained and her breath caught. He wasn't a coddler. It wasn't his style. He'd absolutely give her what he thought she needed, but he knew she didn't want to be babied. She smiled at him then because damn. Damn, she could really fall for him.

Not that she was going to. Nope. No way, no how. "You have any tips for how not to do that again?" she asked.

"Yeah. Keep your mouth closed so you leave some of the snow for the other skiers."

"Haha."

He grinned and gave her a very gentle push off. "Again," he said. "Without the sliding on your face part."

She sighed and hunkered into her ski pose, trying to concentrate.

"Lean forward," Hudson said from right behind her. "Turn into the fall line."

She did and immediately saw the difference. For once she actually felt in control and adrenaline surged in her veins. She loved the wind hitting her face and loved the feeling that she was flying—

"Bend your knees," he said.

"I am."

"More."

"My thighs are burning."

"Which means you're doing it right."

"Maybe I should rethink this," she said. "And become a ski bunny who gets to sit all nice and warm and toasty in the lodge."

"I'll make you nice and toasty later," he promised. "Watch your skis. When you traverse across the slope, your skis need to be more parallel."

She was about to parallel him upside the head when a little girl called out to him.

"*HudsonHudsonHudson!*" The cutie pie swooshed around him on her tiny skis, beaming wide as she came up alongside.

She was missing both her front teeth.

"Emma," Hudson said with a chuckle. "You escape from your dad again?"

"Yes!" She giggled. "Race me!"

Hudson turned to Bailey.

"I don't mind," she said. "I'd love to see her kick your butt."

"Ready, set, go!" Emma yelled, and took off.

Hudson easily got ahead of her and turned to face her, skiing backward like it was no big deal.

But Emma was no slouch. She might be tiny, but she was very good. Her little body moved with easy confidence. But then she dove into a turn and—in Bailey's humble opinion, because she bent her knees too much—fell...right into Hudson.

He dropped his poles to catch her in midair, twisting so that as they tumbled to the snow in a heap, he was on the bottom, not crushing her.

Emma immediately sat up, grinning wide. "That was fun! Can we do it again? Can we?"

From prone on the ground, Hudson lifted Emma off of him. "No, you little rug rat. Some of us are too old for this."

Beaming at him again, she took off. "Gotta go," she yelled back. "Mom and Dad are waiting for me at the bottom."

And then she was gone.

Bailey came to a careful stop next to Hud. "You're supposed to stay on your feet," she teased, tossing his own lesson back in his face.

Not afraid to laugh at himself, he snorted as he got to his feet. They took off in tandem.

"Uh-oh," she said, moving in closer. "You have a little..." Pretending she was going to brush some snow off of him, she instead smacked his ass in the same way he'd done to her. Except maybe harder. Or, you know, a lot harder.

Hudson's eyes lit with a heated challenge as he gave her a look that had every bone in her body melting. It was the only reason that she plowed right into him, taking them both back down to the snow.

This time everything flew off, her skis, her poles...her good wits, scattering along with her equipment.

"And *that's* what you call a garage sale," Hudson said.

"I'm sorry," she gasped, sprawled out over the top of him. She pushed up off his chest and stared down into his face. "I didn't mean to—"

"Wait." He cupped the back of her head, his gaze dropping to her mouth. "You have a little something..."

She touched her face. "Where?"

"I've got it." And he pulled her face down to his, kissing her long and wet and deep.

"Get a room," someone yelled from the ski lift above them.

Bailey ignored it and so did Hudson. Only when he was apparently finished thoroughly ravaging her mouth did he let her go. "Ready?" he asked.

Ready? For what? She no longer knew her name. That she was still on a ski slope shocked the hell out of her. She looked down at herself to make sure her clothes hadn't melted off. "I'm always ready," she said.

He grinned. "That's what I like about you." He got to his feet in one move that made it look easy.

It wasn't. First off, her legs still weren't working, so it took her a minute to get them beneath her. Hudson patiently straightened her out.

Dazed, she stared at his mouth, which she knew could drive her halfway to orgasm with just a kiss. She let out a rough laugh and shook her head. "Hudson?"

"Yeah?"

"I know I'm the one who put limits on this...this *thing*," she said, and bit her lower lip, suddenly nervous. "But I'm pretty sure we're not quite done with each other."

He looked at her for what felt like a long time. "You want another night."

Still unable to take her eyes off his mouth, she didn't muzzle herself. "I want as long as it takes."

He cupped her jaw, lifting her head up so that she was looking into his eyes again. "Don't make promises you can't keep."

"What makes you think I can't keep it?"

"Because you seem to like things one night at a time," he said in that low, sexy voice. "But no way is one more night going to be enough."

Again, her heart skipped a beat. "Cocky much?" she managed.

His smile was slow and sexy as hell. "That wasn't bravado, Bailey. That was fact."

Chapter 19

At the base lodge, Bailey removed her skis next to Hudson. He scooped up all of their skis and poles and set them over his shoulder.

While she gaped at the easy strength, he held out his free hand for hers.

"What?" she asked.

"You have a promise to fulfill."

Oh boy. Everything was about to change, and she could feel it. She'd had a lot of changes in the past few years. More than most had in their entire lives. Was she ready for another?

No way is one more night going to be enough...

At just the memory of his words, she quivered, even as she knew he was right. With Hudson, one night would never be enough. Waiting patiently while her mind sorted through all of this, Hud merely kept his hand out.

When she took it, his eyes heated. A sexy smile curved his lips as well, and then he was pulling her through the crowd in the lodge, past an EMPLOYEES ONLY door, down a hallway of offices...

A few people looked up or said something briefly to Hud. He nodded and responded in kind, but Bailey couldn't keep track of any of it, and then Hudson had opened a door and pulled her inside. Completely lost in thought, she stumbled. He used her momentum against her, tugging her so that she fell into him, and the two of them tumbled into his office.

She knew this room—intimately.

Hud kicked the door shut, slapped a hand out to lock it, and then dropped his jacket and pressed her into the wood.

She smiled but as Hudson took her hands and slowly slid them up the wood on either side of her face until they were over her head, her amusement died. It was replaced by sheer, unadulterated lust. Body vibrating with need, she tried to reach out to kiss him but he held her off.

"You still want this?" he asked in a low and gravelly voice.

He was vibrating, too, and that gave her a surge of feminine power. She tugged her hands free and set them on his chest, letting them trail down his rock-hard abs.

"Bailey."

"Yes," she said, loving the feel of his six-pack. She let her hands drift down to the waistband of his ski pants, and the question of the day became what to touch first.

Everything, she decided, and grabbed a handful of his shirt, yanking it free of the pants. "Yes, I still want this," she said. "I want you. I want you now. Please, Hud—"

His mouth came down on hers hard, locking them in a battle to get closer, then closer still. A battle fought with hands, arms…tongues. Still not feeling close enough, she squirmed and Hud responded by tightening his grip on her, deepening the kiss ever further.

She could feel every part of him plastered against her, and there were some really great parts she wanted to get up close and personal with. She'd been so nervous their first time, but ever since then her nerves had been replaced by a bold need to know every inch of his glorious body. To that end, her hands found their way beneath his shirt. Her fingers retraced the path they'd taken a moment before up his chest, stroking over one side and then the other, thrilling to his sharp intake of breath and the way his nipples tightened into little beads—

The knock at the door made her jump.

"Hud." The male voice that came through the door was Gray, she thought half hysterically, and started to pull away. Hud made a low male sound, gripped her harder, and kept kissing her.

Oh, thank God, was all she could think. This was going to happen, hopefully before she combusted. But then the door handle rattled at her hip and she gasped.

Gray was trying to let himself in!

"Dammit, Hud!" Gray muttered. "Open up!"

Hud didn't answer. Couldn't, seeing as his tongue was currently caressing Bailey's in a delicious fight for sexual dominance that had her whimpering and trying to climb up his body.

She'd never felt so electrically, erotically charged. Never. This was *not* the cozy sex she was used to. She loved cozy sex, at least as much of it as she could remember. But this…this was in a whole other league from anything she'd ever experienced.

"Asshole," Gray said from the other side of the door. When silence followed this, Bailey hoped that meant Gray had walked away.

Hud's hands came up to cup her face and his lips found hers again. "I can't get enough," he whispered huskily against her mouth. "I can't get enough of you."

She nodded because she couldn't get enough of him either.

"Say it," he said.

She swallowed hard and stared up at him. "I can't get enough of you. I wanted to but I can't."

He closed his eyes for a beat and then scooped her up. Turning with her in his arms, he swiped an arm across his desk, sending everything flying to the floor.

She nearly had a mini-O on the spot.

At the whimpering sound she made, his gaze turned to her, hot. Hungry. He set her on the desk, pushed her legs apart, and stepped in between them. He stripped off her jacket. Her shirt and bra took even less time, and he shook his head.

"What?" she asked, lifting her hands to cover herself.

He caught her hands in his and held them out to her sides. "I thought maybe I made some of this up in my head," he murmured.

"Some of what?"

"How beautiful you are." He shook his head again. "I didn't. You undo me, Bailey." And then, still holding her hands in his, he kissed his way down her body, paying special homage to each spot. When he licked her nipple before very gently biting down, she barely held back a cry for more. Needing a handhold, she sank her fingers into his hair, holding him to her as he sucked her into his mouth. She tried to squeeze her legs together to alleviate some of the ache between them, but he stood in the V of her thighs, holding her spread open. He rocked into her, pressing into her right where she ached the most.

Not wanting to be a slouch, she shoved his shirt up and undid the button on his ski pants.

And then the zipper.

Their gazes met.

"Condom," she whispered.

He pulled one from somewhere just as a sudden and firm pounding at the door had her nearly jerking out of her skin.

"Hud!" A woman's voice came through the wood, sounding stressed. "Half your guys screwed up their time cards *again!*"

Hud lifted his head from Bailey's breast and gave her a slow headshake. He wasn't going to fix the time card problem, at least not right now. And then he went back to driving her crazy with that tongue. When she gasped again, he reached up and covered her mouth.

Right. Quiet.

But how was she supposed to be quiet? Especially when—oh, sweet baby Jesus—he crouched low, undid her ski boot, and slipped it off, careful to set it on the floor instead of letting it hit with a *thunk*. Then he lifted his head and met her gaze. His head was level with her crotch.

It was a shockingly intimate position and her body liked it.

A lot.

He did the same for boot number two and then unbuttoned and unzipped her ski pants, and he wasn't nearly as slow as she had been. In two seconds she was sitting on his desk in nothing but her leopard-print bikini panties.

Chapter 20

Hottest sight Hud had ever seen. Fantasies set aside, he'd never had a woman sitting on his desk in just her panties before. And that this was Bailey...damn. Better than any dream. Better than any of his wildest dreams.

"Your turn," she whispered, and slid her hands into his pants to lower them to his thighs. He expected a reaction from her but he didn't expect her to freeze in shock.

Which was when he remembered—he was wearing the Big Dog briefs from Aidan, the ones with the words CHOKING HAZARD written in bold block letters down the fly.

Jesus.

She blinked and then read the words to herself. He knew this because he watched her lips move and form the words *choking hazard*. She then made a rough sound that please God was a laugh and not a horrified sob and covered her mouth with her hand.

"Fucking Aidan," he muttered.

She made the sound again and yeah, it was most definitely a laugh. He looked into her smiling eyes. "You think this is funny?"

Hand still on her mouth, she nodded.

He blew out a mock sigh, but God he loved her smile and her laugh. "Not exactly the mood I was hoping to set here, Bay."

She dropped her hand and gave him a look from beneath her lashes. "You set the mood just fine." And then she slid off his desk to her knees on the floor in front of him. Her mouth headed south down his abs. When the briefs impeded the process, she tugged them out of her way.

He sucked in a breath and tipped his head down to make sure this was still Bailey because the whole thing felt surreal. His Bailey was sweet and maybe even a little introverted. Hell, she still blushed when he kissed her. She wasn't a woman who—in his office, no less—would drop to her knees in nothing but skimpy panties and— "Oh, Christ."

She pressed a hot kiss about an inch to the right of where he really wanted her and then slid her gaze up at him and smiled.

"You like this?" she whispered. Not being coy, genuinely wanting to make sure.

In spite of himself he let out a rough laugh. "Keep that up and you'll see just how much in about sixty seconds," he managed.

Her grin widened.

"I'm just amusing you all over the place today," he said.

"Maybe I just like the idea of making a big, tough guy weak in the knees with nothing more than a kiss."

He didn't tell her that she'd made him weak in the knees from their very first moment together, with one wide-eyed look on the top of the mountain.

She slid her hands up his thighs, licked her lips, and then licked *him*—

"*Hud!*" someone yelled through the door. Aidan, this time. "A surprise storm's moving in by nightfall."

Used to people pounding on his door day and night, Hud didn't so much as flinch. But Bailey—her mouth on her admittedly favorite part of his anatomy—nearly went through the roof.

Ignoring Aidan outside the door, Hud pulled Bailey back up. "When I die," he whispered against her lips, "I want to go just like that, with your mouth on me."

She smiled and kissed him deep and hot, and from very, very far away he heard his brother mutter "shit" through the door.

Hud didn't respond. Instead he kissed Bailey, his hands slipping into the back of her panties, feeling nothing but smooth, velvet-soft ass. Cupping a cheek in each hand, he lifted her back up to his desk and pressed his hips hard into hers.

Her eyes were worried. "But people keep coming—"

"The next person to come is going to be you," he said. He dropped to his knees then and hooked his fingers into the lace on her hips. "Lift up, Bailey."

"Um," she said even as she lifted up for him.

He slowly slid her panties down her legs and then held those legs open with his shoulders.

He lifted his head from the gorgeous sight of her all soft and wet. Very wet. "Okay?"

She bit her lower lip. "I don't know yet."

He leaned in and kissed her inner thigh. "You just let me know when."

Eyes wide, she nodded slowly, clearly unsure. So he bent his head and did his best to make her very, very sure.

It took less than three minutes, and by the end of those three minutes she'd squeezed his head between her thighs like a grape, sunk her fingers into his hair, and nearly made him bald.

He'd loved every second.

She was still panting when he rose up to his feet. She stared up at him in dazed shock. "I liked that."

He grinned. "I know."

"No, I mean I *really* liked that," she said. "We need to do that again."

"Yes. After this." He pulled her off the desk and then turned her to face it. "Bend over," he murmured, pressing the front of his body to the back of hers and running his hands down her arms. He used his fingers to guide her palms flat to his desk so that her ass pressed into his groin.

She went still. "Hudson—"

"The desk isn't the right height when you're sitting on it," he whispered. "This will be a better angle for you, I promise." As he spoke, he pressed open-mouthed kisses to the sweet spot just beneath her ear as his hands found her breasts. When his rough fingers teased her tight nipples, she went soft and compliant.

Very gently he inserted a foot between hers and urged her legs farther apart. Keeping an arm around her waist to cushion her from the edge of the wood, he trailed a hand between her trembling thighs.

She moaned and squirmed, and he sank his teeth into

the nape of her neck. "Shh," he reminded her, loving the scent of her—coconut shampoo, soft and willing woman, and maybe a tinge of apprehension. She shivered and pressed back against him.

Nope. Not apprehension. It was arousal, in every beat of her heart and every hitched breath.

"Please," she breathed, and pushed her hips back into him, gripping the edges of his desk and quivering like a bow strung as taut as it could get. "Oh, Hud, please…"

Making quick work of a condom, he thrust into her and she came. Instantly. Barely managing not to do the same, he held her through the tremors and stroked her up again. He was trying to slow her down, trying to slow them both down, but she kept rocking those hips back for more and he lost himself, just completely lost himself in Bailey.

When their frenzied need overtook them both, they detonated. Hud just barely managed to keep them both upright in spite of the fact that his legs weren't a solid bet. He was still working on that and also trying to catch his breath—*and* come to terms with what had just happened. He was pretty sure that what happened was his heart had just rolled over and exposed its tender underbelly—when there was another knock at his door.

"Hud?" It was Penny this time. "Hud, have you seen Bailey? Her car's in the lot but no one's seen her. I just want to make sure she's okay."

Penny was smarter than both of his brothers. In fact she was smarter than all of them added together. "She's okay," he said to the door.

There was a beat of silence from Penny. Never a good sign. Then, "So is that 'she's okay' as in you just want me to go away and leave you the hell alone?" she asked.

"Or 'she's okay' as in you've got her in there with you and you're making good use of your desk the way I do with Gray's?"

Bailey squirmed. "Door number two!" she said.

Jesus. Hud dropped his forehead to Bailey's shoulder. "Now you've done it," he murmured. He could feel her shaking with laughter and it occurred to him that any other woman might have been pissed. And with good reason. He'd just bent her over his desk and taken her. And also, his family was certifiable. Completely. "Now that you know she's okay," he said to Penny through the door, "you can go away."

"Will do," Penny said, sounding very amused. "I'll retract the search party. Hey, you guys want to come for dinner tonight?"

Hud closed his eyes. "Penny?"

"Yeah?"

"Go away. And if you tell, I'll let Gray know you're the one who put that dent in his precious truck."

There was a shocked beat of silence and then "I was never here!" This was followed by the sound of her footsteps hurrying away.

"Shit," Hud muttered, turning Bailey in his arms to face him. "She'll have told everyone by the end of the day."

Bailey, looking soft and dazed and sated, smiled and he gave her a kiss. Then he propped her up against his desk and picked up her clothes for her. Since she still looked boneless and adorably wobbly, he ended up helping her get back into them. He added his own sweatshirt to the top of her ensemble to keep her warm.

Bullshit. You just like the way she looks in your clothes...

When yet another knock came on his door, he just about blew his gasket. Since they were both put back together, more or less, he yanked his office door open and was prepared to blast whoever stood there.

It was Penny again. He'd have to kill her. He'd have to kill Gray, too, of course, but Hud thought he could easily learn to live without them both—

These thoughts collided on themselves when he realized that Penny was looking extremely sorry to be interrupting, and also that she wasn't alone.

Behind her was a fiftyish woman—

"Mom?" Bailey asked, sounding shocked as she came up to Hud's side and peered around him. "What are you doing here?"

The woman looked at Bailey with such shocked horror that Hud turned to look at Bailey too.

Shit. The sweatshirt she wore—his—was on inside out, her ski cap was askew—from his hands—and she was hopping into her other ski boot without a sock since they'd been unable to locate it.

"What's going on here?" Bailey's mother asked dramatically, slapping a hand to her own heart as she divided a gaze between Hud and her daughter.

"A meeting," Penny said smoothly. "Just an everyday old average meeting. Isn't that right, Hud?"

But Bailey's mother's eyes ignored Hud entirely, locking on Bailey. "Then why are you all flushed and sweaty? You're either running a fever or you were just—"

"Mom," Bailey said, righting her cap. "Just give me a minute here to finish up and I'll take you to the cafeteria where we can talk—"

"I came up here to see the mural you're always talking

about. I wanted to take pictures for all my friends who are constantly asking me how you're doing and if you're needing any more help, financially or otherwise. I thought—" She broke off and shook her head, and turned her hard, angry eyes on Hud.

He held out his hand. "It's nice to meet you, Mrs. Moore."

She stared at his hand and then whipped back to Bailey. "We've been worried sick about you. You've been putting so many hours into work, and then on top of that coming up here to work some more—or so I thought."

"Mom," Bailey said with quiet reproof. "You're being rude."

"*I'm* being rude? I thought—" She broke off and shook her head. "Well, it doesn't matter what I thought. I was wrong. You've been up here cheating on poor Aaron!"

Bailey stepped forward to take her mom's arm and steer her out the door, carefully not meeting Hud's eyes.

Which, for the record, Hud hated.

Bailey's mom tugged herself free and shook her head again. "No. I'm not staying."

Bailey sighed. "Mom—"

"I can't," her mother said, voice quavering. She took a step back, eyes shimmering. "I don't even recognize you," she said, and then she was gone.

Bailey started to go after her, but Hud caught her and held on when she tried to break free. He bent a little to look into her eyes.

Yep. Filled with humiliation.

Dammit all to hell.

He easily switched his anger from Penny to Bailey's mother. But much as he'd like to, he couldn't strangle the woman. She was Bailey's mother. "Hey," he said softly, holding her gaze and wishing she'd let him console her, wishing she'd acknowledge that what they'd just shared was worth fighting for. "That was pretty rough. Take a minute."

She turned her head away from him so he couldn't see but it didn't matter. The stricken look in her eyes was now burned in his brain.

"I have to go after her," she said, her voice thick with emotion. "I don't want her on the curvy roads upset."

And he didn't want Bailey upset at all, but this wasn't Christmas and wishes didn't come true. "Bailey. Bay, look at me a minute."

She turned back to him, eyes downcast. He waited and she finally lifted them up to his.

"Don't let her cheapen what just happened," he said quietly.

"You can't cheapen a one-time thing," she said just as quietly.

"This has never been a one-time thing."

She shook her head, pulled free, and walked away.

Chapter 21

Bailey followed her mom to the parking lot. "Mom," she said. "Please don't leave like this."

Still wearing the scrubs from her nursing job at Denver Urgent Care, Terri Moore turned back to Bailey, her eyes shimmering. "What was going on up in that office with that man, Bailey?"

"Mom, I love you, you know I do, but that's none of your business."

Her mom crossed her arms and inhaled sharply—a sure sign of defense that meant she knew Bailey was right but she wasn't ready to give up the point. "I wanted you to end up with Aaron," she said.

"I know you did."

"He's so perfect for you, and I thought after you had some time you'd see that and go back to him."

"Mom." Bailey reached for her mom's hands and held them in her own. "I do love Aaron."

"Well you sure have a funny way of showing that."

"I love Aaron," Bailey repeated. "But I'm not *in* love with Aaron."

Her mom stilled and then sighed. "Oh, Bailey. He's always been there for you, always. You're going to break his heart."

"We've talked," Bailey said. "We're okay. And if we're okay, I need you to be okay. I need you to be happy for me."

"But you're alone!"

Bailey let out a breath. Her dad hadn't exactly been a model husband. Her mother had never forgiven the male race. But for some reason, she'd loved Aaron since day one. "Being alone doesn't scare me," Bailey said.

"Well it should!" Her mother looked horrified. "I understand feminism and I can appreciate the sentiment, but that won't keep you warm in the stormy times." Her mom's voice wavered. "And there are stormy times, Bailey. There are always stormy times."

"Mom." Bailey stepped in closer and pulled her into a hug. "That's just life. There's good and there's bad. My happiness and safety won't come from having a man. It comes from me."

Her mom sniffed and pulled back just enough to meet Bailey's eyes. She cupped her daughter's face and sighed. "When did you get so wise?"

"I had a really great mom."

Her mom's eyes softened. "As long as you're okay."

"I'm okay."

"And happy."

"I'm happy," Bailey said. "I'm so very happy, Mom."

"Because of that man I saw you with?"

"Because I'm free," Bailey said. "I get to wake up

each day and know I've got a bunch more days in front of me now. I get to do the things I've always wanted to do, like—"

"Sleep with strangers?"

"Like paint a mural," Bailey said firmly. "And if a hot stranger comes into my life, I can stop to smell the roses. So to speak."

Her mother blinked. "Does he have a name?"

"He tried to introduce himself to you. Hudson Kincaid."

Her mom covered her cheeks with her hands. "I was rude to him."

"Yes, very. You can make it up to him next time you see him by being nice," Bailey said.

"There's going to be a next time?" her mom asked, sounding worried again.

Bailey sighed.

"Right. Minding my own business." She nodded and then shook her head. "I don't think I will be very good at that, Bailey."

"For me, you're going to try."

Her mom nodded and then her eyes filled again.

"Mom," Bailey said, pained.

"Did you hear back from the doctor?" her mom asked. "Is that what this is all about?"

"No," Bailey said. "You know I'd have told you immediately if I'd heard anything. Results won't be in until Monday or Tuesday, but I'm still clear. I know it."

Her mom studied her face for a long beat. "You're sure?"

"*Yes*," Bailey said with a smile. "The doctor said I looked good, remember? She even threw out the R word." *Remission.* Not cancer free, that would take longer, maybe even five years longer, but Bailey knew it would come. "These are just tests that I do every three months to make sure," she said. "You know all this."

"Yes, I just like to hear it."

A few flakes began to drift down, reminding Bailey a storm was moving in and they were on borrowed time. "I'll follow you down the mountain, okay? We need to stay ahead of the storm."

"I'd like that." A look of guilt flashed across her mom's face. "But it means you have to leave a day early."

Bailey nodded. "I know. It's okay."

"The mural is beautiful." Her mom reached for her hand. "So beautiful it stopped me in my tracks. I'm so proud of you, Bailey. I hope you know that. And how very much I love you."

Her throat went a little tight and she squeezed her mom's hand. "I do know it. And I love you too."

Her mom gave a little smile. "Once we're out of the storm's reach, let's stop and have breakfast for dinner at IHOP, like the old days."

The old days. When Bailey had been dying. They'd go and have her treatments and then stop at IHOP on the way home, where Bailey would always order the same thing every time. Strawberry pancakes.

She didn't ever want to see another strawberry pancake again. But she smiled. "Sounds great, Mom."

After Bailey left, Hud got two consecutive calls, both involving injuries that required his immediate and full attention.

And he'd given it.

But in between, whenever he had even two seconds

to breathe, his mind replayed Bailey on her knees in his office, her mouth—

"Hud."

He was running a training exercise in the dark, stormy evening. Evacuating lifts—never easy in the best of conditions, which these weren't.

"What are you smiling at?" Gray asked. "I said your name like ten times to get your attention."

Hud gestured for Mitch to take over the training exercise and moved aside with his brother. "What are you doing up here?"

"Needed to have a meeting with you," Gray said.

"About?"

"About that smile you're wearing, seeing as it's been awhile since anyone saw that look on your face."

Hud looked around and was relieved to find no one paying them any attention. "Are you kidding me? This is what you interrupted a training session for?"

"I never kid about meetings," Gray said. He pulled out two bags of M&M's from his pocket and handed one over to Hud. "So...the smile. 'Splain, Lucy."

He shook his head. "I'm not smiling."

"Mitch," Gray called out.

Mitch turned their way. "Yeah?"

"What's on Hud's face?"

"Uh...a smile?" Mitch guessed.

"Bingo." Gray beamed at Hud like, *See?*

Hud shook his head. "This meeting isn't all that much fun."

"It's a lot of fun to me." Gray tossed an M&M up in the air and caught it in his mouth.

"So smiling's against the rules now?" Hud asked.

"Man, you're not just smiling. You look completely wasted."

"Maybe I had a really great lunch."

"You locked yourself in your office for lunch."

Hud lifted a shoulder.

Gray stared at him for another beat and then sighed. "I wouldn't mind a lunch like that."

"Exactly what do you think I had for lunch?" Hud asked.

"Bailey."

Hud, who'd just tossed an unfortunate M&M into his mouth, choked on it. "Penny is dead to me."

Gray grinned. "You going to deny that you banged Bailey in your office?"

"Jesus."

"Listen, you bang on the clock, you have to talk about the bang."

Hud drilled his finger into Gray's chest. "Say 'bang' one more time and I'll kick your ass."

Gray grinned wide. "Fine. I'll stop saying it. But not because I'm afraid of you. Because I have to go."

Hud caught him by the back of his jacket. "Who else knows besides you and your big-mouthed wife?"

"About the banging?" Gray wisely shook free and took a couple of steps back as he spoke, counting off on his fingers. "Lily, Aidan, Kenna..."

"So everyone," Hud said, annoyed. "Everyone knows. Shit." He looked at Mitch, occupied with running the training session. "Don't let anyone tell Mitch."

"Why not?"

"Because he's got a bigger mouth than you and Penny. He'll tell everyone else."

Gray shrugged. "Should've taken her someplace more private."

"Like you do?"

"That's right," Gray said. "I take Penny some place real private. Like my office *closet*." He grinned. "Have to, she's noisy so we need the extra buffer."

Hud resisted stabbing himself with his ski pole while Gray finished his bag of M&M's and eyed Hud's.

Hud tightened his grip on his bag. "What do you want?"

"Confirmation on the you-and-Bailey thing."

Hud stared at Gray. "Tell me you didn't really come up here just for that."

"Hey, it's big news."

"How so?"

Gray shrugged. "Maybe I'm just curious whether you're going to find your happy or not."

Hud blinked. "Why are you talking like Penny all of a sudden?"

"What do you mean?"

"Asking me about my feelings and shit."

"Because that's what we do," Gray said.

"We do that never."

Gray scratched his head. "No?"

"No, and you're full of shit. You're not up here for you. You're up here for Penny. She made you."

Gray grimaced. "Lily too. So you've got to give me something," Gray said. "I can't go back to those two empty-handed."

Hud ran a hand down his face. "I can't believe how afraid of two sweet, adorable women you are."

"Are you kidding me?" Gray asked. "Those two aren't

sweet, adorable women! They're hormone driven, crazy, and obsessed with curiosity about you and Bailey. I can't go home until I get the scoop."

"Well you should get comfortable in the doghouse then, cuz I'm not giving you the scoop."

Gray blew out a sigh. "At least tell me how the choking-hazard Underoos went over."

Hud choked on another M&M. *"Dammit."*

Gray grinned from ear to ear. "So you *were* wearing them. And you got laid anyway? Man, she's a total keeper, just sayin'."

Hud lunged for him but Gray was nothing if not quick as hell. Laughing like a loon, he twisted away.

Hud blew out a breath. "I've got a question."

"What?" Gray asked.

"You said I'd know when it was time to open up and let her in." He paused, hating that he had to ask. "But I don't."

Gray straightened, his eyes going serious. "Holy shit. You love her."

Hud froze and looked around. *"Who told you that?"* he hissed.

"You just did." Gray smiled and clapped a hand on Hud's shoulder. "And you'll just know. I promise." And with that, he pushed off on his skis and was gone in a blink.

Bastard.

Hud reached for his phone to call Aidan and tell him that his fiancée was every bit as crazy as Penny.

And that's when he realized he didn't have his phone.

He slapped his pockets, searching, before flashing back to slipping his sweatshirt over Bailey's head. Damn. *She* had his phone.

Back in Denver.

"Mitch," he yelled. "Need your phone."

Mitch pitched it over and went back to training.

Hud dialed his own phone and held his breath. Would she answer it if she saw a number she wouldn't recognize? Would she answer at all? They hadn't exactly parted on rosy terms. One minute he'd been inside her in more ways than one, having unarguably the absolute best time of his life, and the next a bucket of cold water had been tossed over their heads in the form of one pissed-off mama—

"Hudson Kincaid's phone."

He felt a smile crease his face at the sound of her voice. Not exactly friendly or open, but he'd take it. "Hey," he said. "You answered."

"Hud? I'm so sorry I ended up with your phone," she said in a rush. "Do you have any idea how many times a day it goes off?"

He laughed a little. "Yeah."

"I saw it said 'Dumb Ass calling' and I figured it was someone you knew pretty well so I answered."

Hud looked at Mitch and grinned. "Fast thinking *and* pretty."

She laughed. "I answered in case it was an emergency. I was going to overnight the phone to you first thing in the morning—"

"I'll text you our courier information," he said. "Use our account so you don't have to pay for it."

"Thank you," she said, her voice softer now.

"You pick up any more phone calls I should know about?" he asked.

"No." She paused. "Mostly because I didn't want to get you in any sort of trouble with...anyone."

"What kind of trouble?"

"You know," she said softly. "Like another woman."

Aw. Look at her fishing. Equal parts heat, amusement, and affection went through him. "If the triplets call, tell them I'm busy this weekend."

She choked out a laugh. "Will do." She paused again. "But are you? Busy this weekend?"

He smiled. "You coming up?"

"Yes," she said.

"Then yeah, I'm busy."

There was a beat of silence at that. She didn't know how to take him. Which made them perfectly even because he had no idea how to take her either.

"What if an important text comes through?" she asked.

"Would it be from you?"

She laughed. "Why would I send you a text when I'm holding your phone?"

"I don't know," he said. "But you should feel free to take lots of pics of yourself with my camera."

"I'm going to hang up now," she said.

"Or videos—" He grinned when she disconnected him. He tossed Mitch's phone back.

"Nice to see you smiling," Mitch said. "More trips to your office with the hottie artist for you."

Chapter 22

On Monday, Bailey worked with one eye on her phone, waiting to hear back from the doctor about her checkup.

She heard nothing.

She finally quit work a little early to package up Hud's phone and get it to the post office for overnight delivery. She was just setting it into the box when it buzzed an incoming text from "Mom." The first few lines of the text showed up on the screen and read:

Need to talk to you. Call me? I think Jacob's got a problem and only you can—

That was it. That was all she could see in the preview. To access the text would require her to swipe her finger across the screen, which was much more of an invasion of his privacy than taking a quick peek at his screen as texts came in. She closed her eyes, feeling torn between guilt for seeing it in the first place and worry.

Worry won.

She called the resort and asked for Hudson. She was sent to his voice mail. The sound of his voice telling her to leave a message sent a low-level sense of anticipation humming through her.

Okay, a high level.

The highest.

She looked at the time. Three o'clock. If she left right now she could get to Cedar Ridge just as dark hit. The weather was clear at the moment, but if the roads iced up later she'd have to spend the night. This should've deterred her in a big way. She had work to do here and she needed the money.

She got into her car anyway.

She got to the resort at five thirty. The lot was nearly empty. The sun had dropped behind the mountains, leaving the kind of dark that a city girl had a hard time getting used to. Up here there were no streetlights, no traffic sounds, no billboards.

The resort offices had a deserted feel. A young woman had a cleaning cart and was working on the floors. "It's a weekday," she said to Bailey's inquiry. "Resort closed at four thirty."

"Is Hudson still here by any chance?"

The woman looked at a wall that was almost entirely covered by a huge dry-erase board. It had a long list of people on the left. To the right you could see if a person was on duty and where they were located on the mountain. Hud was listed third after Gray and Aidan, and, no surprise, he was on duty. But his location box was empty.

"He's probably somewhere around here," the woman said. "He's in charge of a lot and is always on the move."

Gray came out from an office and went brows up at the sight of Bailey.

"I came to bring Hudson his phone," she explained.

He blinked. "You have his phone?"

"Yes, it was an accident. He gave me his sweatshirt on Saturday and his phone was in the pocket..." She trailed off at the look on Gray's face. "He didn't tell you?"

"Can I see it?"

She handed the phone over and Gray slid his thumb across the screen.

"You think something's wrong?" she asked him.

Gray didn't answer but worked his thumbs furiously for a moment, then handed her the phone.

She stared at him. "You don't want to give it to him?"

He grinned. "Hell no, I don't want the evidence anywhere near me."

"What?"

He just patted her on the arm. "You can leave the phone on his desk. Or if you want to deliver it in person, he's visiting his mom tonight."

She bit her lip.

"Ah. You're as chickenshit about this stuff as he is, huh?" He shook his head. "I'm disappointed."

She had no idea what that meant, but she headed toward the door.

"You two are perfect for each other," he said to her back. "Both stubborn as hell. You need to figure out how to portray that on the mural. Maybe label beneath his picture: 'Mr. Obstinate' or something."

She laughed and turned back. "And what would be your label?"

"Mr. Hot-ass Troublemaker." This from Penny, who

came in from outside. She pushed back her hood and met Gray's eyes.

Gray immediately dropped his amusement and strode straight for his wife, pulling her into his arms hard.

"I'm all wet," she murmured.

"Just the way I like you." His voice was low and soft with affection and a lot more. "Missed you today, babe."

Their embrace was incredibly intimate, and feeling like she was intruding on a private moment, Bailey let herself out into the night.

She drove into town and a few minutes later knocked on Carrie's door.

"Two birthday visitors in one night!" Carrie said, happy.

"Birthday?" Bailey asked.

"It's my birthday," Carrie said, and beamed.

The first time Bailey had been here, all those weeks ago now, Carrie had told Bailey that her birthday had been just the week before. But not wanting to upset Carrie, she just smiled. "I'm sorry, I didn't bring you anything. But I will next time."

"I love presents," Carrie said. "And cupcakes. Hud's here too. He's chatting with the gals in the front office. Said he had some paperwork."

Paperwork could mean anything, but not for the first time it occurred to Bailey that Carrie's stay here had to be expensive for Hud and Jacob, very expensive.

"It's a Monday," Carrie said. "Not that I'm not thrilled to see you, but what are you doing here tonight?"

Not wanting to admit that she'd accidentally read her private text to her son, she smiled. "Just wanted to check in on things. How are you?"

"I've got one of my boys here tonight," Carrie said simply, "so I couldn't be better. Now you."

"I'm good."

Carrie smiled. "Because you're here visiting my boy?"

Bailey laughed. "Are you matchmaking?"

"If you have to ask, I'm not doing it right," Carrie said. Her smile turned sly. "Just seems like there's a little something there, don't you think?"

Bailey had been thinking of nothing *but* that very fact. Whether she admitted it out loud or not, there was more than a "little something there" between her and Hud. And it only strengthened with time. She could close her eyes and see his slow, lazy smile, hear his sexy voice...feel him buried inside her.

"You look happy, you know," Carrie said. "He's made you happy, hasn't he?"

Bailey opened her mouth and then closed it, making Carrie laugh. "Oh, ignore me," Hud's mom said. "I like to butt in where I'm not welcome. Lifelong habit."

"It's not that you're not welcome," Bailey assured her. "It's more that it's been so long since I could just enjoy myself that suddenly I'm not sure what to do with all the emotions."

"You could just let them come," Carrie suggested with brilliant simplicity. "Let things happen."

"I'm not all that good at that," Bailey admitted.

Carrie tilted her head to the side. "That's okay. You might've noticed my son isn't very good with it either."

"No," Bailey said on a short laugh. "He's not."

"It's because he has so much on his plate all the time and he always has. It's a heavy weight, all that responsibility, although he's pretty comfortable wearing it. He ever tell you about the well?"

Bailey shook her head.

Carrie sighed. "He and Jacob were born feral. Wild to the core. I couldn't corral them. Hell, I don't know if anyone could have. They needed a father, but that wasn't going to happen. They were ten years old when they were playing with a friend on an abandoned property near where we lived. Stevie fell into the well and couldn't get back up on his own. The water was deep enough that he had to tread water to keep his head free. The twins knew he wasn't going to be able to keep that up for more than a few minutes in the cold water so Jacob went for help while Hud found a rope and lowered it down the well. But he wasn't strong enough to pull Stevie up. He had to hold on and wait for Jacob to come back with help."

"Oh, my God," Bailey breathed. "How long did that take?"

"They were four miles away from the road and then Jacob had to hitchhike back into town. Took him two hours to get back to the well. Hudson waited two full hours holding on to the rope the whole time, promising Stevie he wouldn't let him go."

Bailey could see the boy Hudson had been, bent over the well to keep eye contact with his friend and uttering assurance for as long as it took.

"He still has the scars on his palms," Carrie said. "All his life, everyone has always talked about good ol' dependable Hud. Couldn't find a more steady, responsible man if you tried. Some of which he took to heart, of course."

"I don't see how he couldn't," Bailey murmured.

Carrie nodded. "Although to be honest, he's used it to his advantage. He lets responsibility always win out over a personal life. It's easier, you see. Safer."

"Safer than what?"

"Putting his heart out there, of course," Carrie said. "It's prevented him from letting go of any responsibility in favor of a life. Instead he holds on to his responsibilities with the same grip he held on to Stevie—at the expense of his own happiness." She paused and met Bailey's gaze. "You know what I'm saying?"

"Yes," Bailey said. "I believe I do." Hud had made it about her, that *she'd* set the one-day-at-a-time rule, that it was *she* who didn't want a real relationship.

He'd hidden behind that.

And she'd let him.

"Don't get me wrong," Carrie said. "You can always count on Hud. That's the point of this story. Always, to the end. He doesn't fail the people he cares about, ever."

"But he gives so much to everyone else in his life that there's nothing left for him to give to someone . . . special," Bailey said softly.

Carrie touched her own nose and nodded. "He shuts women out," she said. "It's a definite fault. And as I've mentioned, he also pushes away those he especially cares about. You might have noticed that as well."

Bailey laughed mirthlessly. "Yeah. Little bit."

Carrie smiled sadly. "Are you going to fall in love with him, Bailey?"

Bailey drew a quick breath. Was she? Was she really going to fall in love with Hudson Kincaid?

She suspected she already had . . .

"Whatever's happening between us," she finally answered, "it's just until the mural is done. We both knew that. I have my graphic design work in Denver—"

"Which could be done from anywhere."

"Maybe," Bailey allowed. "But Hudson's pretty busy here with the mountain and..."

"Looking for his brother," Carrie said.

"Yes."

"And taking care of me."

"He would never say that was a burden," Bailey said.

"True," Carrie agreed. "But we both know different."

Bailey shook her head. "No—"

"If it wasn't for me," Carrie said, "they'd still be together. We'd never have left Jackson Hole. But we did, and that's on me. Now Hudson's alone and sad." She broke off and bowed her head a moment, rubbing her temples.

"Carrie?" Bailey rose from her chair. "Hey, you okay?"

"Just a headache. Raising twins will do that to you. They're hell on wheels." Carrie sighed and lifted her head. "Hudson broke Jacob's arm, did I tell you that? He was riding his bike on the back roads with Jacob on his handlebars when he hit a bump and sent Jacob flying to the moon. He hit a tree on the way."

"That must have been a long time ago," Bailey said.

"Just last week. Jacob's in a cast. Hud grounded himself."

Bailey blinked at the sudden change in Carrie. Obviously something had switched and she was no longer in the present but once again locked in the past. Bailey reached for Carrie's hand. "Maybe it's time to rest."

"Nonsense," Carrie said. "A mom with two wild heathens has no time for rest. No one else blamed Hud, of course, but he can't be talked out of feeling responsible for Jacob. He never can. It's the well all over again, only this time his scars are on the inside not the outside—"

"Mom."

They both turned in surprise to the door.

Hud stood in the doorway. Bailey couldn't read his expression. He was really good at hiding his thoughts when he wanted to. In any case, he wasn't exactly broadcasting good humor at the moment.

"Excuse us a minute, Mom," he said, and wrapped his hand around Bailey's wrist.

Nope, definitely not happy, she thought as he pulled her from the room. "I'm sorry," she said quietly. "We weren't gossiping about you."

"No?" he asked mildly as he pulled her out of hearing range of his mom, nudged her up against a wall, and leaned in close to kiss all the good sense out of her.

Chapter 23

When Hud pulled back, Bailey let out a breath. "I always forget things when you do that," she said.

Hud had his forearms flat on the wall on either side of her face and let his fingers cup her head. She was wearing a sky-blue ski cap today. The cap was rolled up at the edges, allowing him to see her new, thin strawberry-blond wisps—a few inches long now—that were starting to frame her face.

The sight of them brought an ache to his chest so strong he couldn't breathe for a moment.

"I really didn't mean to be talking about you with your mom," she said. "But she was confused."

"She's getting lost," he said. "Lost to all of us and she's right here."

Her eyes held a well of empathy. "She was telling me stories about you," she said. "Good stories. Stories that made me..." She shook her head.

"Made you what?" he asked, tilting her face up to his.

She stared into his eyes and then dropped her gaze

to his mouth before nibbling on her own. Unable to stop himself, he bent his head and brushed his lips over hers. "Made you what?" he asked again.

"You know what," she whispered, clinging to him.

Yeah. He figured he did. His mom had a way of making him look like some damn hero when he wasn't. Not even close. "You can't believe everything she says," he reminded her. "She gets a lot of things mixed up."

Bailey shook her head. "No. She *never* gets mixed up on how much she loves her boys. You're her life, Hud. She's quite clear on that. And I'm glad you're not mad at me, but you are...*something* at me—" She broke off when her phone buzzed.

She turned away slightly to answer the call and he thought about what she said. He was *something* all right. Although what that something was couldn't be easily defined.

Unsettled?

Yeah, that was it. She was visiting his mom, which felt a whole lot...intimate. When had they gotten intimate?

After you stripped her naked and licked her up and down like a lollipop...

The memory of each and every time he'd had her in his arms burned bright in his brain, and he spent way too much time bringing out the memories to replay them in his head. Hud couldn't erase thoughts of the way she opened up to him and gave him everything she had. And she did so with a heart-stopping generosity and vulnerability that slayed him even now.

Still, by her own decree, those times had been just that. No strings attached. He was damn lucky enough that she wasn't finished with him yet, and he was just selfish enough to take what he could get from her.

Bailey disconnected her call and slid her phone away. There was an odd stillness to her and her shoulders seemed to carry far too much weight. Reaching out, he turned her to him.

She was pale, too pale, and her eyes shimmered brilliantly from unshed tears. His heart dropped to his toes. "What is it?"

She shook her head and tried to turn away again but he held her firm. "Hey," he said. "Talk to me."

Taking a shuddery inhale, she pressed her fingers to her mouth. "I'm still clear," she whispered. "I had all those tests last Friday and the results are still clear. It was a milestone. Three straight months. On top of the first three months this makes six. I'm done with chemo, radiation, all of it. Really done."

At the words, a knot loosened in his chest, one he hadn't even realized he'd had. "That's the best news I've had in a long time," he said, and reached for her.

She sagged into him and cuddled in tight, wrapping her arms around his waist and pressing her face into his chest with a shudder. In return he closed his eyes and just held her, absorbing the overwhelming relief coursing through him. This amazing, warm, irresistible, irreplaceable woman was okay. She was going to stay okay.

That's when he realized she was trembling. He pulled back slightly to look into her face.

She shook her head. "Don't ask me—"

"What aren't you telling me?"

"Nothing, I just—" She shook her head again. "The call came from my mom. The doctor's office called and since I wasn't there, she gave the message to my mom."

"They're not supposed to do that," he said.

"I'd given permission for my mom to get any information regarding my care and treatment and condition," she said. "This is good news, it's *great* news, but my mom said…"

"What?" Hud asked a little tightly, already not liking what was coming next. If that woman had taken away the joy of this moment, he was going to have to strangle her.

"She just wanted to remind me that I'm still in the danger zone."

Yeah, he was going to have to strangle her.

"And it kinda just sucked a little bit of the joy out of it." She sniffed and swiped at a tear like she was mad to find herself crying. "Three months ago I got the first clear I've ever had and to get it again now…It's a great sign," she said.

"It's a hell of a sign. And you're going to keep getting clear results. You have to." He smiled. "There's no other option."

At that, she gave him a tremulous smile in return. "Thank you."

"For what? You're the one who's amazing," he said.

"For believing in me."

Like a punch to the gut. He didn't break eye contact as he pulled her back in. "Always," he whispered.

"You're so lucky," she said, cheek to his chest. "Don't get me wrong. I love my mom. I do," she said, "but I don't have the kind of bond with her that you have with your family—" She stopped abruptly when her voice broke.

Ah, hell. "Bailey," he breathed, dropping his forehead to hers, tightening his grip on her, and stroking her back when she let out a shuddery sigh.

"It's okay," she whispered. "I'm okay."

"I know," he said, and kept hold of her.

"It's just that the weekends are becoming so much

more real to me than the rest of the week." She pressed her face into his throat. "And so much more important."

He tried not to react to that. Part of what had allowed him to let her in as much as he had was the hard reality that being here in Cedar Ridge wasn't her life and never would be. Harsh as it sounded, it'd made her safe.

But if she turned that upside down, if she stayed, he wasn't sure what could possibly happen. He didn't have the room in his life—or his heart—for one more string.

He had too many strings now.

"I'm just so grateful for this second chance," she said. "So damn grateful. I want to make good use out of it, but it's hard because I don't know who I am or who I'm supposed to be." She lifted her head and stared at him. "I made that list thinking it'd give me direction, but instead all it has done is confuse me. I don't want to be just the list, you know?"

"You're not," he said firmly. "You're a beautiful, smart, wonderful, warm woman who brings heart and soul into the lives of everyone you meet. You're not the list at all. You're far more."

She pulled it out of her pocket, that damn little notebook. "I made a promise to this thing."

"That's fine," Hud said. "But that doesn't mean it gets to define your life. *You* get to do that, Bailey. Only you."

She stared at him and nodded. "Yes, you're right."

He cocked his head as if he couldn't hear her. "What was that?"

"You're right." She gave him a little push and he had to laugh.

"I heard you the first time," he admitted. "I just like the way that sentence sounds on your tongue."

She rolled her eyes. And then blinked. "Oh! I nearly forgot the reason I'm here tonight." She pulled his phone from another pocket. "Gray's the one who told me I could find you here."

Hudson grimaced. "You saw Gray?"

"Yes, I went to the resort first," she said. "To bring you the phone."

As she said it, his phone buzzed an incoming call. He took it from her and looked at the screen. Gray. Might as well get it over with, he thought, and answered.

"You should probably stay off Facebook," Gray suggested, and disconnected.

The phone immediately buzzed again. He answered with a curt, "*What?*"

"Check out Facebook," Kenna said gleefully.

"Delete it," Hud said. "Whatever you dumbasses have done, delete it or I'll find you and it won't be pretty." He disconnected and stared at Bailey.

"Um." She blinked. "Problem?"

"You told Gray I lost my phone?"

"No, I told him I got it by accident," she said, and then paused. "What's going on? Who was that?"

He was scrolling through Facebook. "Gray," he said, distracted. "And then Kenna."

"You threatened your sister?"

Hudson looked at her. She was shocked and horrified. "You don't have a sister," he said.

"No. No siblings period, you know that."

"Which means you wouldn't understand the occasional need to strangle someone who shares your own blood. *Shit*," he muttered. "Here it is."

"What?"

"What Gray and Kenna are so gleeful about." He turned his phone screen so she could see. He had the Cedar Ridge Resort's Facebook page up. There was a post there from Hud.

"I didn't know you posted on Facebook," she said.

"I don't," he said. "Ever. Gray went on as me."

She started to read it.

"Out loud," he said.

"Okay." She turned the phone to a better angle. " 'Did you see *Dancing with the Stars* last night?' " she read. " 'The dancers were so beautiful it brought a tear to my eye…' " She stopped and stared up at him, and then laughed.

"You think this is funny?" he asked. "You gave Gray access to my phone and he's a dick."

"And you're upset that people will think you love *Dancing with the Stars*?"

"I've never watched a single second of that show," he said stiffly. He'd cop to *Say Yes to the Dress,* but not this. No way. "And that's not my point," he said. "He's just screwing with me. And *that's* the point."

She bit her lower lip.

He narrowed his eyes and considered retribution. Because there *would* be retribution. "The messee is about to become the messor," he said.

"Was that in English?"

"You're going back to Denver tonight?" he asked instead of answering her question.

"Yes."

"Maybe you have time to pick something up for me."

"Sure," she said. "What?"

"Just a little something for Gray." He pulled out a credit card and gave it to her. "Something special. I'm thinking sheer lace. A woman's extra-large."

She blinked.

He smiled.

And then so did she. "You want to get back at him for the Choking Hazard briefs."

"No, that was Aidan," he said. "Gray deserves worse. Much worse."

"Is it just me, or do you Kincaids spend most of your waking days trying to mess each other up?" she asked.

"Yeah," he said. "And?"

She laughed and slipped his card into her purse. "Nothing. Will do."

He walked her outside, where they both stared up at the dark night sky, from which heavy lines of white were falling to the ground in eerie silence.

Snow. Dumping snow. So fast it had already accumulated several inches.

"That wasn't supposed to hit until midnight," she said at his side, her voice sounding a little small.

"There's something else that wasn't in the forecast," he said.

"What?"

He reached for her gloveless hand and tugged her into him, wrapping her shivering figure in close. "The fact that you're not going home tonight."

Chapter 24

Hud watched as Bailey gave him a long considering look.

"You're supposed to ask a woman to stay with you, not tell," she said.

"And normally I would ask," he said. Maybe. "But you're not taking your car over the summit in this." He tugged her in a little closer because she seemed more than a little pale—except for her nose, which was bright red. Leaning in, he kissed her cold lips until she relaxed into him.

"Not fair," she whispered, slipping her frozen arms under his clothing to touch her even-more-frozen fingers on the bare skin at the small of his back.

He grimaced. "Holy shit, woman."

"My parts are cold." She paused. "Some more than others."

He manfully sucked it up and let her fingers stroke up and down his back. "Can't have you suffering from cold parts," he said. "I've got a hot shower and an even hotter bed only ten minutes from here."

"Hotter bed?"

"It's got a heater in it."

She narrowed her eyes. "It does not."

"Hand to heaven," he said.

She narrowed her eyes. "Does this 'heater' run on electricity?"

"Nope." He grinned. "Animal magnetism." He rubbed his hands up and down her arms and met her gaze, his amusement gone. "I'm serious about the roads, Bay. I want you to stay. If you'd rather, I'll call and see if there's any employment housing open tonight. Or you can have my place and I'll bunk with Aidan. No pressure."

She touched his face lightly. "I wouldn't mind a little...pressure."

He smiled and turned his face to press a kiss to her palm. "Come home with me. I've got all the pressure you'll need."

They'd just gotten into Hud's truck when Hud took a call on his Bluetooth. Bailey could hear Gray's voice, tinny, through the phone.

"Alarm just went off at the cafeteria," he said. "I'm two hours out, in Denver with Penny at some fancy dinner for her work."

"On it," Hudson said. He hung up and sent Bailey an apologetic look. "I've got to go check this out. I'll drop you off at my place—"

"Just go straight there," she said. "It'll be faster."

When he started to shake his head, she put her hand on his arm. "You don't have time to deal with or worry about me, so just get there. I'll stay out of the way."

In the end, he dropped her off in the resort offices,

refusing to leave her in the dark in his truck because she would be alone in the parking lot.

Lily was in the office as well, having been similarly dropped off by Aidan. They sat at Hud's desk in front of the radio and listened unabashedly.

Two local high school kids had broken into the resort's cafeteria and set off the alarm. Surveillance cameras showed them carrying fistfuls of candy bars out of there with their snowboards strapped on their backs.

"High as kites," Lily guessed, shaking her head. "Going to be a long night." She helped herself in the supply closet, coming out with a bottle of Jack.

Bailey went brows up.

"I've had a long day," Lily explained. "And now our significant others are on the mountain in the dark looking for two walking DUIs." She stuck her head into another closet and came up with Dixie cups.

"What happened today?" Bailey asked as Lily poured them each a drink. "I mean, if it's not too personal."

"Oh, it's personal." Lily tapped her cup to Bailey's. "It's also a long story. Drink first."

They each drank and Bailey promptly choked.

Lily too. "Holy shit," she wheezed.

Bailey nearly coughed up a lung and pounded her chest.

When they could breathe, Lily spoke. "So I had a... scare," she said.

Bailey involuntarily gasped and clasped a hand to her heart because a scare to her meant a health scare, a bad one.

"Oh no," Lily rushed on when she saw Bailey's reaction. "Oh, my God, I'm so insensitive! No, nothing like that!" She grimaced and then rolled her eyes. "It's just that I thought maybe I was pregnant. Accidentally."

"Oh," Bailey breathed. With all the treatments she'd had over the past ten years, she wasn't at all sure she'd be able to have babies, though she wanted them. Someday. She didn't feel her biological clock ticking or anything, but when she pictured her future—which was something she actually did now, and often—she liked to think there was a man in it, one who'd promised to love her forever. And a baby. Or three. "I see."

"No," Lily said. "I don't think you do." She paused. "Aidan and I aren't married. We're not quite there yet. I mean I know he's the one for me and I know I'm the one for him, but we aren't rushing anything, you know? There's no need to rush. I was never the woman who dreamed about babies, or a husband. I just…" She shook her head. "I always buried myself in work and never went there. Now I'm not buried in work and I'm…enjoying us. A lot. I like being a twosome. A tight little unit, just us." She paused and then laughed. "Well, us and the rest of the Kincaids." Her smile faded. "But then I didn't get my period and I got scared." She let out a breath. "More like terrified."

"Did you tell Aidan?" Bailey asked.

"I did." Lily shook her head. "I was so upset. Cried all over him and he was…" She shook her head.

"Mad?" Bailey whispered, unable to picture Aidan— who she'd seen looking at Lily like she was his entire universe—mad at Lily for anything.

Lily shook her head. "Happy," she whispered back. Her eyes glistened. "So happy." She smiled. "God, he's amazing. He calmed me down. And somehow it just happened. I got on board. By the time I bought the stick to pee on this morning, I was convinced I was preggers and already in love with our baby." Her smile faded. "But I got my period on the way home from the store."

"Oh, Lily," Bailey breathed, reaching out to squeeze her hand. "I'm sorry."

Lily lifted a shoulder. "It's silly. I mean how can you miss something you never really had in the first place?"

"It's not silly," Bailey insisted. "When the time is right, you'll make a great mom."

Lily sniffed. "Thanks. Now tell me about your day."

"I got my second all clear from my doctor today," Bailey said softly, not used to being able to share good news. For so long the news was always bad. People would ask her how things were going and she never knew what to say because there was nothing worse than saying the truth and having to bum people out. "It's a milestone. A six-month milestone."

Lily squeaked and grabbed her, giving her a big bear hug. "That's wonderful! *Now* we have something to toast to. Another single? Or should we make it a double this time?"

"Um…"

"Double it is." Lily carefully filled their cups to the brim. "To today's all clear and many more." Once again they tapped their paper cups together and drank.

"Holy crap," Bailey gasped, and proceeded to cough up her second lung.

Lily snorted hers out her nose and they both starting laughing.

"I was trying to be cool," Lily said, swiping a hand over her face. "But seriously, how does anyone drink this stuff?"

"No idea," Bailey said in a hoarse whisper, having

burned her vocal cords down to nubs. "Maybe we need to drink it faster."

"You think? Let's try that." Lily poured them each another shot and lifted her cup. "What are we drinking to now?"

"To you peeing on a stick and getting the positive sign real soon," Bailey said.

Lily smiled and they both tossed back and...once again choked.

"Jesus," Lily managed, and pushed the Jack away. "I don't think there's a good way to do that."

Bailey swiped her eyes and nose. Since she still couldn't talk, she shook her head. And anyway, she didn't need any more. The alcohol had burned a warm path to her belly and she was feeling...damn good. She smiled. "I like the aftereffect though."

Lily grinned back. "You're all blurry. Like, there's kinda two of you, and also kinda none of you at the same time." She closed one eye and then the other. "Nope, there's *three* of you!"

Bailey snorted. "Does Aidan drink this stuff?"

"Yeah, once in a while he and the others drink together after a long day on the job."

"Do they have a lot of long days?" Bailey asked, already knowing the answer. The Kincaids played hard and worked even harder.

"They're good guys," Lily said. "Which you already know. Take Hud, for instance."

Bailey tried not to look fascinated and nearly fell off the desk.

Lily grinned. "Or maybe you've already *taken* Hud..." She tried to waggle a brow and went cross-eyed instead.

Bailey laughed. "Do you have a point?"

"I do," Lily said. "But the alcohol is making it hard to keep on point. Where was I . . . ? Oh yes! You and Hud. He's a rock, you know. When he loves you, he's in one hundred percent. His brothers and sister. His mom. Me and Penny. He's in all the way and never wavers. And the same with this mountain, this resort, and every other thing in his entire life. He's loyal and smart, and"—Lily pointed at Bailey and nearly poked out her eye—"he's also hotter than sin on a stick."

Bailey blinked. "What does sin on a stick look like?"

Lily paused, her forehead wrinkled in deep thought. "Hud?"

Bailey laughed. "Not Aidan?"

"Yes but see, Aidan is *my* sin on a stick."

The radio crackled and then Hud's voice came on, calm and sure. "Got one of them. Need assistance. Over."

Both Bailey and Lily gasped and leaned into the radio.

"Two minutes out," came Aidan's reply, also calm and sure. "Do we need to call the police? Over."

"I am the police," Hud responded. "This one's taking himself on a joyride in the terrain park. He's about three-quarters of the way down the run. I've got eyes on him from the bottom and I'm watching him hotdog it while holding lit sparklers in each hand, having a party of one. No visual on the other. Over."

"I'll go to the top," Aidan said. "Maybe he's still up there. Over."

Two minutes later, Hud was back on the radio. "Got idiot number one," he said, sounding slightly strained. "He says idiot number two crashed and needs assistance. Heads up, idiot number one's impaired and was combative. Over."

"Was?" came Aidan's voice.

"He came around to my way of thinking. Over."

Lily and Bailey stared at each other. Lily poured them each another shot.

"What's this one for?" Bailey asked in a stage whisper, although who she thought was listening, she had no idea.

"If you're going to love one of the Kincaids, you should know, sometimes alcohol is necessary."

Bailey blinked. "Who said I was going to love one of the Kincaids?"

"It's all over your face." Lily knocked her cup to Bailey's. "It's okay, honey. They're worth it. They're worth every second of this crazy, topsy-turvy, wonderful ride."

Bailey drank to that. Was she going to love him?

You already do, a very small voice whispered, way, way, way back in the depths of her brain. No, make that her heart. Her brain most definitely hadn't caught up yet.

And how could it? Her heart and brain had never, not once, *both* been in love. She'd never really been a whole person.

Hud was most definitely a whole person. He had a very full life of his own making. But her life wasn't full at all and never had been. She was starting to get that *that* was what her list had really been about. "You're easy to talk to," she told Lily.

"It's the alcohol."

"No, I mean it," Bailey said. "This is nice for me. I don't have a lot of close friends." She never had, because she'd never been a part of any sort of normal life, nothing even close. And she'd seen what her mom and Aaron had gone through, preparing themselves for her death. She'd never been able to bring herself to get close to people just to cause them pain.

Lily reached out and squeezed her hand, seeming to understand without having to be told. "I'm always here. And since I'm relatively new to being back in Cedar Ridge, I'd be thrilled to consider you a good friend."

Bailey might have embarrassed herself by getting choked up, but the radio squawked.

"Need backup," came Aidan's voice on the radio. "Handcuff your idiot to a rail and come to me one hundred yards to the west. Over."

"Ten-four," was all Hudson said.

Ten minutes later, Hudson's voice came over the radio again. "In sight. Over."

"Confirm visual," Aidan said.

"I see a guy hanging off the rails by his homeboy boarder pants," Hud said. "Which are hooked on his ankle, his credentials dangling in the breeze. He's yelling something about losing his sparklers and suing us. Over."

Lily and Bailey gaped at each other.

"That's him." Aidan's cool, calm voice had a sliver of humor in it. "I just thought you'd want to see this. Kinda makes the past hour worth it."

"Kinda does," Hud agreed.

And then five minutes later came Hud's voice: "Who the hell goes snowboarding commando?"

"This guy apparently," Aidan said. "And you're not the one standing beneath him. Every time he moves I get to meet Jim and the twins all over again."

Inside the warm office both Lily and Bailey snorted and choked on their shocked laughter.

Thirty minutes later their two men walked into the offices.

"The menfolk returning home from the hunt to collect

their women," Lily whispered to Bailey and giggled. She covered her mouth with her hand.

Bailey grinned too. She was absolutely drunk. But then she got a good look at Hudson's beautiful face and the black eye, and her grin faded.

Chapter 25

Hud walked into the offices where he'd left Bailey an hour before. Aidan was right on his tail, trying to get an ice pack on Hud's eye. Which wasn't going to happen.

"Hud, man, you need to ice it."

"It's fine." Okay so it throbbed like a bitch and so did his knuckles from where he'd punched the idiot after getting sucker-punched himself, but hell if he'd admit that.

"It's going to swell," Aidan said.

"Back off." All he wanted to do was to collect Bailey and get the hell out of work mode for half an hour. Hell, he'd take ten minutes. But since Mother Nature had granted him a stay of execution with a glorious storm, he was thinking he might actually have all night.

And he wanted every single minute of it.

Aidan was hovering again, still trying to get the ice pack on Hud's face. Hud pushed him away. "If you don't get the fuck away from me with that thing right now, I'm going to shove it so far up your ass you'll be shitting blue gel for the rest of your natural life."

"If you won't let me look at it," Aidan said tightly, all pissy as he always got when he didn't get his way, "we'll need to have medical look at it."

"Man, we *are* medical."

"But—"

"Jesus. I'm an EMT and I say I'm fine," Hud snapped.

"I'm an EMT, too, jackass, and I overrule you."

"How the hell do you figure that?" Hud demanded.

Aidan looked smug. "I'm older than you."

"Oh, shut up." Hud turned to face the room and found Lily and Bailey sitting on his desk with their legs folded beneath them Indian-style. The radio sat between them, as did a bottle of Jack—which if he wasn't mistaken was nearly empty—and two Dixie cups.

He went brows up. "Ladies."

Bailey looked at his face and gasped. She went to hop down off the desk but got tangled in her own legs and would've fallen on her face if he hadn't caught her.

When she got her sea legs, she blinked up at him. "You're hurt."

"And you're tipsy." Hud turned to look at Lily, who was beaming dreamily at Aidan. "You were supposed to watch her, not get her drunk."

"Hey," Lily said, slurring her words a little bit. "She's a grown-up. She didn't need a babysitter."

"Nope," Bailey said, popping the *P* sound. She reached up and touched Hud's eye.

He sucked up a wince and caught her hand in his because she was more likely to poke out his eyeball than gently touch his bruise.

Aidan scooped Lily up off the desk and gave her what looked like a bone-crunching hug.

"You okay?" she asked him.

"I'm perfect," he said, sending a smug smile in Hud's direction. "No one got a shot in on me tonight." He kissed her and tossed the ice pack to Bailey. "Good luck with that," he said. "He's a terrible patient." And then he carried Lily right out of the office. Given the giggles coming from the latter, he wouldn't be bothered by Hudson's countenance again until at least tomorrow.

"Does it hurt?" Bailey asked him softly.

"No." *Liar, liar...*

Reaching back, she locked the door and turned to him. He stepped into her at the same moment and they reached for each other. The kiss started out gentle but didn't stay that way. Finally she stumbled back a step and gave him another of those brain-melting looks that made him want to beat his chest and drag her off to his cave like the Neanderthal he was.

Still smiling at him like maybe the sun and the moon rose and set in his eyes, she slowly lifted his hand... and very gently guided the ice pack in to his goddamn throbbing eye.

He opened his mouth, but she set a finger over his lips.

He stared at her as the cold absorbed into his skin, soothing the ache as surely as having her pressed up against him soothed the rest of the world away, back behind a brick wall where nothing could get at them.

"Better?" she asked, her hand over his on the ice pack.

"Yes, but that's because you're pressed up against me," he said. "It's not the ice pack."

She shook her head. She was onto him. Then her smile faded. "What happened?"

He shrugged. "He got in one good punch before I restrained him. It happens."

But not to him. It'd been a damn long time since anyone had gotten the jump on him, and he had no idea why it had happened tonight.

Don't you? a voice asked inside his head.

Yeah, okay. So he knew exactly what had happened. Bailey. He'd gone into that call thinking about her, soft and warm in his bed for the whole night. And suitably distracted, he'd been taken by surprise.

That shit had to stop.

But now here he was with a soft, warm, sweetly sexy woman in the circle of his arms, and not just any woman but the one he hadn't been able to stop thinking of since he'd first seen her on top of the mountain.

An instant connection, his first in too damn long.

Somehow she got him. She got him on a level that no one really had, not since...Jacob.

And even knowing that this was going to come back and bite him on the ass at some point didn't stop him. He drew her close and breathed her in and said her name on a shaky exhale.

"Yes," she murmured back, her fingers sinking into his hair, answering the question he hadn't voiced out loud.

As Hudson's arms tightened around Bailey, she became aware of the closeness of their bodies. No, that was a lie. She was *always* extremely aware of Hud's body.

He walked her backward and she came up against the credenza. He dipped his head and even as her brain screamed, *You need to think this over*, she was lifting her face and parting her lips to accept his.

Once his mouth fastened on to hers, she was lost. It had seemed so complicated, but when he was with her like this, it was suddenly the opposite. It was the simplest thing she'd ever done to pull him in and give him everything she had. She arched her back to get even closer. He was hard.

Everywhere.

Her heart had gone haywire and she was already breathing in little gasps as they broke apart to stare at each other and then dove back in. Desire was a living thing within her, coiling out from her core and bringing a warm tingling wave of pleasure with it.

Hud's hands slid up from her hips to cup her breasts. Making a sound of low male appreciation, he slid those hands down again and then back up, beneath her shirt this time. His thumbs glided softly over her pebbled nipples standing at full, happy attention.

She was still fully clothed and she was seconds away from an orgasm...And then he stopped. She moaned in protest but he was firm. "Let's go," he said.

"Where?"

"Much as I've enjoyed the memories we've made here, I'm not doing it in my office again. I still have rug burns—" He broke off at her laugh and narrowed his eyes. "You think that's funny?"

She made an effort to stop smiling but couldn't pull it off. "You weren't the only one who got rug burns," she reminded him.

"Yes, but yours are on your back and hidden," he said. "Mine are on my knees and we wear shorts when we train in the gym."

She clamped a hand over her mouth. "Oh, my God."

"Uh-huh—which is exactly what you were moaning when I got those rug burns. That and a bunch of 'oh please' and 'yes, there, oh, Hud, *there*!'"

She couldn't really object to the truth...

Hud poured Bailey into his truck and gave her a quick once-over. She was definitely tipsier than he'd thought. "You okay?"

She gave him a long look. Right. That question was not allowed. "Okay," he said, "how about—are you going home with me?" He held her gaze, watching her reaction closely. Any hesitation, even a flicker, and he'd tuck her into his bed and walk away, no qualms.

But she didn't hesitate. She blinked slowly and smiled at him, a little goofy. "Yes, please."

He grinned. "How many shots did you have?"

"Um...one."

Okay, one was good. One wasn't drunk—

"Plus three," she said, and then looked confused. "Or four."

Ah, hell. That was most definitely drunk. Which put her in the off-limits zone.

She smiled at him. "You're pretty. Anyone ever tell you that?"

He had to laugh. "You're completely shit-faced."

"Am not." She flashed another silly grin. "I know you probably think 'pretty' is an insult to your manhood, but I've seen your manhood and it doesn't have any reason to be insulted."

He scrubbed a hand down his face. She was a happy, silly, sexy adorable drunk. And one hundred percent irresistible. And damn, his phone was buzzing in his pocket.

He pulled it out and looked at the screen. Aidan. He hit ANSWER. "Yeah?"

"Lily's bombed."

"I know."

"I'm getting lucky tonight," Aidan said.

"And you're calling me why?"

"Because *you're* not," Aidan said. "Getting lucky, that is. If Lily's this far gone, so's Bailey. You can't tap that tonight, man."

"You think I need you to tell me that?"

"Just making sure you're thinking with your big head and not your small one." Aidan laughed a little and started to say something else but Hud disconnected him. He looked at Bailey.

She blew him a kiss.

Damn. Only a real asshole would take advantage of her tonight. The question was, was he that asshole? He took her hand in his.

She brought it up to her mouth and kissed the scars on his palm. "You're a good man," she said softly.

Was he? At the moment, he didn't feel like it. He parked at his place and when they walked inside, he saw neither hide nor hair of any annoying Kincaids.

A miracle.

He took Bailey into his bedroom and she sighed dreamily at the sight of his bed. "Looks nice," she said, and walked toward it.

"Take off your shoes," he said.

"Mmm, I like it when you get all commanding and bossy," she said with a wicked grin.

Jesus, she was killing him.

She laughed a little at his expression and kicked her

first shoe off. It flew across the room and nearly gave him a second black eye.

"Ohmigod," she gasped when he caught it in midair an inch from his face. "You've got good reflexes."

That he did. Which was how he managed to control his expression when she bent to more carefully remove her other boot and fell over.

"Whoops." She laughed. "I swear I'm not a walking DUI. I'm just a lightweight cuz I never drink alcohol."

He scooped her up off the floor and set her on his bed. He yanked the comforter down and pointed for her to scoot in.

With a laugh, she tugged him down over the top of her and then wrapped herself around him like a monkey. "You smell good," she murmured, face plastered to his throat. "You always smell so good. What is this stuff you wear?"

Her entire body was glued to his. He could feel her soft breasts pressing into his chest, her thighs cushioning his, and between those thighs the heat of her drawing him in like a bee to honey—

"Hud, are you listening?"

"Of course I'm listening." He totally wasn't listening. He was thinking about how she'd look if he stripped her naked. She'd be all flushed and gorgeous, and he wanted to taste every inch of her and then nibble some of those inches. Just thinking about the sounds she'd make as she got closer to orgasming made him painfully hard.

It required every ounce of control he had to break free of her and get off the bed, but he did it. He tossed his blanket over her.

"But I have all my clothes on," she said, blinking

confoundedly up at him, then rolling over to try and get off the bed.

"No," he said, tucking her in. "Stay."

"I can't sleep with my clothes on, silly." Wriggling free of the blanket, she unbuttoned and tugged off her sweater, which somehow got caught on her knit cap.

This left her in just a little lacy-nothing bra and jeans, arms up over her head, fighting the sweater that was covering her face. Every panicked move she made had her breasts jiggling, and he couldn't tear his eyes off of them.

"I'm going to suffocate!" she gasped.

Shaking his head, he put a knee on the bed and bent over her to free her. She was warm and soft, and her cap came off. Her very short hair was strawberry blond and baby fine. Soft. The scent of the silky strands had him inhaling her like she was crack. He'd noticed every time his fingers brushed the nape of her neck, she shivered. So he did it on purpose now, stroking his fingers over her soft skin, and a low moan escaped her, which didn't help his situation any. He finally freed her from the sweater.

"My hero," she said with huge relief. She went to work on her jeans. Not easy since they were snug. When she shimmied them down past her hips, her panties started to go with, giving him a heart-stopping view of the promised land.

He abruptly turned away.

"Hud?"

Killing him. She was killing him. It wasn't the first time she'd shortened his name the way everyone in his world always did, but she didn't do it often. On her tongue it sounded...perfect. Which was why, against his better judgment, he turned back.

She was sitting in the middle of his bed in just her undies, his comforter clutched between her breasts. "Is that okay?" she whispered. "That I call you Hud?"

"Yes." His voice came out unintentionally husky and a little thick, and she dropped the comforter. Her bra wasn't doing much in the way of hiding her from him. The skimpily cut cups had most of her spilling out. She was either cold or turned on, and that question was answered when she spoke.

"I want you," she whispered.

Oh, Christ. He didn't have enough control for this. Not even close. He backed to the door and ran right into it. He turned to face it, his fingers on the handle.

"Hud?"

"We can't," he said to the door.

"Because you're a good guy. Lily said that I was falling for you because you're hotter than sin on a stick, but I don't think that's it. I think I'm falling for you because you're everything I want in a man: strong from the inside out, steady, calm, smart...sweet."

While he grappled with that—*sweet?*—she went on. "I know I said I didn't want The One," she said. "That I had a lot to do before I found The One. Like the stuff on my list." She sighed. "I know I also said that you weren't The One, but I think that was me just trying to protect myself."

Oh, Christ. "We shouldn't talk," he said desperately. "Until no one in this room is sloshed, we should have some quiet time."

"And you," she went on. "I was trying to protect you too. Against my feelings."

"Bay." He *thunked* his forehead to the door.

"Because the truth is I know you don't have time for

anyone, even The One. You've got a full plate. And I don't want to be someone's...something, a something that they don't have room for on their plate. That would make me...broccoli." She shuddered. "And no one wants to be broccoli, you know?"

Drunk Bailey had her head on straighter than Stark-sober Hud. He turned to face her and found her struggling out of her bra, which she flung across the room. It landed on his lamp. "I'm going to get you some water," he said. "Do you need anything else?"

She blinked and smiled and the blanket slipped out of her fingers to pool at her waist, revealing all that creamy, soft skin that he knew would be warm and welcoming. She patted the bed beside her, those amazing breasts shimmying. "Just you," she whispered.

Jesus.

She reached down and hooked her fingers into the sides of her panties.

"Wait." Good God. "Bailey, this isn't going to happen."

"I know," she said, and he started to breathe easier. But then she spoke again and lassoed his heart. "I know what you're going to do next," she whispered.

Shoot himself?

"You're gonna push me away. You're going to do that because you care about me." She swallowed hard. "I don't know when, but I know you will. Because that's what you do when you care too much. And I know you care about me because I can feel it in every look you give me, in every touch. So I guess what I'm saying is that I'm just trying to make the most of it before you do."

Jesus. She slayed him. "You're so sure of that, huh?" he said softly, not sure if he was teasing or stalling.

"Yep. Your family helped me get there."

"What?"

She blinked, looked a little worried, and said . . . nothing.

"Bailey." She tightened her lips. Oh, great, so *now* she was going with the fifth. "You've been talking to my family about me?" he asked with what he thought was damn good restraint.

"Not in the way you think."

"How many ways are there to talk about someone?"

"Okay, first of all, you're taking this wrong," she said. "And second of all, you're misdirecting, purposely picking something out of that conversation that you can get all self-righteous about so you can ignore the real issue."

You know what? Maybe he didn't like drunk Bailey so much after all. "You're the one who said you didn't want a relationship," he said carefully. "You're the one who put it out there."

"Didn't mean I didn't want to know you."

"People who are not in a relationship don't need to know each other's deep, dark secrets," he said.

She stared at him. "You're twisting this whole relationship thing around and out of proportion," she said with the very purposeful speech of the heavily inebriated. "And I think you're doing it on purpose."

"Why would I do that?"

"So you can do what everyone said you would, push me away. For real."

Direct hit. "You think you're in my head," he said. "But you're not."

That apparently stopped her cold. She opened her mouth and then shut it. And then, dammit, a flash of pain crossed her face. "Bailey—"

"I think I'll go home now," she said, and started to slide out of the bed.

"No," he said sharply and she stilled. "You stay," he said. "*I'll* go." He hesitated but she didn't try to stop him.

Congratulations, idiot, he told himself bitterly. *You got what you wanted. You pushed her away.*

Chapter 26

Bailey had never experienced a hangover, so it took her by surprise. Actually, it took her head by storm— pounding, drumming, beating behind her eyes, reverberating off her temples, throbbing mercilessly at the base of her skull. If she got lucky, she thought with a groan, if she got very, very lucky, her head would just blow right off her shoulders.

She didn't get lucky.

Instead she opened her eyes and realized it wasn't even dawn yet. She lay on soft sheets in a bed that wasn't hers.

Alone.

She sat up, having to hold her head to do it. Someone, God bless them, had put a glass of water and a bottle of ibuprofen on the nightstand. She made liberal use of both and took stock.

Hud's bedroom. The evidence of last night's activities was strewn about the room. The most damning was her bra, hanging haphazardly off a lamp.

And then there was the fact that she was in Hud's bed. She lifted the covers and stared down at herself. She was in a very large black T-shirt and her panties. One sock.

But the most troublesome was Hud's absence. She'd never scared a man off before. Another first...

She slid out of bed and pulled her bra off the lamp. A flash of memory came at that, the memory of trying to do a sexy striptease for Hud and nearly knocking his face into next week with her boot.

And then another. She remembered telling him things. *I think I'm falling for you because you're everything I want in a man; strong from the inside out, steady, calm, smart...sweet.*

She'd told him he could be The One.

Oh God. Why had she done that? The answer was painful. She'd told him because it was the truth. "Clearly he'd like me to go away," she said aloud, her voice dry and rough.

Which was just what she suddenly needed to do because now he knew. He knew exactly how she felt and that was her own fault. Especially since in return, she had no idea how *he* felt. The heat of embarrassment flamed her cheeks. Yep, she needed to be gone and she suspected he wanted that as well. She wrangled on her knit cap, slipped into her jeans, and stuffed her feet into her boots. Then she snagged one of Hud's shirts—which smelled like heaven—and made her way out of the bedroom to hopefully find a ride to where she'd left her car and get the hell off the mountain, where she could lick her wounds in private for the week.

Luckily, Hud wasn't anywhere to be seen so she ventured out farther and found herself standing on the main floor in a huge open room. One wall was all windows, leading out to the still-dark morning where a small sliver of the black sky was lightening.

In front of the window stood a tall, broad shadow sipping at a steaming mug.

Her heart stopped.

"Just me," Aidan said mildly.

"Oh," she said on a breath of relief, and then hoped her sheer relief wasn't too obvious. "I was just hoping to get a ride to my car."

He turned and looked at her for a long moment. "I could do that. You know Hud's downstairs, right?"

Bailey blinked. "I thought this was the bottom floor."

"There's a basement. We have it set up as a gym. He's been at it for a couple of hours now. You might want to get down there and put him out of his misery."

"How do you know it was me who made him miserable?"

Aidan laughed low in his throat, his smile real and genuine, and suddenly Bailey knew exactly what Lily saw in him. "I didn't suggest *you* made him miserable," he said. "I'm suggesting that your presence might chase away his misery."

She managed a small smile. Because she remembered throwing herself at Hud last night and he'd . . .

Resisted.

Easily.

Aidan looked down at his mug and then back into Bailey's eyes. "He ever tell you why he doesn't easily get attached to people?"

"Because his plate is full," she said. "He doesn't have room. Especially since he's determined to find Jacob."

Aidan's smile was humorless. "Yeah, he talks a good game, doesn't he? He's full of shit, Bailey."

"So he lied to me?"

"He's lying to himself. He blames himself for our dad leaving his mom—which, don't even get me started. He blames himself for his mom not being well—more ridiculousness. He blames himself for Jacob leaving—a whole new level of ridiculousness."

Bailey's heart squeezed. "That's a lot for him to put on himself."

"No shit. But our boy likes to blame himself." He took another drink from his mug. "The stairs at the end will take you down to the gym."

"Oh. Well, actually, I think I'm just going to…" She gestured to the front door.

Aidan just looked at her for a beat. "My mistake then," he said coolly. "Do you still want a ride?"

She looked at the door and paused. The silence in the room was deafening. "Dammit," she whispered.

I'm falling for you because you're everything I want in a man…

She closed her eyes. What if she did go see him? What would that accomplish? It's not like she could take the words back. Nope, they were out there now taking root, making a life of their own.

Maybe he'd just shrug it all off as the ramblings of a cheap drunk…

No. No, she'd seen his face, had seen the regret, and worse, she'd seen the horror.

He didn't want her to feel these things for him. Which made two of them. But if she left now, she knew she'd kill whatever this was. If she left now, she would be taking them down a path she couldn't retrace, sending the message that she was ashamed of what she'd said last night.

She wasn't ashamed. She'd meant every word.

And yet to stay and face him...That was definitely the tougher route. But last night he hadn't done anything wrong. He'd kept her off the roads. He'd allowed her to stay. And more than all of that, he'd taken care of her.

She needed to thank him. It was just good manners. Turning, she glanced at Aidan where he still stood watching the dark night slowly turn into a glorious morning.

He'd let her have her inner battle in private.

"I'll get my keys," he said.

She drew a deep breath. "Not necessary. Turns out we were both wrong about what I'm doing next."

He turned then and met her gaze, a small smile on his mouth. "Not me," he said. "I had money on you and I never lose."

She let out a shaky breath. "Well you could've saved me some time and anxiety if you'd just said so to start with."

White teeth flashed. "Where would the fun be in that?"

The stairs did indeed lead to the gym. The only windows in the place were high, up close to the ceilings, and set in the concrete walls. The moon was still up and beaming ghostly slants of light across the hardwood floor, casting the room in a patchwork of luster and shadow.

Hud was indeed there, shirtless, sweatpants dangerously low slung, working weights. As she moved across the floor to the weight bench where he was mechanically lifting, she shifted in and out of the moonbeams. Dark. Light. Dark. Light.

Matching the flip-flopping emotions churning through her. Stay. Go. Stay...

Hud continued to silently hoist weights in perfectly timed repetitions like some dark superhero, and she took a moment to appreciate the beauty of the man and how much she ached just looking at him.

She leaned over the bar and smiled at him.

He didn't look surprised to see her. Nor did he return her smile.

"Right," she murmured. "Because *you* remember everything about last night."

He settled the bar into the rack and sat up as she moved around to straddle the bench facing him. "You don't remember?" he asked with a whisper of disbelief.

"Not at first, but it's all coming back to me." Determined to keep the tone light, she tried smiling again. "So. I threw myself at you. Should I apologize for that?"

The false stillness in his face told her that he wasn't going to let her keep anything light and he wasn't going to smile this away either. "Absolutely not," he said.

Okaaaaay. "And the things I said," she managed. "How about that?"

"You shouldn't apologize for what you feel," he said carefully. "Ever."

With a sigh, she scooted forward and invaded his space. When he didn't make a move to get away, or make any move at all in fact, she splayed her hands on his chest. "I wanted to thank you."

"For which part?" he asked, staying on his side of the bench, not making a move to touch her in return. "Letting you drive up here into an oncoming storm to give me my phone back? Or maybe for being so nice to my mom. Or hell, how about having to keep Lily company when I ditched you for a robbery call?"

"All of it." She let her hands drift a little because she couldn't help herself. He was warm and hard and a little sweaty. It shouldn't have been such a distraction but it was. He was one big distraction. "I meant I wanted to thank you for *everything*," she said. "Allowing me to paint the mural, which gave me time on this mountain. Teaching me to ski better. For the friendship that had nothing to do with having cancer." She paused because this one was harder. "For making me feel whole again," she said softly.

He stared at her for a long beat and then leaned forward. The burgeoning daylight softened his features from a superhero to a mortal man, one with weaknesses and hopes and dreams like any other. She liked the superhero. After all, he'd given her chills and excitement. But she loved the man.

When he reached for her, she slid her arms up and wrapped them around his neck, sighing in pleasure when he leaned in farther to press his forehead to hers. "That sounded like a good-bye," he said.

"It was." Her voice was a whole lot firmer than her heart. "I've got to get home."

His lips moved down to hers and he hovered there as he whispered, "I didn't peg you for a runner."

"I'm not running."

"Feels like it," he said.

The temptation to kiss him was strong and she was weak, so she gave in, pressing her mouth to his. Their mega attraction exploded between them, as always. Before she lost herself to him fully, she pulled away and stood up, determined to keep her resolve. "I can't think when we do that."

He stood up too. "What do you need to think about?"

She met his gaze. "Work. I've got to go, Hud."

"Okay. But you'll be back this weekend," he said. He didn't word it as a question, but it was one.

"Yes," she said. "For the mural."

"Bay."

He said her name softly, with so much feeling her throat tightened. She stepped back into the shadows, relieved to have them.

"If this is about last night—" he started.

"No." She closed her eyes. No, she didn't want to go there. He didn't have time for her, for this, and she needed to protect herself. Besides, this wasn't exactly in her plan either. She wanted to go out and see the world, and it wasn't as if he'd drop everything to go with her. "I'm sorry," she whispered. "I did a foolish thing, letting this go so far."

He was silent, and she took that for her answer. Unable to look at him again, she kept her eyes closed, the memory of his regret burning in her brain. Backing away, she struggled to keep her voice even. "Good-bye, Hud."

And then she ran up the stairs.

Chapter 27

Bailey ran up the stairs and down the hall, hoping like hell Aidan was still in the living room and still available to take her to her car in town. A good cry was all she needed, she assured herself, but it was going to have to wait until she was alone. It was a matter of pride that Aidan not see what a baby she'd become.

She made a quick pit stop back in Hud's room for her phone, which she'd left on the nightstand, and then hit the living room.

No Aidan.

Of course not, she thought bitterly. Heaven forbid a Kincaid fall into line.

No problem, she decided. She'd just call a cab—she sincerely hoped they had one in town!—and wait outside. Pulling out her cell phone, she moved, head down, to the front door.

And ran right into a brick wall. Or rather Hudson Kincaid. He stood there with his feet braced apart, his arms folded across his chest, and his gaze inscrutable.

"Move," she said, and then her good manners couldn't be held back. "Please," she added but not contritely.

He broke his stance to take the purse from her shoulder and transfer it to his. Then he took her phone and shoved that into his back pocket.

Stunned, she scrambled for something appropriately scathing to say.

But he beat her to it. "You want it both ways," he said. "You want this to be just an item on your list as you're spreading your wings and enjoying life, and that's perfectly fine with me. I get it. I'm happy to be that guy for you. But on some deeper level you're also playing at wanting something more, flirting with it when it suits you but running away when it doesn't."

"I'm not . . ." she started, indignant and furious. How dare he tell her what she was thinking? But . . . dammit. She couldn't deny that there was some element of truth to what he was saying. After all, it *had* been her who said that she didn't want this relationship and that she wasn't ready. He'd been onboard with that because his life was full. He didn't have room for love.

It'd made him the perfect man for her.

The problem was that she hadn't counted on falling for him. That had been a mistake, her first of many. Like keeping that fact from him. Or assuming that he'd fall too—and then keeping *that* to herself as well. She'd told him to keep it light and she'd gone ahead and done the exact opposite. *She'd* been the one giving mixed signals, screwing this all up.

Her experiences had changed her. In fact, they had made her grow up to be someone more independent, more sure of herself. That had been so difficult for Aaron to accept that he'd tried to change her back. It had cut right to the bone.

And yet here she was, trying to change Hud. God. She gasped at the pain of it and pressed a hand to her heart.

She felt Hud slip an arm around her and lead her to a chair. He crouched in front of her with his hands on her knees, staring into her face. "What just happened?"

She shook her head. "I'm trying to change you, change what you want, what you need." She squeezed her eyes shut, horrified at herself.

"Bay. Bay, look at me," he said, a quiet demand.

She opened her eyes, a little amused in spite of herself that his tone of authority still got her.

"You didn't try to change me, you simply told me how you felt," he said.

"Under the influence," she reminded him.

"It was still the truth," he said calmly. "You didn't ask me to change a damn thing. You were open. That's the way it's supposed to be between two people who are—"

"Sleeping together?"

"It's a little more than that," he said dryly, even though he looked a little surprised to hear himself say so.

She heard a half laugh, half sob escape her, and she slapped a hand over her mouth. "How much more?" she asked from behind her fingers, unable to help herself.

"A hell of a lot." He was gracious in defeat, standing and offering her his hand, pulling her to her feet and straight into his arms.

His kiss, deep and full of emotion, sealed the deal. No, he didn't say the three little words *I love you*, but she didn't need them. Words weren't needed in moments like this, especially as he carried her to his suite, where he kicked the door shut and hit the lock.

"Be sure," he said quietly, letting her slide slowly down his body until her feet touched the floor, looking into her eyes, his own dark and intense and serious.

She wrapped her arms around him tight, one hand reaching up to slide around the back of his neck, pulling him down to her.

He hesitated for a beat and then came willingly, crushing her to him, burying his face in her neck. "Bailey," he whispered. "You deserve better."

"Sorry, but we're going to have to agree to disagree on that."

He opened his mouth but she put her finger over his lips. She knew he was mixed up about his past, how he felt it tumbling into his present, making his future hard to imagine. He hadn't heard about Jacob. He had no idea how fast his mom was going to deteriorate.

It weighed on him. She got that.

And maybe she couldn't help the boy he'd been, and she'd never been one to look to the future since, until recently, she hadn't even *had* a future.

But the present... That she could handle. She had the present right here in her arms, and fears and worries aside, she couldn't imagine ever letting go. "You know what I think?" she whispered. "I think you're about fifty percent tough alpha male, thirty percent bravado, and twenty percent bullshit."

He laughed. "In this case, bravado and bullshit might be the same thing."

"Fifty-fifty then," she said, unconcerned. She lifted a hand to his face, letting her fingers linger over the scruff lining his jaw. "I think you take what you want when you want it. Except when it comes to things that might actually want you back."

He stilled and his muscles bunched, like maybe he was going to pull away. She wasn't a match for him on the best of days, of which this wasn't one, so she just wrapped herself around him like a monkey on a tree. Because if he thought he was going to bow on this conversation, he was sorely mistaken.

Instead, he backed to the chair in the corner of his room and sat, and because she was still wrapped around him, she ended up in his lap.

His hands went to her hips. To hold her there or to shove her free, she had no idea so she kept her grip tight just in case.

"You keep saying shit like that," he said. "Like you know me to the core."

"Maybe I do. Or I'm coming to."

"It hasn't been long enough."

"What's long enough?" she asked. "Life is in the moment, Hud. Life isn't always eighty plus years, not for everyone. And besides, some things take only a blink. Maybe we've not dated in the traditional sense, but we've spent a lot of time together. On the scaffolding. On the mountain. On skis. Off skis..." She smiled. "Hours that add up to days. We've been in the trenches, hung out with your family. You've seen mine in action too. I know where you've come from and where you want to go. You know the same about me. If you add up all those parts and put them together, including the times when we were flirting while pretending not to even like each other, we've been together for a good long time."

He stared at her. "That's some creative accounting," he finally said.

She smiled demurely. "I can be very creative, it's true."

He laughed, low in his throat, the sound sexy as hell and also...familiar. It made her warm from the inside out. "Do you want me to make the first move?" she asked. "Because I'm good at that too. I'm fearless these days." She smiled. "Creative, fearless, and hungry for you. So hungry I'll even beg." She softened her voice, low and husky. "I'll do whatever you want, Hud."

She'd absolutely meant to seduce him, but she'd meant to do it while keeping the upper hand. Wrestling that from her, he surged upward, knocking them both out of the chair and onto the soft, thick carpet. Sprawled and knocked breathless, she stared up at him.

He gave her a smile that was so wicked and full of naughty intent, she felt herself go damp. Then he scooped her up and tossed her to the bed, following her down and pinning her to the mattress, his eyes heavy-lidded and sexy as he watched her reaction.

From flat on her back, weighed down by one hundred and eighty pounds of hard muscle, she tried to figure out how to wrestle the control back. She arched up into him.

"You're a menace," he said fondly, and pressed her deeper into the mattress, rubbing the neediest part of her to the hardest part of him, wrenching a moan from her throat.

"A gorgeous menace," he murmured, and held her still, making her take what he offered.

And what exactly is he offering? a little voice asked. Nothing yet...

But then he rocked against her with the exact right pressure and rhythm, and she gasped.

"Kiss me," he demanded.

Well, finally. She obliged, kissing him with all the pent-up heat and hunger in her heart. She'd been craving this, starving for this with a man. This man.

They went nuclear then, tugging at clothing, their hands battling each other to get skin to skin until with a frustrated growl Hud drew back and ripped her—*his*—shirt open, sending buttons flying across the room.

She moved against him, trying to get him inside of her. But he held her off, his mouth moving from her mouth to her throat, to the curve of her exposed shoulder and then her breast. He teased her nipples, sucking them into his mouth, then pulling back to blow on them so that they tightened even further, making her writhe beneath him.

When he seemed satisfied that she was completely out of control, he shifted down her body. With a whimper of gratitude she threaded her hands into his hair, trying to guide him to the spot where she needed him, but he pulled her hands free and held them in his, one on either side of her.

"Hurry," she demanded. Nicely of course.

He flashed her a hot smile. "We're not on my desk or on the floor," he said. "We're in my big, comfy bed. You're not going to hurry me."

Damn. Had she actually thought she liked his alpha side?

Ignoring her plaintive whimpers, his big hands slid to her inner thighs. He held them open for his mouth, which made its torturously slow way from her stomach to her hipbone and then finally headed south.

She quivered and felt him smile against her. "Patience," he said.

Not her strong suit. In fact, words like *hurry*, *now*, and *faster* were running through her mind and as if he could tell, he let out a huff of laughter against her skin.

"Dammit, Hud—" She broke off as his tongue flickered out and touched her, and she moaned shamelessly.

Then his mouth descended and she lost herself. Just as, when she was with him like this, she was found. Simple and terrifying as that.

When he'd peeled her off the ceiling, he came up with a condom and slid into her, making her cry out his name.

"So good." His voice was low and rough in her ear. "You always feel so good wrapped around me." Pushing up to his knees, he lifted her along with him so that she straddled him now—which seated him even more deeply within her—and she gasped.

He slowly rocked his hips against hers. "Okay?"

So okay she couldn't speak, she could only nod and clutch at him. Every time he ground into her she whimpered for more. He crushed his lips to her and she plastered herself to him, unwilling to let him go. *Ever.* Needing to maintain contact with his skin, to feel the heat of his desire, to hear him groan her name as he pushed deep inside her, she held on tight, so tight.

But then he pulled away—just far enough that their lips were no longer touching and their eyes could meet— and held her gaze as he moved slow and steady, his chest brushing hers with his every thrust, his big hands hard at her hips, holding her where he wanted her.

Staring into his eyes, she searched but didn't have to look far to see everything she felt for him mirrored right back at her.

After, he tucked her into his side and covered them both up. She thought she could be happy in the warm, strong circle of his arms forever. There was no doubt in her mind. She'd fallen in love with Cedar Ridge, with the people in it, with the life she'd made for herself here...

With Hudson Kincaid.

She'd experienced a few epiphanies in her life, but right there in Hud's bed with a new day dawning, she had another. She'd been given a new lease on life and she was so grateful. But now she dared to hope for more, that she could have that new lease on life *and* love.

Don't worry about if you can do it, Bailey-Bean, just pretend you can. Pretend enough and it becomes real.

And thinking it, hope blossomed.

Because yes, this whole thing had started as a line item on a list of things she wanted to do to fulfill her life, and yet instead Cedar Ridge had become that life.

But Hud had been right. She wasn't the list. Not even close. For the first time, she wasn't worried about what happened next. She could actually control that and she knew what she wanted.

To be here, with Hud, for as long as he'd have her.

Yes, there were a whole lot of things she didn't yet know, such as whether she would continue to go back and forth, or move here and freelance from Cedar Ridge. But the beauty of her job was she could do whatever she wanted. It'd take some work and it would also involve a lot of compromising, but it would be worth it.

So worth it.

All that was left was to find a way to tell Hud what she was thinking so they could talk about it. Plan. She couldn't think of a better time than right now, lying in his arms as she was. She'd just come right out and say it. *Hud, I'm in this, all the way.*

But Hud hadn't moved, not so much as a muscle twitch. His breathing came slow and deep and steady—he was out. She knew how exhausted he had to be and the truth was, she wasn't that far behind him. She could wait. They could wait. There was no hurry, no need to rush this at all. In fact, she should do the opposite of rush, since she now had all the time in the world.

The thought made her smile. She had two weeks of work left on the mural. She would just enjoy those two weeks and enjoy Hud. And let things happen. She had other jobs on the horizon, things she needed to firm up. There was a possible graphic arts job for a pub in London, which, if she was lucky, she could also finagle into a trip over there to see them in person and knock something else off her list. She also had things cooking closer to home. She'd line them up and see where things took her.

And then, when she finished the mural, if Hud hadn't said anything about them in the meantime, she would. She'd tell him how she felt about him—while sober this time—and they'd go from there.

Yeah, she thought with a yawn, that worked. And thinking about it all with a smile on her face, she followed him into dreamland.

Chapter 28

As often happened during the ski season, the following two weeks came and passed in a complete blur for Hudson. He spent every second during the day on the mountain, whether on the ski runs or in the office, and plenty of graveyard shifts in town on the police schedule to boot.

But it was the weekends where he found himself thriving, able to feel Bailey's presence in his life even when she was working on the mural and he was in uniform or on the mountain.

They'd claimed the nights for themselves though, and had made the most of every hour, every single moment.

And all those moments had him both flying high and also on edge.

Because it was almost over.

They spent a lot of time with each other's tongues down their throats but not a single moment discussing what happened next.

Because Hud knew.

He'd heard her on her phone several times in the past weeks making plans for future graphic design jobs, which he got. Her job was fluid. She had to always be looking for the next job. And one of them was in England, where he knew she wanted to knock out another item on her list—taking a walking tour of English and Scottish castles.

She'd even talked about making a side trip to Paris, taking ballroom dancing lessons while she was there just because she could. He was thrilled for her, sincerely to-the-bone thrilled.

As for how he felt? He told himself it didn't matter, that this was about Bailey, not him.

The mural itself was the talk of the resort. It was nearly done now, the colors vibrant and gorgeous against the lodge, a set of siblings whose stories seemed bigger than life.

And it was almost done. He'd always known he was on borrowed time but that point hit home hard. And suddenly all those times when he'd changed the conversation or steered it away from what would happen when Bailey finished came back to bite him on the ass.

At the end of the day he walked into the offices. It was Saturday and his mom's real birthday. The plan had been for Kenna to drive into town, pick Carrie up along with her favorite meal—loaded pizza—and bring her back to the resort for the evening. Everyone would make their way to the conference room for a dinner celebration.

Hud got to the offices a few minutes early, his mind busy with calculating how fast he could get himself and Bailey in and out and then up to his place for a quickie without anyone noticing.

And that's when he got the text from Max regarding
Jacob.

> *Our boy's finally confirmed safe and sound. Or at least
> as sound as he gets.*

Hud let out a breath and felt a slight release in the knot
in his chest as he entered the conference room. It was
empty except for Aidan, who was pulling sodas out of the
small refrigerator on the other side of the room.

Aidan straightened at the sight of Hud and gestured to
the table. "I caught Gray and Penny on the table in the
staff room last week. You don't think they've been in here
too, do ya?"

They both eyed the table and shuddered.

"They need to keep it to his office," Aidan said. "Like
normal couples."

"Is that why your office door's always locked now?"
Hud asked.

Aidan smiled. "Hell yeah. And you're one to talk.
There's been plenty of times when your door's been
locked over the past two months."

Yeah, the best two months of his life, which were just
about over.

Aidan, taking in his expression, got serious. "What?
What did I just say?"

Penny came into the room. "Looks like you've just told
him that Santa isn't real."

"I was ragging on him about Bailey," Aidan said.
"Which started, FYI, because of you and Gray."

"Aw," Penny said. "Using us as sterling examples of
being the perfect Kincaid couple?"

"Bailey and I aren't like that," Hud said, finding his voice.

"Really?" Penny asked, tongue in cheek. "So when you're holed up with her in your suite or your office, you're what, just checking each other for ticks? Because the couple who fights off Lyme disease stays together? Is that it?"

"We're not like that," Hud repeated. "Not in the way you seem to think."

"And which way is that?" Penny asked.

"Married." Hud looked at Aidan. "Or nearly married."

"Okay," Penny said slowly. "So for the record, what would you say you and Bailey *are* like? And be careful here, Hud, because I've seen how she looks at you. She's not just messing around. She's a keeper for you."

Hud took that in and told himself Penny was wrong. Because Bailey was just messing around. That was the whole point. "She's not a keeper to me," he said. "She's not staying around after the mural is finished. There's no reason for her to."

Because he hadn't given her one and he knew it. He opened his mouth to correct himself, and maybe to throw himself on Penny's mercy and ask her how the hell he might turn this around when a sound had him looking to the doorway.

Gray and Kenna stood there holding pizza boxes. Just behind Kenna stood Lily and Hud's mom.

And with them, holding Carrie's hand, was Bailey.

Gray cleared his throat, gave Hud a you-are-such-an-idiot look, and strode in, setting the pizzas on the table.

Kenna did the same and looked at Gray. "If you and

Penny have messed around on this table like, *ever*, I want to know right now."

"The table is a messing-around-free zone," Penny said, voice too bright.

Hud hadn't moved. Neither had Bailey. But she moved then, taking Carrie to a chair and gently setting her up with a soda and a paper plate for her pizza.

"Thanks," Carrie said and hugged Bailey tight. "I hope you're not going to let my idiot son ruin your appetite."

"No," Bailey said, voice quiet but calm. "But I can't stay. I have to . . . go."

Hud closed his eyes because he truly was an idiot. When he opened them again, Gray had moved to Bailey and was hugging her. "You should know that the Kincaids have a brain/mouth disease," he said to her. "It makes us say stupid shit we don't mean."

Bailey managed a small smile that made Hud feel even worse.

Aidan said nothing at all but kissed Bailey gently on the cheek.

Hud finally found his feet, which took him to the door, getting there just as Bailey did. He studied the emotion swirling in her eyes. "Leave," he said.

Bailey took a step back but he caught her hand. "Not you."

"Us," Penny said and nudged Gray and Aidan to the door.

"But there's pizza," Gray complained.

"No," Bailey said. "No one's leaving except me." She held up a hand when everyone protested in unison. "I've got some colors already mixed up. I need to use them before they dry."

And then she was gone and everyone left in the room glared darts at Hud.

Or so he assumed since he stood there facing the door where Bailey had vanished. He could feel the weight of his family's various emotions behind him—anger, disappointment, frustration—all stabbing him in the back. "Well?" he said. "Someone say something. I know you're dying to."

"Fine," Gray said. "I'll go first. Good going, Ace—you're even more of a dickwad than Aidan here was when he met Lily."

"Hey," Aidan said. "I wasn't a dickwad." He turned to Lily. "Was I?"

She patted him on the arm.

Aidan blinked. "Is that a yes?"

"Well..." she said evasively.

Hud was still staring at the door. He shook his head. *What just happened?*

"In a nutshell?" Gray asked, making Hud realize he'd spoken out loud. "You told the woman you love that you don't love her."

"And then you missed your opportunity to take it back," Kenna said. "The window for those things is really short. It's like the three-second rule when you drop food. You have three seconds to pick it up and eat it or you have to throw it away, even if it's a cookie." She shook her head. "You threw it all away, Hud."

He opened his mouth and then shut it and turned to Penny, the only logical one in the room.

She smiled at him sadly. "I'm afraid they're right this time. This *one* time..."

Bailey went straight to the mural. Her security blanket. She'd just gotten to the base of the wall and climbed up to the second level of scaffolding when she felt someone right behind her. She turned and faced—*perfect*—Hud. Because what had just happened wasn't humiliating enough.

"Bailey—"

"No," she said, pointing at him, voice shaking with the depths of her fury. "Don't. You don't have to say anything, I get it."

She was just glad she hadn't spilled her guts in the past two weeks, revealed any more of her feelings for him. That was her saving grace, she told herself. He had no idea how much he'd hurt her and it was going to stay that way.

He studied her for a beat and she didn't know what she expected, but it wasn't the words that came out of his mouth.

"I told you I wouldn't regret what we shared," he said, his words insidiously quiet, his voice flat.

She hated that most of all. "That you did," she agreed. Hell if she'd thank him for it. She had to fight to keep her expression just as nonexistent as his—not easy when her heart had been cracked in half. "How nice for you to be able to turn your feelings on and off so easily," she managed coolly.

He didn't answer, not that she'd expected him to. She concentrated on dragging air in and out of her lungs until she no longer had the urge to cry. Because no way would she allow him to see her weak. She was going to stand strong if it was the last thing she did. Turning away from him, she faced the mural.

But Hud didn't go. She ignored him for as long as she could, which wasn't very long. The weak winter sun behind them cast their shadows on the mural, his a lot taller and broader than hers. "You're in my light," she said.

"We need to talk."

She glanced over her shoulder. He was in ski patrol gear, dark sunglasses hiding his eyes. His expression was dialed to dark and brooding, and his shoulders were set in grim determination. "I think we've talked enough," she said.

His jaw tightened. "You misunderstood what I was saying to Penny."

"No, I'm pretty sure I didn't," she said, concentrating on her painting. She was on the very last part, finishing up the caricature of Jacob. She'd decided to put him in an airplane, flying past the mountains painted behind him with his eyes on the horizon, a very small smile playing about his mouth. Then she spent some time filling in the heart and soul to the piece.

Her heart and soul.

"You said you couldn't be pushed away," he said quietly. "You said that to me. Was it a lie?"

She stilled and stared sightlessly at the mural in front of her, telling herself not to react to the...disappointment?...in his voice. "I need you to move a few feet to the left," she managed.

"That would take me right off the scaffold."

"Yes," she said.

And then she went on painting, her heart in her throat. She heard his radio go off at his hip, then heard him respond that he was offline.

She sucked in a breath at that. But whoever was calling for him was insistent and the call was an emergency, which had her sucking in another breath.

Someone was hurt.

"Bay," he said quietly. "I have to go."

"I know."

"I don't want to."

This she didn't answer. She told herself she was absolutely not listening for him to climb down and leave her alone. Not even a little bit. To ensure it, she pulled her earphones from her pocket, slid them into her ears, cranked the music on her phone, and tried to cancel out the real world.

But two minutes later she couldn't stand it anymore and turned to face him.

He was gone.

She forced air into her lungs and nodded to herself, acknowledging that she'd done this, and kept painting. When it got dark, she didn't stop. She didn't go to bed.

She kept painting. She figured she had maybe six hours left on the mural and she was going to finish tonight if it killed her.

It nearly did. She stayed up all night and finished just before dawn, and it was worth it. As she stepped back to take it all in with the day's first light, it caught her breath.

It'd come out better than she could have imagined.

Which didn't ease the pain in her gut.

Or her heart.

Just as the first of the sun's rays peeked over the mountain, she got into her car. She pulled the list from her pocket and crossed off the mural.

She eyed the rest of the list, trying to force her mind to settle on one item because she needed a direction now, more than ever, something to jump right into and take her mind off what had happened.

Skydiving?

No, she decided. She'd just discovered she was going to get to live, no sense in tempting the fates.

London maybe... Yes. That would do nicely. And she put her car into gear and headed off the mountain, not looking back.

Okay, she totally looked back, taking in the glorious colors of the new day in her rearview mirror.

Wishing...

But even as she let herself half hope, the words replayed in her mind. *She's not a keeper to me...*

As the words washed over her again, she strengthened her resolve and hit the gas.

Chapter 29

Hud almost always knew what to do. On the mountain. On the job. With his mom. With any of his family, really—with the sole exception of Jacob—he knew what to do. And he did it.

A dad who'd walked when Hud had been so young he didn't remember much of him at all? He'd handled it.

A mom who had a little problem sticking to reality? He'd handled it.

Having to move around because of poverty as a child due to said mother not being able to hold down a job for long? He'd handled it.

Finding out at twelve that he had siblings who wanted him in their lives? He'd handled it.

But then Jacob had left him. Walked away like their dad and never looked back, and Hud had finally come up against something he couldn't handle.

So he'd faked it. He'd faked it pretty damn well too. He'd faked it for so long now that he'd given off the air of handling it just fine. And it had become true.

But losing Bailey? No, he couldn't handle that. Wouldn't. He'd make sure of it. He had no idea how, yet, but he'd figure it out and handle it like he had everything else.

If he ever got off work. The call that had taken him away from her last night had originated when a woman called the police because her boyfriend and his best friend hadn't come back from skiing at Cedar Ridge for the day.

Dispatch had called Hud and put him on it. He'd done a quick sweep of the parking lot for any cars that didn't belong to staff.

There were zero.

When he called the woman directly, she'd told them that she'd dropped the guys off that morning with the directive to call her when they'd finished skiing.

That call had never come.

The mountain had been swept at closing, as always. All of ski patrol skied the entire mountain at dusk yelling, "Closing," checking every nook and cranny.

They never left anyone on the mountain.

But at the very end of the phone call the woman had admitted that the two men had been talking about going off-trail to ski, in an area clearly marked NOT CEDAR RIDGE PROPERTY.

Hud had been forced to call back all the staff who'd already left for the day, and they'd spent the long hours of the night combing the out-of-boundary areas along with search and rescue.

It was five in the morning before the woman called dispatch again to tell them she'd heard from the guys. Apparently they'd left the mountain at closing and had gone to the Slippery Slope and gotten drunk. They'd hitched a ride and had just showed up at home.

Unbelievable.

Penny had taken Carrie to the Kincaid lodge, where she'd fallen asleep on the couch waiting for Hud. He'd walked in at five thirty in the morning, bleary-eyed, knowing he had to take her home for her meds before any-thing else—including going to Bailey. He got his mom up and out to the parking lot, where he discovered Aidan's truck blocking his.

Aidan waved them into his vehicle saying he was headed to McDonald's for breakfast and it wasn't out of the way. He didn't say another word on the ride, but Car-rie had woken all the way up and had plenty to say.

"It's not too late to make things work with Bailey," she started.

Hud had spent the entire night out in the cold on the mountain searching for dumbasses, so he'd had lots of time to replay what had happened in his head. He didn't need to discuss. He'd screwed up, big time. And the worst part was, his life was so crazy he didn't even have time to fix it. "Mom—"

"No, I know you. You're stubborn. So determined to be a damn island. But you can do this, baby. You can stop pushing away people who care about you. You can learn to accept love. You accept mine, you accept your siblings', why can't you accept anyone else's?"

Aidan snorted beneath his breath and turned Hud's way for his response.

Hud didn't have one. He put on his sunglasses and stared out the windshield. A storm was blowing in, a hell of one given the gunmetal-gray clouds pouring in over the mountain peaks like smoke coming out of a cauldron. He hadn't had a spare second to check the weather so he turned on the radio now, which was predicting the storm of the season, maybe the decade.

Perfect.

Carrie sighed from the backseat. "You going to talk any sense into him, Aidan?"

Aidan laughed a little and met Carrie's gaze in the rearview mirror. "You ever had luck talking any sense into him?" he asked.

"No. He's pretty hardheaded."

Aidan chuckled.

Hud rolled his eyes.

"This is important," Carrie said to Aidan. "This is his life he's messing up. We can't let him do that. Can you try harder?"

Aidan shifted his weight in the seat, looking uncomfortable. The Kincaids didn't do well discussing feelings. "I'm not really authorized to talk on this issue," Aidan finally said. "It's above my pay grade."

"You think Lily would agree to that?" Carrie asked.

"Lily's smarter than I am," Aidan said. He looked at Hud. "And I'm pretty sure Bailey's smarter than your son. No insult intended."

"None taken," Carrie said, and sighed as they pulled into her home. The guys got her inside and settled.

Hud leaned over her to kiss her good-bye. "Missed you, Mom," he said quickly, wondering how long she'd stay lucid, if it would stick this time. "It was good to see you."

Carrie cupped his face and looked him in the eyes. "You've always said there were things you wished you could take back," she said, voice earnest. "When you crashed your bike and sent Jacob flying over the handlebars and straight to the hospital. Or when you cheated and took Jacob's multiplication test for him and got both of you suspended from third grade for a week."

"Mom, it's going to be okay."

"How?" she asked. "Your dad's gone, Jacob's gone, and now Bailey too? How much loss can you take, Hud? Don't let her go, baby. Please, don't." She started to cry. "The principal and school counselor once told me they were worried about you because you didn't let yourself get attached. And it's all my fault. Please don't let this be all my fault, Hudson."

"It's not," he said, destroyed. He sat on her bed and pulled her into his arms. "This isn't your fault. None of it is your fault."

"It is! If I'd loved you better, if I wasn't bats-in-the-belfry crazy like everyone says, if I'd been less of a coward to let love back into my life and given you the right example, if I'd been a better mom—"

"No," Hud said firmly. "This is on me. Not you. I know how to love, and I know it because you taught me."

Carrie's eyes filled. "You're trying to make me feel better and that's sweet, but—"

"No buts," he said firmly, suddenly everything clicking into place for him. It wasn't his mom who was the coward—it was him. Love terrified him and that was bullshit, complete bullshit. He hugged her hard and kissed her on top of her head.

She clung to him tight. "You've always been a good son to me, Hud. Always. You and Jacob—"

"Took care of what we could, I know, Mom."

"No. Well, yes, you did. Always. And the promise in

you as a young boy… Well, you've kept it as you grew up. You're a wonderful man, Hud, and I'm so very proud of you."

He met her gaze and was gratified to see that she was still one hundred percent lucid. She knew exactly who she was talking to. She was talking to Hud the man, not the boy.

"You've shouldered so much responsibility," she said, "staying here and doing what was right for the family. I don't know a better man. Well, except for you, Aidan. You're a good man too."

Aidan winked at her.

Carrie smiled and turned back to Hud. "And because you *are* such a good man, you know that you deserve love. But I still want to hear you say it."

"Mom—"

"Hudson Edward Kincaid," she said, her voice wavering but her tone utter steel. "Say it. Say you deserve love."

He sighed. "I deserve love."

"Well then what the hell are you still doing here? Go get her!"

Back outside, Hud looked at the sky. Shit. Their "storm of the season, maybe the decade" was moving in faster than he'd thought. He tried to take the driver's seat.

"No way," Aidan said. "No one drives this baby but me."

"You let Lily drive it."

"Yeah, and sometimes I let her drive in my bed too," Aidan said. "But not you." Using his big body to edge Hud out of the way, he grabbed the driver's seat. "Get in or stay here," he said out the window. "Doesn't matter to me."

Hud swore and got in the passenger side a split second before Aidan hit the gas. "I don't know what crawled up your ass but I'm in a hurry."

"Why do you think I'm driving?" Aidan asked. "You drive like a grandma."

Hud narrowed his eyes at him.

"Oh, excuse me," Aidan corrected. "You're a cop, not a grandma, and you're required to drive within the limits of the law." He flashed a grin. "I'm not."

"Fine," Hud said. "But haul ass, you hear me? Lights do not exist."

Aidan's look to Hud said his intelligence had been insulted as he tore out of the parking lot. "You got your head on straight then?"

"Yeah," Hud said.

"You sure? Cuz I could knock you around a little to make sure."

"Thanks," Hud said dryly. "You're a giver but I'm good now."

"You got a plan?"

"No," Hud admitted.

"Groveling usually works. You hit your knees and you grovel like there's no tomorrow. I'm talking until you have rug burns, man."

"I've got time to figure it out. I've got until she finishes the mural to convince her that I'm worth a real shot."

"How long is that?" Aidan asked.

"She's close… At least today, hopefully one more weekend, I don't know."

They drove up to the resort. It was six thirty. The lot was still mostly empty except for staff vehicles, the groomers, ski patrol, cafeteria workers…

Bailey's car was nowhere in sight.

Aidan caught that too. "I don't see her, man—"

Hud slid out of the truck and went running to the mural site. Halfway there, Marcus tried to stop him to talk.

"I'm late," Hud said.

Marcus looked surprised, as well he should. There were no lifts running, no staff still waiting on him for anything, and no meeting for another half hour. "But—"

"Sorry, I'll get back to you," Hud promised.

Four minutes later he stood at the base of the mural as the first snow fell. The *complete* mural, which meant she'd stayed up all night to finish it.

It was gorgeous. He and his siblings in larger-than-life form, taking on the world together.

Their world.

It took his breath away. But everything was gone. The scaffolding remained, nothing else. No brushes, no paint, no rags.

No Bailey.

Chapter 30

That's what I was trying to tell you," Marcus said as he came to a stop next to Hud. "She was packing up and fretting about taking down the scaffolding. I offered to do it for her so she wouldn't have to."

Hud scrubbed a hand down his face.

"Is that a problem?" Marcus asked.

"Yeah, but only because he's a dipshit dumbass," Aidan said, coming up behind them both.

Gray and Penny as well.

"You missed her?" Penny asked with some incrimination in her tone.

"Yeah," Hud said. "I missed her. Between that all-night call and making sure my mom got back home and medicated, and dealing with the latest news on Jacob—"

Everyone gasped.

"He's okay," Hud said quickly. "I got the email just before you all showed up at the conference room last night and then everything went to hell and I forgot to tell you. He made it back, his entire unit did. All is okay." He shoved his hands through his hair. All was okay, except for himself...

"Man, this is not what any of us want for you," Gray said. "Get the hell out of here and go after her. We'll hold the fort down."

"I can't let you take it all on," he started.

Gray was already shaking his head. "Listen, we're not being martyrs here. You'll be back with her. Bailey loves it here and she belongs here every bit as much as you do."

"And even if that's not true," Penny said, chiming in, "even if she doesn't want to live here with all the crazy, so what?"

Gray looked at her. "So what?"

"Yeah," Penny said. "So what?"

"So this is Hud's home," Gray said. "You don't just leave your home."

Penny shook her head at him. "You're missing my point, babe."

"You're telling him it's okay to leave."

"It is," Penny said, more gently this time. She looked at Hud. "She's worth it. Love is worth it." She turned back to her husband and looked at him until he sighed and nodded. Penny gave him a warm smile and met Hud's gaze again. "Go wherever the love takes you," she said.

"Yeah," Aidan deadpanned. "Because Hud's the go-where-love-takes-him, hippy-dippy one of the family."

Penny glared at him and Aidan lifted his hands in surrender. "Okay, okay, so maybe he can learn..."

Hud ignored all of them. "I thought I had more time to get her to stay," he muttered to himself.

"Just how much time did you need?" Gray asked. "You knew this day was coming."

Yeah, he had. But he'd kept thinking that falling in love was the last thing he needed to be doing, that it was ridiculous, and that he didn't have time for it.

But watching Bailey attempt to carve out a life for herself from nothing, continually picking herself up by the bootstraps and doing her best in order to give life everything she had, made him realize something. Something big.

He really had shut himself off.

And Aidan was right. He was a dipshit dumbass.

"Hud," Penny said gently. "We're all here. We'll cover for as long as it takes. Go after her. We've got your back." She paused. "Do you need me to say it again?"

"Probably should," Aidan piped in. "I mean, you had to tell me about a million times and he's even slower than me, so..."

Penny rolled her eyes at the love of her life's other brother and then met Hud's gaze again.

He shook his head. "I can't just leave. I've got a staff debriefing in twenty minutes. We've got a massive storm moving in, two patrollers on leave, and—"

"You leave because love is all that matters and you love her, you sorry ass," Penny said.

So much for her being the nice one.

"Haven't you done enough for all of us?" she demanded. "The answer's yes, by the way. So do not use us as an excuse to stay. Your mom wouldn't want that, and Jacob, well he'd just beat the shit out of you for even thinking it."

Hud nodded and whipped out his phone. He hit Bailey's number.

He went straight to voice mail. "Bailey," he said. "Call me." He paused. "I'm coming to you, okay? So call me. *Please*."

Bailey drove away from Cedar Ridge, the storm on her tail the entire way. Halfway, she thought she would have to stop and wait the weather out, but luck was on her side, leaving her just ahead of the road closures. It took her a nerve-wrecking four hours to get home though, and by the time she pulled up to her apartment complex, she was a shaky mess. She looked at her phone, which beeped a voice mail from Hud.

She's not a keeper to me.

The words were still reverberating inside her head. When she'd first processed them, her heart had leapt into her throat, and there hadn't been enough air for her to breathe ever since.

When she heard Hud's voice saying, "Call me," she sucked in a breath. Nope, she couldn't do it. So she deleted the rest of the message without listening to it. She got that he was probably worried about her. But she didn't want his worry.

She wanted what she couldn't have. His love. She sent him a brief text that said: *I got home safe.* And then she turned off her phone.

On top of her nursing job, her mother was the building super and had the first apartment. Bailey let herself in and found her mom in the kitchen pulling frozen cookie dough out of the freezer. She took one look at her daughter and turned on the oven. "We're going to need the cookies cooked, not just raw dough," she guessed.

Bailey nodded wordlessly.

Her mother's welcoming smile faded. "Oh, baby. He hurt you. Dammit, I knew this would happen."

"No." Bailey shook her head. "I hurt myself."

Her mother turned to the phone on the wall. "I'm going to call Aaron."

"No! I don't need Aaron."

"What do you need?"

"Cookies." She gulped some air. "And you."

And then she burst into tears.

The snowstorm that blew in was indeed massive, closing most of the highways and causing havoc from one end of Colorado to the other.

Thirty-six hours went by and for each of those hours Hud grew more impossible to live with, or so each of his family members told him.

"You want to change your tone, or I'll shove it down your throat," Gray suggested mildly when Hud told him where to shove it after Gray had dumped a bunch of paperwork on his desk.

"You kiss your mama with that mouth?" Aidan asked when Hud had to pull one of their snowcats out of a ditch, which took all night.

"Just because I'm a chick doesn't mean I can't kick your ass," Kenna said when he snarled at her for drinking the last soda in his place. "And I could totally do it too," she told him, "since you're still pouting over letting the love of your life get away—which, by the way, is your own damn fault, so you might want to stop taking your dumbass moves out on the people who actually still like you."

That night Hud stood in his kitchen staring out at the

storm that wouldn't end. Every year for as long as he could remember, a storm like this had been a dream come true. It meant feet of fresh powder that, at first light, he and his brothers could plow through, racing each other through the trees, hip deep in snow the consistency of sifted flour.

In more recent years it also meant good business. People flocked to Cedar Ridge from far and wide for snow like that, snow that only came along like this once or twice a season.

But right now he'd give anything for it to be summer.

"Want to talk?" Gray asked, coming into the room.

"Hell no." Hud let out a breath. "I waited too long to tell her how I felt. You warned me and I still waited too long."

Gray waited until he turned to look at him. "It's never too late."

Hud hoped like hell that was true.

The next day finally dawned clear and bright, and Hud did something he'd never done before. He took himself off the schedule on a workday.

"Thank God," Penny said fervently, and took the dry-erase pen from him and marked him off for the rest of the week. "Don't take this personally, but no one wants to see you back here until you've handled your shit and have the girl."

Hud followed the GPS to Bailey's Denver address and found himself in a neighborhood that had seen better days. Snow covered the yards in huge berms, but he'd bet even in spring there wasn't much landscaping going on. There were few cars in the building's lot, which suggested this was a hard-working area and everyone was on the job.

When he parked and walked the not-quite-shoveled path, a woman stuck her head out the first apartment, which had MANAGER printed on the door.

"Can I help y—" She broke off at the sight of him and narrowed her eyes. "*You.*"

It was Bailey's mom. "Me," he agreed. "Is she here?"

She slammed the door on his nose.

He dropped his head, studied his shoes, counted to five, and knocked on the door.

It opened slowly. "I don't talk to heartbreakers," Bailey's mom said.

"Mrs. Moore, I screwed up with your daughter, but I'm here to tell her I was an idiot and that if she'll let me make things up to her, I'll never be an idiot again."

She sniffed. "No man can promise to not be an idiot. It's in your blood. You're cursed."

"Okay, true enough," he allowed. "I'll probably be an idiot several more times this week alone, but if she'll let me, I'll love her for the rest of time in spite of it."

She stared at him for a long beat. "She won't let you love her," she finally said, but her voice was warmer and hey, she hadn't slammed the door on his nose in a whole minute now.

Both good signs. "Why won't she let me?" he asked.

"She talks a good game, wanting to live the life she could only dream about before," she said. "But she's not all that good at putting herself out there. She used to do that with her dad. He'd promise to come visit and she'd get all ready for him, using energy she didn't have to waste, making him cards and stuff. And then she'd sit in the window in the living room and wait for him."

Hud's gut tightened for the little girl she'd been.

Her mom made a noise of anger and remembered frustration. "He'd show up just enough to completely mess with her head, but more often than not, he'd forget."

Hud knew that feeling. His dad had been no better.

Bailey's mom hesitated. "And then there's Aaron. I love that boy as if he was my own, but he screwed up once and Bailey's..." She shook her head. "She's used to a black-or-white world. Sick, not sick. Alive, making plans to not be alive. No gray. No middle ground." She paused. "When she was so sick, forgiving came easy. Too easy. She was way too kind. But now..." She smiled a little. "Healthy Bailey isn't quite as forgiving. It's as if getting to live made her more human. And we all know humans are flawed. She's working on that. She's working on a lot of things. And she's forgiven her father and Aaron, but she hasn't forgotten. Karma or fate or God, whatever you want to believe, gave my daughter a second chance at life and she's taking it. Thank God. But I've influenced her decisions enough. And I learn from my mistakes. She makes her own now, with only loving support from me."

And with that, she pulled her head back inside her place and shut the door.

Hard to argue with that.

Hud continued along the path, winding his way until he found 10A, which was the address Bailey had listed as hers. Heart pounding against his ribs, he knocked.

No answer.

He knocked again and would've sworn he felt someone watching him. "Bailey," he said, hand flat on the door. "Listen to me, I was wrong, okay? About a lot of things. But mostly about us. I want an us. I always did, I was just..." He sighed and set his forehead to the wood.

"Scared." He blew out a breath. "Bay, I need you to open up the door now and forgive me."

Her door didn't open.

Instead the door across the way did and…shit… Aaron stood there. "Nice on the spilling your guts," he said, "but typically an apology involves more 'I'm sorry' and 'please' and question marks, not a demand to forgive."

Hud ground his back teeth. "Where is she?"

"Not here."

Hud blew out a sigh. "You all live in the same building?"

"Yes." Aaron paused and his voice warmed slightly. "When someone you love gets as sick as she was for as long as she did, it takes a lot of care, twenty-four-seven sometimes. She and her mom had to downsize, sell the family house. The medical costs devastated them. They moved here and so did I, to be around to help when she needed it." He paused. "She hasn't needed it for a while," he admitted.

"Where is she now?" Hud asked.

"Your guess is as good as mine."

Hud stared at Aaron, who stared back, eyes clear. "You really don't know," Hud said.

"I really don't know," Aaron agreed. "She might be mad at you, but she's even madder at me."

"If you had to take a wild guess…" Hud said.

"I'd say she was after something she always wanted." He shrugged. "You've seen her list. She could be anywhere."

"You saw her leave, don't tell me you didn't. You see everything when it comes to Bailey."

Aaron gave a barely there, slight nod. "So?"

"When?" Hud demanded.

"An hour ago."

Ah, hell. One hour. He'd missed her by one fucking hour. "Did she have suitcases or duffel bags? Do you know if she had her passport?"

"You mean for a cruise through the Greek Islands, touring the castles in Scotland, visiting the glaciers in Greenland, whale watching…"

The list that had once thrilled him was now terrifying him. "Yes," he ground out.

Aaron paused and then shook his head. "You know, I really want to be a dick here and tell you yeah, she was packed and loaded for bear, but she only had her back-pack. There's no way she went anywhere on a plane, because trust me, if she had, she'd have packed a huge bag. Or ten." He paused. "She did say something about having a few things she wanted to say to her last ski instructor."

Hud nodded. Breckenridge. That he could deal with. "Thanks."

"Oh, don't thank me," Aaron said. "We're not on the same side, you and me."

Hud ignored this and drove to Breckenridge.

Chapter 31

Six hours later, Hud had to admit defeat. He'd been to Breckenridge. He'd scoured the entire town.

Not a single sign of her.

Frustrated, out of options, he drove back to Cedar Ridge. It was midnight when he pulled in and parked. He didn't pay much attention as he let himself inside the place that had always been home to him.

Every light was on.

The first thing he saw was Kenna sitting Indian style on the island eating from a huge pizza box. This was unusual because one, she was actually smiling instead of snarling, and two, she was looking happy, and three...

His entire family was there, crowding in his kitchen, sitting on every available counter or chair—or in Aidan's case, leaning up against the sink inhaling a huge piece of pizza standing up.

And then his heart stopped because as everyone turned to him in unison, shifting, the person sitting on the table came into view.

Bailey.

"What took you so long?" she asked, and took a bite of her piece of pizza.

"What took so long?" he repeated dumbly.

"Yes," she said, chewing, swallowing. "*I* figured out almost as soon as I left here that leaving was a mistake, that I never should have walked away like that without at least giving you a shot at groveling. It's taken you *days*."

Aidan snorted and then turned it into a cough when Hud looked at him. Suddenly everyone was busy staring at the ceiling or their shoes but no one, apparently, was leaving the show.

Hud let out a breath and pushed them all out of his mind, concentrating on Bailey. "I've been one step behind you for… Shit." He laughed mirthlessly and shook his head. He was so stupid. *He'd* been her last ski instructor. "Hell, Bailey, I've been one step behind you for months."

She swallowed hard, eyes a little wide, and full. So full of things it almost hurt to look at her, but he managed as he tossed his keys aside and walked into the kitchen. He strode straight to the table, took her wrist, and directed the piece of pizza in her hand to his mouth.

Not nearly as calm as she clearly wanted him to believe, she stared at him, her eyes suspiciously bright. "Hi," she whispered.

"Hi." He swallowed the pizza, decided that wasn't even close to what he was hungry for, and took it out of her hands, setting it aside. He wrapped his hands around her ankles, uncrossed her legs, and dragged her to the edge of the table, pulling her body flush with his.

Obliging with a gratifying rush of air from her lungs, she wrapped her legs around him and then her arms. "I was wrong to leave," she whispered. "I didn't really want to leave, not the town, not the people in it, and not you." She stared up at him accusatorily. "How could *you* leave?"

"Because you were gone." He lifted his head to give each and every one of his siblings and their significant others a hard, dark look for not taking mercy on him and calling him with her location.

Not a single one looked particularly sorry, the assholes. He turned his attention back to Bailey. "I couldn't be without you," he said. "I couldn't breathe here without you, I couldn't think without you. I couldn't... *be* without you. Without you, I wasn't me."

"True story," Gray interjected. "You know those commercials where people turn into bitchy divas when they're hungry? Hud here took bitchy diva to a whole new level, trust me."

Penny elbowed him in the gut. With an *oomph*, Gray stopped talking.

"What were you going to do if I'd moved to New York?" Bailey asked Hud. "Or London? Or Timbuktu?"

He thought about that. "I don't know about Timbuktu," he finally said. "But New York has great food and Europe has some pretty cool skiing."

"You'd have left here, moved somewhere with me?" she asked doubtfully. "You'd have left your home?"

"Don't you know?" He set her hand onto his chest, right over his heart. "Home is wherever you are, Bay."

"Okay, that's a good one," Gray whispered. "That's going to get him laid— Ouch! Christ, woman, watch the goods."

Bailey stared at Hud and shook her head in disbelief. "But this mountain is everything to you," she said softly.

"*You're* everything to me."

"What took you so long?" she asked again.

Her voice killed him. Her tone suggested that she'd nearly lost faith in him.

"I was worried," she said. "I was worried you didn't care—"

"The thought of you leaving and staying away made me want to drop to my knees," he said. "How's that for someone who doesn't care? It's been three days, twelve hours, and six minutes without you."

She blinked. "You kept track of the minutes?"

"No, I made that part up," he said. "I was trying to load the evidence in my favor."

Aidan snickered. "Rookie."

"Shh," Lily said. "He's being romantic."

Hud did his best to ignore their obnoxious audience. "I called you, told you I was crazy for you."

She closed her eyes. "I deleted your message. I'm sorry, I shouldn't have done that."

"I got held up by the storm but went after you as soon as I could. You'd left this huge Bailey-size hole in my heart, but the storm—it was the only thing that could've stopped me."

"Oh, good save," Gray muttered. "Makes up for him being so slow on the uptake."

Penny smacked Gray lightly on the chest. "Shh. And it wouldn't hurt you to be taking notes here, Mr. Not Romantic. You might actually learn something."

Gray sighed and reached for another piece of pizza.

Hud lowered his head and brushed his mouth over Bailey's. "I knew my mistake instantly," he murmured, "I don't know why I resisted."

"You were hoping I'd be scared off."

"I was," Hud admitted.

She nodded. "You about done with that?"

He pressed his forehead to hers. "Yeah."

"*Good.*"

Hud couldn't believe his luck, that she was really here looking at him like she always did, as if he was the most important thing to her. He'd never get tired of that, and how he'd thought he could live without her, he had no idea. "I love you, Bailey. So very much. I have since I first laid eyes on you."

"On Devil's Face," she said softly. "When you inferred that I was a very stupid woman for being somewhere I didn't belong."

"If anyone was stupid that day, it was me," he said. "But that wasn't the first time I saw you. It was earlier that morning. You were in the parking lot, sitting on your back bumper putting on your boots. Your cap was so bright it made me need sunglasses. You were singing Ed Sheeran. Your eyes were shining with…" He closed his own eyes. "Happiness," he said. "You were incredibly happy, and what I didn't know then but know now is that you were just feeling lucky as hell to even be breathing."

She inhaled, slow and deep and a little shaky. "Yes," she whispered.

"I took one look at you and you—"

"—made you want to run in the opposite direction?"

"Smile," he said. "You made me smile. I wanted to know who you were. I wanted to breathe your air and take in some of your glow and feel everything you were feeling because I wasn't," he said. "Feeling. I'd closed myself off and yet one look at you and I knew what I was missing."

"Oh, Hud," she whispered.

"I have this recurring nightmare," he said. "You take off with your list and vanish, and I never see you again."

"I'd never do that," she said.

"I know, and I realize now that's not even what my real nightmare would be. My *real* nightmare would be if you never spoke to me again."

"*C-H-E-E-S-Y*," Gray stage-whispered to Penny.

"I took one look at you," Hud said to Bailey, "and control went flying out the window. You tore down the brick wall around my heart one smile at a time."

"Oh, for God's sake," Gray stage-whispered again. "Really? Women buy this shit?"

"*Yes*," Penny and Lily said in sync. "*Shh!*"

Kenna shrugged and kept eating pizza. "Depends on what comes next."

Hud let out a shaky breath and didn't take his eyes off of Bailey. "I'm not saying we need to buy rings, but I think we owe it to each other to see where this goes. And I want you to know, I'm all-in."

"What if I get sick again?" she asked with a casualness that didn't fool him.

His lungs squeezed out all the air so he couldn't breathe. "I'll still be all-in," he managed. "Whatever you need, I'm in."

"What about if *you* get sick?"

"I'm not going to," he said.

"But what if?" she asked stubbornly. "You going to try to push me away again?"

"Never," he promised. "Never again." He pulled a small, black velvet box from his pocket and she gasped.

The entire room gasped.

Hand to her heart, she stared at it. "I thought you just said—"

"I wanted to give you an optional ending."

"Okay," Gray whispered to Penny. "*That's* a good one. I'll give him that."

Bailey stared at the box and surprised Hud when her eyes filled. "But seriously, what if?" she whispered softly, her hand over the port scar on her chest.

He tipped her chin up to look into his eyes. "Listen to me carefully, Bay. You're so incredibly strong, and I love that about you. I love you."

Her eyes filled. "I love you too."

"So you get that the best part about being one-of-two is that if something happens and your strength fails you, *I'll* be strong for *you*. I'll never let you down again."

She stared at him for a long time and he waited, trusting her to come to the same conclusion, that together they could face anything. "I signed up for the duration," he said. "For the good, the bad, the ugly, everything. I'm in this, *all* the way in, Bailey. The question is, are you?"

She shifted, a barely there movement, but it brought her even closer to him and she smiled, letting him see what he meant to her. Holding his gaze, she finally took the box and opened it—and gasped again at the diamond ring.

"Options," he murmured. "That's all it is."

She nodded and then shook her head. "I don't need options," she whispered. She slid the ring onto her finger and then tilted her head up to his. "I just need you."

Epilogue

Three months later...

Bailey stood on the bow of the boat, toes over the edge, arms out, head back, eyes wide open on the huge, unbroken sky, having her *Titanic* moment.

She'd passed another round of tests with flying colors. The words *cancer* and *free* were starting to really take root, the reality being that the future she'd spent so many years never daring to hope for was really hers for the taking.

Her heart felt so full it might burst at any second.

She and Hud hadn't set a date. They'd made no wedding plans at all, or further discussed it. She was very, very happy with that, happy and content to just be for a while—with the man she loved.

He'd taken her to the glaciers in Canada last month. They'd climbed them and she'd stood on the top of the world and had grinned from ear to ear. They'd gone dogsledding—the thrill of a lifetime.

And then they'd made love in the hot springs beneath gently falling snow.

They were working their way down her list. This month was the Greek Islands.

"Good?" rumbled a sexy low voice in her ear.

"So good." She sighed, utterly content. Hard not to be with Hud standing just behind her, bracing her body safely in the haven of his, his arms wrapped firmly around her. He wouldn't let her fall.

Not ever.

Of course it also helped that there was no wind and... the boat was moored. They'd been in the islands for a week, since the day after the resort's ski season had ended.

Before they'd left, Carrie was good, Jacob reportedly was still on tour and safe for the time being, and all was as good as could be.

Penny had been making noises about adding a baby to their insanity, and Gray had brought her home a puppy to practice on.

Aidan and Lily were looking at dates for a wedding.

Kenna hadn't gone off the rails.

And best yet, Bailey had never felt better.

Knock on wood. Everything was okay in their world. Hence the long, lazy days at the beach spent snorkeling with colorful fish that poked her face mask and made her gasp and laugh and nearly drown herself. Luckily, she had her own personal rescue squad in the form of one tall, dark, and relaxed Hudson Kincaid.

He nuzzled his face at the back of her neck and made

her squirm in the very best of ways. When she snuggled her butt into his crotch, she felt him smile against her— he hadn't shaved all week and the delicious scruff he had going, along with a dark, perfect tan, damn him, made him her very own pirate, and he had pillaged and taken and conquered her, heart and soul.

"Again?" he murmured, his hands sliding up from her hips to her breasts, barely contained in the itty-bitty bikini she wore.

"Yes." Knowing that their captain and staff had discreetly vanished to give them a private picnic dinner at sunset, she only gasped when his fingers slid beneath the triangles covering her breasts. Gasped and then moaned. "Here?" she whispered hopefully, turning in the circle of his arms, moaning again because the sight of him in nothing but low-slung board shorts stopped her heart.

"The Greek Islands," he murmured, cupping her ass, lifting her up so that she could wrap herself around him. "That's on your list, and never let it be said that I'm not a thorough man." He turned them and laid her out on their towel.

"I do love a thorough man," she managed breathlessly, and reached up for him.

Towering over her, he smiled. Lowering himself to her, he stroked back the wispy and completely uncontrollable hair that had grown in. She was a little self-conscious about it but Hud seemed to love it, always sifting his fingers through the wayward strands. "We're going to do this," he said. "And it's going to be good."

She smiled and welcomed him into her arms. "It's going to be wonderful."

Please turn the page
for a preview of the next book in
Jill Shalvis's Cedar Ridge series,

Nobody But You!

Available Spring 2016

Chapter 1

Sophie Marren parked her ex-husband's boat, tied it up to the deck with knots she copied off a YouTube video on her phone, and flopped to her back on the fancy sundeck that she couldn't afford, willing the seasickness away.

And yes, she was well aware that "parked" wasn't the correct boating term, but then again, neither was the word *husband*, at least not as it had pertained to her marriage.

She'd made vows and kept them, but her ex? Not so much...

Old news, she reminded herself and let out a long breath. That was something she was working on, new choices—such as living without the fist of tension in a vise around her heart, the constant fear and pressure to try and be something, someone, she wasn't.

Her glass was going to be half-full from now on, dammit, even if it killed her. And it might.

"And yet you now live on a damn boat." She shook her

head at herself. Day one of the new digs and it looked like she wasn't going to make it to day two.

The early morning was quiet, the only sound being the water rhythmically slapping up against the hull of the boat, and then the dock. Boat…dock…boat…dock— "Dammit!" she cried, quickly sitting up before she got even more seasick. She had to get ready for work. But the air was cold, she was cold, and with the boat rocking as it was, she hadn't yet risked losing an eye to put on mascara.

From somewhere nearby came the song of the morning birds, all chipper and happy, and it made her wish for a shotgun. She put a hand to her stomach, but it kept on doing somersaults. This was because she could get seasick in a bathtub.

She groaned, hoping death came quickly. Cedar Ridge Lake was one of the larger high-altitude Colorado lakes, and it didn't help that the winds had kicked up this morning, causing rolling waves across the entire surface.

When yet another gust hit, brushing the strands of hair from her damp face, she risked cracking open an eye. From her vantage point, she could see the impressive Rocky Mountains shooting straight up to the limitless, shocking azure sky. A single white fluffy cloud resembled a pile of marshmallows.

Her stomach, normally in love with marshmallows, turned over again. "Gah," she managed and quickly squeezed her eyes shut just as from the depths of her pocket, her cell phone buzzed. She pulled it out and hit answer without looking, because looking would mean opening her eyes again and facing that this all wasn't just a bad dream but her life. "Hello?"

"I just wanted you to know I had your car towed to the scrap yard."

Lucas, ex-husband and the bane of her existence.

"And I had a bonfire with whatever clothes you left in your closet too," he went on. "So I hope it was worth taking my boat."

She knew neither of these things were true because he was too cheap and also a little bit lazy. He simply wanted to punish her for taking his boat. The irony was that she'd wanted nothing from the divorce. Nothing but out. Nothing but the chance to find herself again and not just be an extension of Lucas Worthington III, hotshot lawyer on the rise.

Hindsight being twenty-twenty and all, she now knew she should've asked for at least some money instead of taking a moral stand and refusing to take a penny of spousal support or any of their assets. But she'd gone into the marriage with nothing and in the end she hadn't wanted anything from Lucas but out. Not a single thing.

When she'd said so to the judge, he'd called her aside and admonished her for cutting her nose off to spite her face because she didn't have to walk away penniless.

Hurt at the realization her marriage had been nothing but a sham from the get-go, she'd said fine, she'd take *one* thing, the one thing she knew Lucas had loved far and above anything he'd ever felt for her—his damn boat.

Petty? Okay, yes. But given that Lucas had managed to have the boat tied up in "renovations" for the entire six months since their divorce—until yesterday in fact—and that he'd also managed to get her fired from her office managerial position at a local inn so she'd had to give up her apartment, the joke was on her.

Karma was such a bitch.

Why couldn't he have loved his huge house or the Lexus . . . neither of which would be affected by the morning tide, bobbing up and down and up and down and up and down—

"Oh God." Clamping a hand over her mouth, she breathed slowly through the nausea.

"I want my *Lucas* back," Lucas said and if she could have, she'd have laughed at the ridiculous ego it'd taken for him to name the vessel after himself, including painting *The Lucas* on the hull of the boat for all to see.

"Are you even listening to me?" he demanded.

Nope. She wasn't. She didn't have to because she had a sheet of paper saying that they were consciously uncoupled, thank you very much. And to prove it, she disconnected the call and then let out a long breath, hoping to die before he called back.

"Hey, what are you doing?" a male voice called out from the direction of the dock.

From flat on her back, Sophie froze. Maybe if she didn't move he'd assume her dead and move on.

"You can't moor here, ma'am."

Right, *moor*, not park. She'd known that. But ma'am? What the heck was that? Her mom was a ma'am. Her grandma was a ma'am. Ma'am was for old people, not for twenty-five-year-old women who were desperately trying to get their lives together. Very carefully, Sophie sat up and then narrowed her eyes at the guy standing on the dock staring at her.

He was tall and broad, and he had the benefit of standing in front of the sun, which meant she could see his outline and little else. But his stance seemed aggressive enough that she felt herself wanting to shrink back a little.

Which, for the record, she hated.

But there was a bigger problem. The motion of the boat bobbing up and down, compared to the guy standing on the end of the dock *not* moving up and down, made her want to toss her cookies. In defense, she lay back down and closed her eyes again. "Did you really just call me ma'am? Because I'm not even close to a damn ma'am."

Nope, ask anyone. They'd tell you Sophie Marren was fun and chill, though she didn't tend to stay the course. She was a starter, not a finisher, as her mom would say, and she was absolutely not grown-up enough to be a ma'am. As proof, she was living on a damn boat, illegally parked while she was at it—oh wait, excuse her, *moored*.

"Fine," the guy said. "You can't moor here...Red."

At the recognition of her long, wavy, deep auburn—okay, fine, *red*—hair, she choked out a laugh. He got a point for having a sense of humor. And ah, finally the wind seemed to be settling down. Around her the morning fell silent again. Even the birds shut up. Had the guy left too? Did it matter? Apparently it did, because she sat up—slowly—to look, and then groaned.

He hadn't left.

He'd shifted though, coming closer, giving her a good look at him. Short, sun-streaked brown hair. Square jaw at least two days past needing a razor. Wide shoulders stretching an Army T-shirt to its limits. Flat belly. Lean hips encased in camo cargoes. As she watched, he pulled off his reflective sunglasses, revealing eyes the color of one of her favorite things when she wasn't seasick—chocolate.

Damn.

But if he felt any insta-attraction for her, he was really

good at hiding it because he looked at his watch like maybe he was in a hurry.

The story of her life, men being in a hurry to get away from her, and she decided right then and there she didn't like him, hot or not. "This is a public lake," she said.

"Yes, but you're tied to a private dock that belongs to that cabin." He jerked his chin to the side, indicating the home just behind him.

The lake was multi-use. The west and east shores were owned by the state and were national forest land. There were public campgrounds on the northeast side, with houses on the north shore only.

The cabin he pointed to was indeed privately owned, but she knew for a fact it was deserted because it'd been up for sale for months. Although—troublesome—the FOR SALE sign had been taken down. Even more troublesome, the shades were raised and the front door was open.

Huh. Her bad.

"I was just taking a short nap," she said.

One of his eyebrows took a hike nearly to his hairline. "At seven in the morning?"

Yes, well, that's what happened when she'd had to keep moving the boat so as to not get cited for illegal overnight mooring. Not that she was about to admit *that*. "Didn't sleep last night," she said. The utter truth. "The winds were crazy and the boat never stopped rocking."

"Using two tie-downs instead of one would help stabilize the boat quite a bit,' he said. "At the bow and the stern."

Something that of course Lucas hadn't bothered to tell her. "Thanks," she said, slightly mollified.

"You can moor overnight, but you have to buy a permit

for one of the public docks at the campgrounds or tie up at a private dock—with permission of the owner."

He was lake patrol, she realized. And a stickler for the rules. Not that she was surprised. The entire male race was on her shit list. Sometimes higher on the list than other times, but that was another story. "I'll move the boat," she promised, hoping to appease him enough to make him vanish.

He nodded and...continued to stand there.

Perfect. Still not feeling steady, she managed to get to her feet and sit behind the wheel. That she did so without puking was somewhat of a miracle. But before she could fumble the keys into the ignition, there came the *click click clicking* of heels running down the dock. Sophie turned her head in time to watch with the same muted horror with which she would've watched a train wreck.

A tall, leggy blonde was doing her best to run in painted-on leather pants and matching corset, vastly hampered by her store-bought double D's bouncing up to her chin with each step of those five-inch stilettos.

"Lucas," the woman called out. "Oh Lucas...I've got the day off, we can play pirate and captive maiden again!"

Sophie managed to stand up and make herself seen over the windshield. Yep, it was one of Lucas's regular sidepieces, which made her see red. On the positive side, though, apparently a brain couldn't be both furious and sick at the same time because she momentarily didn't feel like puking up her guts.

"Whoops," the woman said, skidding to a halt, tugging down the corset a little and very nearly causing a wardrobe malfunction of epic proportions. "I'm looking for Lucas."

What was her name? Sophie wondered, trying to remember. Brandy? Candy?

"I'm Mandy," Ms. Camel Toe said, sliding a side glance at Mr. Lake Patrol, who actually scored another point in Sophie's eyes when he took a quick, dismissive glance and then refocused on Sophie.

"I don't understand," Mandy said, confused, staring at Sophie now too. "Who are you? And don't even think of moving in on me. Monday mornings are mine and Lucas's. Well, every other Monday because he has very important meetings on the other Mondays. But he's going to leave his wife for me, so back off."

"Okay, I've got both good news and bad news for you," Sophie said. "The good news is that he did indeed leave his wife. Me."

Mandy did a double-take. "*You're* the coat hanger he dumped?"

Jeez, give up college and then your own life to run your husband's busy schedule for him and suddenly people see you as a worthless extension of the man instead of your own woman.

Good thing she was over that and back at work on herself.

Having no idea what she wanted to do for a living had her in temporary stall mode, but she was working on that too. She was doing the best she could at every job she tried, and so far things hadn't exactly panned out, but all she could do was keep looking forward.

Mandy crossed her arms. "So where the hell is Lucas?"

Later Sophie would feel bad for what popped out of her mouth. Much later. "He...passed." Which actually, wasn't a total lie, because if a Mack truck didn't run her ex over by week's end, she might just do the deed herself.

Mandy blinked. "Passed as in...*passed*?"

You're helping her out here, Sophie told herself. *Saving her future heartbreak*. So she did her best to look suitably grief stricken as she nodded and braced for hysterics.

But instead Mandy got all red in the face and stomped a stiletto on the dock. "Why, that bastard! He said that he'd had a lot of personal growth lately and he'd come to some life-altering decisions about us! And then he up and dies? *Are you kidding me?*"

Sophie didn't think that a hard-on counted as personal growth. She also felt she deserved a medal for sainthood for refraining from mentioning it.

"I had the diamond ring all picked out with a matching necklace and bracelet and everything." Mandy blew out a sigh. "Men suck."

Now *there* was something they could agree on.

"I need to board the boat," Mandy said, her breasts quivering in indignation. "I left a few things down there that the asshole doesn't deserve, even in death."

"Such as?" Sophie asked.

"Lucas gave me a drawer."

Sophie stared at her for a beat and then whirled and went below deck. She indeed found the drawer filled with lingerie and…ew…something in fluorescent pink that required batteries. Rather than touch anything, she yanked out the entire drawer and stormed above deck.

And tripped.

The contents of the drawer flew free and scattered across the dock. Lacy thongs, garter belts, skimpy bras… And last but not least, the fluorescent-pink battery-operated toy, which rolled to a stop at Lake Patrol Hottie's feet.

And then began to vibrate.

Lake Patrol Hottie stared down at it. "You have a license for this?" he asked Sophie.

"It's not mine!"

Mandy gave a big huff and gathered it up along with the rest of her lingerie, glaring at Sophie like this was all her fault. "I'll have you know, Lucas loved me *and* my Rabbit more than you." Then she whirled and headed up the dock, her heels *click, click, clicking*, her vibrator humming along in accompaniment.

Sophie sighed into the awkward silence between her and Lake Patrol Hottie. Actually, it was probably just her who felt awkward because he stood there looking perfectly comfortable and at ease.

"I'm sorry for your loss," he said.

"Don't be. He didn't die." She backed to the bench next to the driver's seat and dropped onto it in sheer woozy exhaustion. "What I said was that he'd *passed*. As in he passed on *me*."

And that was all she planned on saying on the subject.

Ever.

But apparently he didn't get the memo because he crouched on the deck so that they were eye level and said nothing.

She ground her teeth. The wind was back, dammit, and the boat began to rock. "Look, I said I'd move. I just need a minute."

He nodded and . . . stayed right where he was.

"You don't believe me?" she asked.

"Just waiting to see if you need any help."

She eyed him suspiciously, but he seemed to mean it. He really would assist her if she needed it. But she didn't need it. Not from him. Not from anyone.

Somehow she crawled behind the wheel. She started the boat before suddenly remembering she had to untie the boat first.

But her lake patrol guy was already on it, handling the ropes like he'd been born to the task, using his foot to push on the hull so it didn't scrape against the dock and get damaged. He then tossed the rope into the boat. "You're good," he said.

She stared at him. Was he kidding? She wasn't good, she was a hot mess and they both knew it, but then again he'd meant the boat, not her, and she knew that too. Still, she appreciated his unsolicited help. "Thanks," she said.

He nodded. Waited a beat. "Need help finding the throttle?"

This actually made her smile. "You're a real charmer, you know that?"

"Yep, I'm fresh off the boat from charm school."

"Where was it, Timbuktu?"

"Close," he said, offering no further explanation.

Fine. Whatever. Over mysterious men, over men *period*, she hit the gas. When she glanced in the rearview mirror a minute later, he was still standing there on the dock, hands shoved in his pockets, watching her go.

Chapter 2

The very last thing Jacob Kincaid had expected on his first day back in town was a run-in with a mysterious, green-eyed, temperamental cutie. Somehow she'd managed to pull him out of his own head while also irritating and amusing him at the same time.

She'd also made him feel alive.

Since that messed with his head more than a little bit, he got in his new Ford truck and took a ride. The truck had been a present to himself for making it stateside in one piece. It drove well, but his attention was distracted by his first view of Cedar Ridge in a long time.

It felt like a lifetime since he'd walked away from his family—his mom; twin brother, Hud; and the rest of the Kincaids—when he'd been an eighteen-year-old hothead. He hadn't been back.

Until now.

He'd been a lot of things in his lifetime. Brother. Son. Friend. Army Special Forces officer.

He was none of those things at the moment, though he intended to change that. He had begun by leasing a small cabin on the lake only a mile outside of town, a place that had once upon a time been the only true home he'd ever known.

Not that he'd admitted this until recently, and then only to himself.

The cabin sat on the northeast shoreline of the lake and was quiet and peaceful—two things his life had most definitely *never* been.

Something else he intended to change.

When he'd arrived late last night, he'd picked up the keys and spoken briefly to the Realtor, who'd tried to convince him to buy the cabin instead of renting.

But Jacob no longer made quick, rash decisions.

Although he had just chased away the first civilian woman he'd had contact with in a while and he'd done so pretty quickly and rashly.

Yeah, he could've definitely done better there, he admitted. Clearly he was *way* out of practice being sociable. Maybe he was more messed up than he'd thought because he'd actually gotten a kick out of the way her eyes had flashed temper at him, at the world. It'd been like trying to deal with a fiercely angry, beautiful, injured feline and in spite of the sharp claws, she'd given him something he hadn't felt in a damn long time.

Adrenaline. The good kind. And after eight years in the military life, also a taste of the real world.

Town was…the same. Small, but geared to the tourists who came through to ski. The streets were filled with expensive clothing boutiques, art galleries, jewelry shops, a few cafes, bars, B&Bs, and the like. At age eighteen,

Jacob had been climbing the walls here, bored, slowly suffocating.

Now, after having been overseas and seeing more shit-holes than he cared to remember, he could see in Cedar Ridge what others did, a unique quaintness and charm.

He didn't want to run the risk of stopping and running into anyone he knew. His estranged family deserved to be told first, but the need for caffeine overruled self-preservation. Striding into a coffee shop like he was on a mission, he bought coffee and a bagel to go, and headed back to the cabin.

Unscathed.

Red's boat was still gone, and relief filled him. And if there was also a twinge of something that felt suspiciously like disappointment, he didn't examine it too closely.

Instead, he found several paddleboards leaning against the side of the cabin and decided, What the hell. He took one out onto the water, paddling himself into oblivion so that maybe he'd sleep that night instead of figuring out how to reach out to his family after all this time now that he was on leave, or thinking about the reason he'd been given a month of bereavement leave in the first place.

The next morning, Jacob woke up to find his arms pleasantly sore from all the paddleboarding he'd done to clear his head. The chilly June air sliced through the window he'd left open and right through him as well, sharp and pine scented. From flat on his back he could see a sliver of the lake, the surface littered with white caps, much rougher and choppier than it had been the past few days.

He lay there a minute, unable to shut off his mind. It kept flashing images. Images of his closest friend,

Brett, dying in his arms in the desolate wasteland that was Afghanistan. Images of the look on his twin's face when they'd fought that long-ago day. Jacob hadn't seen Hud since. Images of his mom, who with her dementia couldn't keep time or place or people straight but never forgot who he was.

Even Red had somehow wormed her way in; tough and snarky, yet she'd shown him a fleeting glimpse of vulnerability too. The combination had caught his interest.

And attracted him.

Not that he had time to go there. Nope, he was concentrating all his energy on figuring out how to approach his family. Day three and he was still drawing a big zero on that front. He'd given no advance warning of his arrival because, hell, what did one say after nearly a decade of radio silence?

But today was the day. He'd stalled enough. And at the thought of what lay ahead for him, his gut tightened.

Nerves. Crazy, since it'd been a damn long time since he'd been nervous about anything.

He rolled out of bed, showered, dressed, and headed out, once again on the hunt for food he didn't have to make himself. Halfway to his truck he glanced through the clump of trees lining his property to the lake.

The Lucas was back, moored on his dock again.

Changing directions, he headed down there and eyed the boat. No sign of Red, but he heard something from below deck. A...moan?

Walk away, soldier.

But hell. He couldn't do it. "Hello?" he called out. "Red?"

The ensuing silence was so thick that he could tell she'd stopped breathing. "I'm boarding," he said and when she didn't respond, hoping she wasn't aiming a gun his way, he went for it. As he did, she struggled above deck.

She wore a white tank top and a short, flowery skirt that flirted with her thighs. She had a forest-green sweater in one hand and a pair of high-heeled sandals dangling from the other.

With one look, she perfectly conveyed her annoyance as she sagged to the captain's chair and dropped her head to her knees. "Why you?" she moaned. "I mean, seriously, what the hell is up with my karma? It's like the bitch went on vacay. On another planet."

"Nice to see you again too," he said dryly. "You wanna tell me what's wrong?"

"Nothing. Nothing at all," she said to her knees, more than a little hint of the South in her tone. "I always talk to my knees while a stranger asks me twenty questions. Nope, I'm great. My glass is totally half-full."

This made him smile. Call him sick but he loved snark on a woman. "Are you okay?"

"Fan-fricking-tastic. Only way today could get better is if I was scheduled for an appendectomy. Without drugs. In a third-world country."

Snark and a bad 'tude, like she wouldn't hesitate to kick someone's ass if she needed to. Didn't get hotter than that. He crouched next to her so that he was level with her face, not that he could see it since it was still pressed into her legs. "You're not supposed to—"

"—moor here," she said, very carefully not moving a single inch. "Yes, you ever so helpfully mentioned that yesterday."

"I was going to say you're not supposed to look down when you're seasick, it makes it worse."

"Oh." She hesitated and then turned her head to look at him. "And you're not supposed to be nice when I'm not. But thanks—oh crap. Oh shit," she whispered miserably as the boat rocked.

Jacob instinctively reached out and rubbed a hand over her back. "Have you tried Dramamine?"

"Yes. It doesn't work. I'm getting a patch today."

"That'll help," he said.

She nodded and sat up. "I'm sorry I'm back here. I just need to stay docked for the day, okay? I know the cabin's for sale and no one lives there, so I don't see a problem with that."

Other than she was getting off without having to pay the fees, which he suspected she couldn't afford. "Just so you know, the cabin's no longer empty," he said, fully intending to also say that she could keep her boat on his dock as long as she needed.

But she made a sound that might have been a snort of laughter or a sob. A little terrified it was the latter, he rose up to his full height just as she gasped, then moaned, and...threw up.

An inch from his shoes.

Welcome home, he thought.

Find more at
http://jillshalvis.com/books/nobody-but-you/

Please turn the page
for a preview of the first book in
Jill Shalvis's Cedar Ridge series,

*Second Chance
Summer!*

Available now!

Chapter 1

After fighting a brush fire at the base of Cedar Ridge for ten straight hours, Aidan Kincaid had only three things on his mind: sex, pizza, and beer. Given the way the day had gone, he'd gladly take them in any order he could get them.

Not in the cards.

He and the rest of his fire crew had finally managed to get back to the station. They'd been there just long enough to load their plates when the alarm went off again.

"What the hell!"

"Gonna break the damn bell and shove it up someone's—"

"This is bullshit..."

Whoever said no one could outswear a sailor had never lived in a firehouse. Ignoring the grumbling around him, Aidan pushed his plate away and met his partner Mitch's gaze.

"Gotta be a full moon bringing out the crazy," Mitch said.

"Maybe the crazy just follows you," Aidan suggested.

In turn, Mitch suggested Aidan was number one. With his middle finger.

They'd been playing this game since first grade, when Mitch had stolen Aidan's lunch and Aidan had popped him in the nose for it. As punishment they'd had to pick up and haul trash for the janitor for two weeks.

The two of them had become best friends and had spent the next decade being as wild and crazy as possible.

Eventually they'd grown up and found responsibility, going through the fire academy and now working as Colorado Wildland firefighters for their bread and butter, volunteering on the local search-and-rescue team as needed. And here in Cedar Ridge they were needed a lot. Lost hikers, overzealous hunters, clueless novice rafters—you name it, they'd been called to save it.

Tonight's fire call came in as a possible suicide jumper off the courthouse, which at five stories was the highest building in town.

As they pulled up, they could see a woman had climbed out a window on the fifth floor. She stood on a ledge that couldn't have been more than a foot wide. Wearing nothing but her bra and panties.

"Well, at least Nicky left her Victoria's Secrets on this time," Mitch noted.

Nicky was a bit of a regular.

And Mitch was right. The last time Nicky had gotten upset was after finding the town's councilman she'd been sleeping with going at it on his desk with his assistant. She'd stripped all the way down to her birthday suit before covering herself in Post-it notes. Aidan wondered what had set her off this time.

"I changed my mind," she screamed, jabbing a finger down at them. "I don't want to die! He's not worth it!"

No Post-it notes this time. A bonus. The police had blocked off traffic, but the scene was still chaotic.

"Somebody get up here and save me!" Nicky yelled. "If I fall and die, I'm going to sue every one of you for being so freaking slow! Honest to God, what does a girl have to do to get a rescue around here?"

"So she's changed her mind," the captain said dryly to Aidan and Mitch. Aidan and Mitch exchanged glances. No one could reach her from inside the window. And climbing out on the ledge wasn't an option; it was too narrow—and decomposing to boot. And thanks to the layout of the building and the hillside, their truck couldn't get close enough to the building to be effective either.

They all knew what this meant. One of them was going to have to follow the half-naked crazy chick out onto the ledge. There were a few problems with this.

Aidan and his team had a reputation for being unflappable and tough as nails, but the truth was, plenty unnerved them—including a half-naked crazy chick on a ledge five stories up. They'd just learned to do whatever needed to be done, no matter what.

"Let the fun begin," Mitch muttered.

Plan A was for the captain to head inside and attempt to talk Nicky back inside the window. Since Plan A had a high potential for going south, Plan B was to be run simultaneously—head to the roof and begin setting up rigging for an over-the-roof retrieval.

Through it all, Nicky never stopped screaming at them, alternately begging them to hurry and hurling insults their way.

Then came the cap's radio message: "Yeah, so she's declining to crawl back in the window because there's no press here yet. Last time she was front-page news."

Onward. The team found a good anchor spot on the roof. As Mitch and Aidan were the two most senior members of the unit, one of them always took lead. Mitch looked at Aidan. "Okay, go make like Spider-Man and rescue the damsel in distress."

"Why me?" Aidan asked.

"It's your turn."

"Hey, you're the one who likes her undies," Aidan pointed out. Not that he objected to a rescue, any rescue, but this one had shit show written all over it.

"I weigh more than you do," Mitch said logically.

Only because he was six foot four to Aidan's six two, but whatever. The team got the line set up, and then Aidan got into his five-point harness and hooked himself to the first of the two lines. Mitch hooked up to the second one just in case Aidan got into trouble, and the rest of the unit prepared for go time.

Aidan dropped over the edge. The plan was to rappel him down until he hung ten feet above Nicky. He'd then kick out from the building at the same time that his team lowered him eleven more feet, bringing him to just below her, putting him between her and the fifty-foot drop. He'd attach a harness to Nicky, and the team would give them enough slack so that Aidan could rappel down with her.

And the team indeed lowered Aidan to just above Nicky. Aidan kicked out. But as usual, nothing went to plan. Just as he started to swing back toward the wall, Nicky leapt off the ledge like some rabid raccoon and wrapped herself around him.

Not more than a hundred and ten pounds, she clung to him like a monkey as they hurtled at neck-breaking speed toward the wall. Aidan managed to grip her tight and twist in midair so that he was the one to slam into the brick.

Even as lightweight as she was, it still hurt like hell.

"Jesus Christ," Aidan heard the captain and Mitch say in stereo as they watched helplessly—one from above, one from below, at the window.

They didn't know the half of it. With Nicky's legs wrapped and locked around Aidan's waist, her arms squeezing his head like a grape and her breasts literally suffocating him, he couldn't breathe. Somehow he managed to turn his head sideways to suck in some air, but he still couldn't see. "I've got you," he said. "I'm not going to let go, but you need to loosen your grip."

Nicky was too busy screaming in his ear to hear him, not loosening her grip at all. "Omigod, don't you fuckin' drop me or I'll sue you the most!"

Mitch had dropped over the edge as soon as Nicky leapt onto Aidan's back. He was rappelling down as fast as he could, laughing all the way. Aidan couldn't see shit but he could hear him clearly, the asshole.

"Got his six," Mitch said into the radio as he came even with Aidan, still laughing. "Though I can't tell where Aidan ends and Nicky begins."

You can kill him later, Aidan promised himself. "Listen to me," he said to Nicky. "I've got you. I need you to stop yelling in my ear and look at me."

She gulped in a breath and relaxed her hold only enough to look at him. Her eyes were wide, wet, and raccooned from her mascara.

"I'm not going to let go of you," he assured her, staring into her eyes, doing his best to give her an anchor. "You hear me, Nicky? No one's falling to their death today."

She nodded and started to cry in earnest at the same time. Aidan preferred her screaming.

"She's not attached to anything," the captain reminded them via radio.

"You don't have to worry about that, Cap," Mitch responded. "She's not letting go of Aidan."

Nope, she wasn't. She'd embedded her nails into him good, and her legs were crossed and locked at the small of his back, but at least he could breathe. "Just get us down," he said.

As the team lowered them, Mitch kept alongside, offering encouragement, cracking his own ass up as they went.

On the ground, Aidan's new companion was peeled off of him and taken away for further evaluation. Aidan took his first deep breath since the rescue had begun. Aching in more muscles than he'd realized he even had, he gathered his gear.

"You okay?" their captain asked. "You took a few hard hits up there."

"I'm fine." He could feel where he'd have bruises tomorrow, and he was pretty sure his back had been scraped raw from the demolition derby collision with the brick wall, but he'd had worse.

Mitch grinned at him. "Man, you just had your bones totally jumped by a nearly naked chick. We almost had to resuscitate you. 'Fireman Asphyxiated by Boobs, news at eleven.'"

Their captain eyed Mitch, and then Aidan. "You remember we have a strict no killing each other policy?"

Aidan reluctantly nodded.

"I'm going to lift that rule for a one-time exception," the captain said, cocking his head at Mitch.

Mitch's smile faded. "Hey."

But the captain had walked away.

"Whatever," Mitch said to Aidan. "If you kill me, you'll never find out what I know."

Aidan gave him a long look. "You never know anything."

"I know lots, starting with a rumor that you're about to get a blast from the past."

"What?"

"Yeah. I hear Lily Danville's back," Mitch said.

Aidan froze at the name he hadn't heard in a very long time. Years. Ten of them to be exact.

Mitch raised a brow. "Gray hasn't mentioned it?"

No, Aidan's older brother had not told him a thing, which raised the question.

Why?

"How did you hear?" Aidan asked.

"Lenny. He caught the gossip at the resort. Your family runs the place, how did you not hear this?"

Lenny had gone to high school with them and now worked at the Kincaid resort as a big-equipment driver. Aidan stared at Mitch, unable to process that everyone had known before him.

Lily Danville...Damn. Turning, he started to walk away.

"It's no big deal," Mitch said. "It's not like you're seeing Shelly anymore, right? You're a free agent, so if you want to try to get Lily back...Hey, wait up."

Aidan didn't wait. And it was true he wasn't seeing Shelly anymore. Technically, they'd never been "seeing" each other. They'd had a satisfying physical relationship whenever they both felt like it, and neither of them had felt like it in over a month now. He hadn't thought about her once since.

But Lily Danville . . .

He hadn't seen her in forever, and yet he still thought about her way too often.

"Hold up," Mitch called out. "Your half of the gear's still—" He broke off when Aidan kept walking. "Seriously?" And when Aidan didn't so much as look back, Mitch swore and worked to gather the load, making some of the newbies help. He was quiet on the ride back to the station but only because they weren't alone and also because he was playing a game on his phone.

Aidan reached over and swiped his finger across Mitch's screen.

Mitch swore, nearly lost the phone out the window, and then turned to glare at Aidan. "You owe me a Candy Crush life."

"Tell me more about Lily being back."

"Oh, *now* you want to talk? You done pouting then?"

When Aidan just gave him the I-can-kick-your-ass gaze, Mitch grinned. "You know you were."

"It's all over Facebook," one of the guys said from the back. "The news about Lily."

"Aidan forgot his password," Mitch said. "A year ago."

Aidan ignored him, mostly because his brain was on overload. Lily. Back in town . . .

He'd long ago convinced himself that whatever he'd felt for her all those years ago had been just a stupid teenage boy thing.

Seemed he was going to get a chance to test out that theory, ready or not.